Dance Night

Dance Night

DAWN POWELL

STEERFORTH PRESS
SOUTH ROYALTON, VERMONT

Library of Congress Cataloging-in-Publication Data

Powell, Dawn.
Dance Night / Dawn Powell.
p.   cm.
ISBN 1–883642–71–X (alk. paper)
I. Title.
PS3531.O936D36   1999
813'.52—dc21   98–51106
                                    CIP

Manufactured in the United States of America

FIRST PAPERBACK EDITION

For my sister Phyllis

*W*HAT MORRY HEARD above the Lamptown night noises was a woman's high voice rocking on mandolin notes far far away. This was like no music Morry had ever known, it was a song someone else remembered, perhaps his mother, when he was only a sensation in her blood, a slight quickening when she met Charles Abbott, a mere wish for love racing through her veins.

The song bewildered Morry reading Jules Verne by gaslight, it unspiralled somewhere high above the Bon Ton Hat Shop, above Bauer's Chop House, over the Casino, and over Bill Delaney's Saloon and Billiard Parlor. It came from none of these places but from other worlds and then faded into a factory whistle, a fire engine bell, and a Salvation Army chorus down on Market Street.

Morry leaned far out the window and looked above and below, but there was no woman in the sky nor any sign of a miracle for blocks around. Girls from the Works in light dresses wandered, giggling, up and down the street waiting for the Casino Dance Hall above Bauer's to open, farm couples stood transfixed before Robbin's Jewelry Store window, the door of Delaney's Saloon swung open, shut, open, shut, releasing then withdrawing the laughter and the gaudy music of a pianola. Everything was as it was on any other Thursday night in Lamptown.

Nevertheless to Morry this had become a strange night and he could read no more. He thrust *Twenty Thousand Leagues Under the Sea* into his washstand drawer, turned down the gas, picked up a pack of cigarettes, thrust them in his hip pocket, and went downstairs. In the dark narrow hallway he ran into Nettie Farrell, assistant in the Bon Ton, her arms encircling a tower of hat boxes. Morry, absorbed in his new and curious quest, had no desire to meet anyone from his mother's shop and he hung back. But Nettie deliberately left the workroom door open and there was his mother, her pale cold face bent over a basket of cotton pansies, a blue-shaded lamp burning intently above her.

"You've been smoking!" Nettie whispered accusingly. "I'm going to tell your mother. And now you're going over to Bill's place! You are—you know you are!"

"I wasn't!" Morry denied everything sullenly.

"Hanging around poolrooms! You ought to be ashamed!"

A bell tinkled in the front of the shop and Nettie, hat boxes tipping perilously eastward, backed into the workroom without another word, only her black eyes blinking reproachfully at him.

Morry hurried out the side door into the little stone court where half a dozen Market Street shops ended in kitchen stoops, and half a dozen lights from these dwellings back and above shops united in a feeble illumination of a cistern, old garbage cans, a broken-down doll buggy, and a pile of shipping boxes.

Where was the song now, Morry wondered, and vaguely he blamed Nettie Farrell and the Bon Ton for having lost it. A freight train rumbled past a few yards from the court, its smoke spread over the Lamptown moon, and then he heard above its roar a girl's voice calling. Though certainly no girl in all Lamptown could be calling Morry Abbott, he was always expecting it, and he tiptoed hastily across rubbish-strewn cinders toward the voice. A flight of steps went up the side of the saloon to where Bill Delaney lived with his mother, and here Morry stopped short for at the very top of these steps huddled a dark figure.

Morry hesitated.

"Did you call me?" he asked uncertainly.

"Yes," said the girl and since Bill had neither sister, wife, nor daughter, Morry could not for the life of him imagine who it was. "I was lonesome. Come on up."

Morry was embarrassed.

"I—I can't." He felt scornful of a girl who would talk to him without even being able to see who he was. If it had been daylight or even dusk a strange girl speaking to him would have meant that in spite of Nettie Farrell's repeated taunts, he was good-looking, his black eyes, his broad shoulders, oh something about him was appealing. But it was clear that to the girl at the top of the stairs he might be just anyone.

"Come on," she urged. "I've got to talk to somebody, haven't I?"

The saloon back door opened and the bartender stood there against a sudden brilliant background of glasses, polished brass, and a rainbow of bottles. Morry ducked up the stairs, and the girl moved over for him to sit down. He could see now that she was a stranger in Lamptown, a queer pointed-faced girl, whose hair, black and tangled, hung to her shoulders. He would see if she was pretty when the next engine flashed its headlight down the tracks.

"There's a dance tonight, isn't there?" she demanded of him. In the darkness they eagerly tried to study each other's face, but all Morry could find in hers was a wildness that made him feel oddly older and more responsible.

"Even if I'm not old enough to go," she pursued, "why won't Bill let me go and watch? You ask him."

This terrified Morry. He didn't want to be teased by the factory girls at the dance, and he certainly didn't want to be ragged by the train men in Bill's saloon. Facing their good-natured challenges on his own account was torture enough, but to take on the added burden of a girl . . .

"We don't want to go to any dance," he said. "It's no fun watching. Look, who are you?"

"I'm adopted now," she explained triumphantly. "The Delaneys took me from the Home. This is where we live and I have a room of my own."

"Well." Morry didn't know why you were glad over being adopted but he supposed you ought to be congratulated. "Do you like it here?"

"I like the trains going by," she said. "I like it in my sleep when I hear them whistle way off. And I like it in my sleep when I hear the piano going downstairs and the men laughing. But I don't like to make beds. I can't make the sheets stay under."

Morry lit a cigarette.

"Let me see if I can smoke," she took the one he had lit, made a few masterful draws on it and then gave it back. "Oh well," she coughed, "I guess I can learn."

"What's your name?" he asked her. He liked sitting there beside her but he was a little afraid of her. He must remember, he thought, to hang on to her skirt if she should take it into her head to jump down stairs.

"Jen St. Clair. Maybe I'm Delaney now, but Bill and his mother say they don't care what I call myself." She casually fished in his pocket and drew out a pack of gum, unwrapped it and carefully stuck the wrappings back into his pocket. "But I'm going back to the Home sometime—when I get money."

"Why?" he wanted to know.

"To get Lil. She's my sister and she's still there."

An engine shrieked down the tracks, then a window flew up in the court, a woman thrust her head out and called, "Billy! Oh, Bill—ee!"

"'You'll come back for me, won't you, Jen,' is what Lil said to me," Jen went on. "I said I would."

The saloon back door opened again and a quiet scuffling noise was heard—the engine's searchlight briefly revealed Bill in white apron, wrestling with a heavy but feebly organized man in shirt-sleeves.

"There!" muttered Bill. "There, damn you. . . . Oh, Shorty! Give us a hand here."

Bill always handled the toughs but Shorty, the barkeep, had to pick them up afterward and start them home. Morry explained all this to Jen. She seemed pleased to hear of her benefactor's power. She stood up.

"Come in the house," she invited. "I want to show you something."

"But Bill's old lady wouldn't like it." It was Morry's experience that you weren't wanted in people's houses any more than they were wanted in yours.

"Asleep," Jen tersely nodded toward the old woman's bedroom. "Come on, I want to show you this."

She softly opened the screen door and Morry gingerly followed her into the dark vestibule. The rooms smelled of laundry and doughnuts. He caught her hand held out to guide him. It was the parlor, he knew, by the damp, musty air. Jen stood up on a chair and lit the gas light over the mantelpiece. With the flare of light Morry could see that although her hair and brows were black her eyes were sky-blue, he saw the patch of new calico on her faded blue dress. But she did not look at him again. It no longer mattered what he looked like since they were already established as friends. She took some little thing from the mantel and held it out to him in the palm of her hand.

"Look."

It was a tiny gold chair, barely an inch high, an armchair with delicate filagree for its cane back and seat. Morry took it and examined it, gave it back to her. Jen let it lay in her palm a moment, then with a sigh put it back on the mantel.

"It's so little. . . . I wish I could keep it in my room," she said. "But I suppose it's all right here. I can come in and look at it every once in a while. She got it at the World's Fair in St. Louis."

"I've got to go," Morry decided, watching the door uneasily.

Jen looked stricken.

"No, you can't—you mustn't go yet. Wait."

She tiptoed hurriedly into the next room and came back with a pair of shining tan shoes.

"I've got new shoes with high heels. See? I wanted pumps, black patent leather, but Bill got me these. Look!" She reached down her blouse and drew out a locket on the end of a thin gold chain. "Asafetida. Smell."

Morry smelled. It was asafetida. But he still had to go. He was already out the door. Jen turned down the gas and ran after him.

"There's duck in the ice box," she said. "We could eat it."

Morry only pulled his cap down with more finality. He was amazed at an adopted girl's boldness in entering parlors, and offering delicacies that were undoubtedly reserved by Bill Delaney for his own midnight supper.

"Well, I guess I'm off," he said brusquely.

Jen hung on to the railing and swung her foot back and forth. She wasn't over thirteen or fourteen, he thought.

"I've got folks somewhere," she informed him rather aloofly now, as if she sensed criticism of her lack of background. "They've got papers at the Home. There's a Mrs. St. Clair somewhere and that's my mother—Lil's and mine."

Morry said nothing, but he was impressed. An unknown mother—a Mrs. St. Clair somewhere who might be a millionaire or an actress.

The window on the court flew open again.

"Billy! Oh Bill- -ee!"

And this must have reminded Nettie Farrell to tell something for the next moment Morry heard his mother on their back stoop.

"Morry! Where are you?"

"You're Morry," Jen whispered, and he nodded. Why not Billy, then he wondered. . . . He did not answer and his mother never called twice. He heard her go indoors and close the door.

"Listen!" Jen seized his wrist. From across the street in front of the building came the sound of a drum, presently joined by a piano. Then a man's voice, rich, resonant—on Thursday nights you heard this voice above all other sounds for a block away; it belonged to Harry Fischer, the dancing teacher.

"ONE and two, and ONE and two and ONE and two and—"

"Can't we go and watch?" Jen appealed again.

Morry shook his head. He started down the steps. She said nothing, just swung her foot back and forth, but when halfway down he turned to look back he was startled at the desolation in her face, as if this parting was forever, and as if he, Morry Abbott, meant everything in the world to her.

"What is it?" he wanted to know.

Jen twisted her hands.

"Nothing. Only people last such a little while with me. There's no way to keep them, I guess. Everybody goes away— that's why I've got to go back for Lil because I know how terrible it is to be left always—never see people again."

"I'll see you tomorrow," he promised hurriedly. "I live over the Bon Ton. Probably we'll always be seeing each other."

Jen shook her head. Morry hesitated a moment, then went slowly down the stairs.

"ONE and two and ONE and two and ONE and two—"

The dancing lesson lasted from eight to nine and then the counting stopped and the Ball began. Morry wanted to tell all this to Jen but it was better not to go back once you had said you were going. He looked up. She sat hugging her knees, leaning against the railing.

"Well—goodnight."

She didn't answer. Embarrassed, Morry stumbled over ash-cans and cinders to his own stone-paved courtyard. He wanted to look back again but he did not dare. He went down the little alley and slipped in the side door. The workroom door was open and his mother was in there arranging her hair before a hand mirror with deep concentration. He wondered if she was going to the dance. Behind her he saw Nettie Farrell's trim plump figure. She was rummaging through a large pasteboard box of ribbons. Morry went upstairs before she saw him.

The gaslight in Morry's room went up and shadows were chased up the low sloping ceiling. Jules Verne emerged from the washstand drawer. Morry, in bed, smoked as he read and squashed his cigarette stubs into a cracked yellow soap dish. The short little dimity curtains at his infinitesimal windows quivered steadily with a busy breeze. Below, on Market Street, a group of factory girls gathered about two trainmen just come from Bill's place, and were convulsed by their masculine wit. The Salvation Army moved up a block; its aim was to reach the Casino and save at least a few of those headed for that modest hell. Tambourines clinked.

Morry jammed a third pillow at the back of his head, absently flicked ashes over the quilt, and turned page after page until words again took living shapes and allowed him to enter the book.

He had forgotten the unknown lady singing in the sky.

❦

"Come to me my melancholy baby," sang Nettie, "Huddle up and don't be blue. So you're going to the dance again, Mrs. Abbott."

Elsinore lowered her eyes over the hat for Dode O'Connell. The factory girls always liked flamboyant trimming and she thoughtfully added a green ribbon to the flowers pinned on the straw brim. This was what Charles Abbott would facetiously refer to as a Vegetable Blue Plate.

"There's plenty of time," she answered Nettie. "I don't want to be there first, besides the lesson is still on."

"Huddle up and don't be blue," hummed Nettie. She watched the street door waiting for customers. She was eighteen, she had been in the shop a year and the importance of her work continued to overwhelm her. Other girls in Lamptown worked in the factory or the telephone office, but God had chosen to favor her with this amazingly attractive niche in the Bon Ton Hat Shop. This must be because she was superior, a cut above the factory type, she was on lodge programs, for instance at the Lady Maccabees' meeting she sometimes sang, "When the dawn flames in the sky—I love you."

"Mr. Abbott ought to be in from the road soon," Nettie said. "What does he think of your going to the dances? I guess he's glad you have a little pleasure, maybe."

"He doesn't mind. He knows I work hard and don't get out much. I don't think Charlie minds." It had never occurred to Elsinore, for ten years self-and-home-supporting, that Mr. Abbott's opinion deserved little attention. She accepted his husbandly domination without demanding any of its practical benefits. If Charles, home for a week from a three months' Southern tour, objected to a gown of hers or a new arrangement of furniture, things were quietly changed to his taste. In Elsinore's scheme a husband was always a husband.

Nettie sat down on a work stool and examined her fingernails. She was a plump, sleek little girl, black hair parted in the middle and drawn back to a loose knot on her neck, her face a neat oval with full satisfied lips. Men followed Nettie on the street but

Nettie's chin went up more haughtily, her hips swung more insolently from side to side because Nettie was better than factory girls or telephone operators, she did not speak to strange men, she wanted to get on. Some day she would have a shop of her own. Mrs. Abbott said she was a good worker.

"I don't care about dancing," she observed to Mrs. Abbott. "That's why I never took lessons."

Elsinore held a straw frame out at arm's length.

"I never cared at your age," she said. "It was only this winter I learned."

The echo of the maestro's voice could be heard again—One two three—ONE two three—One—and Elsinore colored ever so faintly. It was easier to wait from one Thursday to the next than from eight o'clock until nine, she thought. She always hoped—yet perhaps not quite hoped, for she was a quiet contained woman, that this night—or next week, then—Mr. Fischer would select her as partner. This had happened once, just last winter in fact, when she had stayed over from the lesson to the regular dance; Fischer had been demonstrating a new dance and he turned to her, "Mrs. Abbott knows these steps from the class lesson tonight. May I ask you to come forward, Mrs. Abbott?"

Usually shy, Elsinore had known no hesitation in going straight across the dance floor to him, aware of her own limitations as a dancer she yet was certain that with him all things were possible. If from a raft in midocean this man had called to her, "Now, Mrs. Abbott, just swim out to me," she would have swum to him without hesitation, safe in her enchantment. A few bars of music, two to the left, two to the right, swing, swing, dip . . . "All right, Mr. Sanderson"—then to the musician.

That was all. It might happen again. Always someone was chosen casually like that for a brief demonstration and even if it didn't happen again, there was that one time to remember.

"The girls are beginning to go up," said Nettie.

Elsinore's fingers trembled arranging the trimmings in their labeled boxes but she said nothing. Nettie drew out a nail buff and polished her nails intently. Her hands were plump, white, and tapering. Nettie greased them and wore silk gloves over them at night.

"Bill Delaney's adopted a girl from the orphanage for his mother to take care of," said Nettie. "Imagine."

"That's no home for a girl," said Elsinore, "over a saloon."

Nettie tossed the buff into her drawer and looked toward the front door. Still no customers.

"Fay's coming for her hat tonight," she said, remembering. "She wants it for the Telephone Company's picnic. . . . She said people thought the girl might belong to Bill—you know men are that way, and Bill used to run around a lot."

"Maybe," said Elsinore but she didn't care. In three minutes more she would go over to the Casino. In three minutes. "Did Morry come in?"

Nettie shrugged.

"How do I know, Mrs. Abbott? Morry never pays any attention to what anybody says. He hangs around poolrooms, he smokes, he sits up late reading and smoking. You ought to get his father to talk to him."

Elsinore's straight eyebrows drew together.

"I must, Nettie, that's quite true. He's just at that age."

"Seventeen-year-old hanging around Bill Delaney's!" said Nettie. Talking about Morry Nettie's face always got red, her eyes flashed, every reminder of this boy's existence subtly offended her.

Two more minutes and Elsinore could stand up and say, "Well, Nettie, I'll leave the shop to you. Shut it up as soon as Fay gets her hat and put the key under the stoop."

Now she said, "He's lonely, Nettie, he goes to Bill's for the company. But it's not a good place for a boy."

She heard a step upstairs and called Morry's name. A sleepy bored voice responded.

"At least he's in," said Nettie.

One more minute. The piano from across the street pounded out the rhythm Fischer had announced—ONE and two and three and FOUR—Come to me my melancholy baby, huddle up and don't be blue. . . .

"Oh it's g-r-e-a-t to be f-r-e-e," sang the Salvation Army, "from the chains of s-i-n that bondage me. . . ."

"Well, Nettie, I'll leave the shop to you," said Elsinore, standing up at last. "Shut it up as soon as Fay gets her hat—and put the key under the stoop."

She did things, rubbed a chamois over her face, patted her hair, adjusted her dress, but these motions were curiously automatic for already she was swimming across oceans to a raft where Harry Fischer stood beating his hands to a dance rhythm—"one and two and three and four—"

"Here's Fay now," said Nettie, but Elsinore was gone. Elsinore gone, Morry asleep upstairs—it instantly became Nettie's shop and Nettie bloomed. She chatted patronizingly with Fay's young man while Fay tried on the hat.

"Smile my honey dear," sang Fay softly into the mirror for the hat was becoming, "while I kiss away each tear—"

Behind her back her young man grasped Nettie's arm. He slid his hand along her biceps and pressed a knuckle into her armpit.

"That's the vein to tap when you embalm people," he said, for he was going to be an undertaker.

꙳

Two floors above Bauer's Chop House fifty pairs of feet went slip a-slip a-slip to a drum's beating. Sometimes a piano melody crept through the drum's reverberation, sometimes the voice of Fischer emerged with a one-and-two and a one-and-two, and when this rhythm stopped suddenly there was a clap-clap-clap of hands, a silence and in this silence the clock sitting on the top of Bauer's cash register marked off the hush into ones and twos and ones and twos and ones and twos.

Behind the counter Hermann Bauer, fat, immobile, leaned on his elbows and looked out of the window without stirring for thirty-nine minutes when a lady got off the Interurban and came in to order a fried egg sandwich. Behind the other counter Mrs. Hulda Bauer, fat, immobile, sat on a high stool and crocheted an ugly but innocent device for a counterpane. Parades of girls from the Works went by and tramped up the stairs behind the restaurant to the Casino. Every Thursday night for six years Hermann had turned from the counter to say to his wife, "Hulda, look how these girls dress! Every cent on their backs. Gott! Silk, satins, and the perfume! I can smell it in here!"

"That will all change when they marry," Hulda answered always, but now Hermann remained silent so that Hulda need not look up from her crocheting. Why shouldn't the factory girls dress well—they made high wages, living was cheap, and nine hundred girls in a town needed to step fast to compete for the stray men. They went down the street giggling and nudging each other, in pink velvets, accordion pleats, lavender and orange satins, their hair peroxided or natural but always elaborately curled, their faces heavily powdered. In front of Bauer's they dallied, waiting for the saloon door across the street to swing open. From behind that door you could hear men's laughter, the pianola, and sometimes a hearty curse, with so much private fun it was amazing that the men should ever come out for a mere dance. But at nine o'clock when the lesson music changed to Dance Number One, a two-step, the saloon door swung open and the men came out—the firemen, brakemen, factory workers—all dressed up to the nines. The girls tossed their heads and hurried up the steps ahead.

"Hello, Jim," a girl leaning out the Casino window upstairs called down to one of the men.

The Bauers had taken in all this play for years but never once had it inspired them to go upstairs to watch as some older people did. It was the duty of one of them to wait for after the dance couples would come in to this place for coffee and sandwiches.

In the kitchen Grace Terris, the waitress, having finished helping the cook with the dishes, hurried upstairs to frizz her hair. She was a thin blonde with a pale face and glasses. She was very neat—her hair and her waist ribbons must always be just so, her outside garments spotless and starched, even though out of sheer love of its texture she sometimes wore a silk chemise three weeks.

Grace brushed past Mrs. Bauer half a dozen times in quest of pins in the cash drawer, a pocketbook left under a serving table, a powder puff hidden under the counter. No matter how busy the place might be on Thursday nights, neither Hermann nor Hulda would ever ask Grace to stay and help. Thursday was her night off—nothing could ever alter that. She couldn't dance but she liked to go somewhere even if she just sat and watched. Presently in a nimbus of azalea perfume, a rose-colored scarf wound around her head as a badge of evening dress, her dark green silk bristling with anticipation, Grace swept through the restaurant and out the front door.

Dance Number Two, a Waltz.

At the dark railroad station just beyond Bill Delaney's saloon Number Eleven drew in and a dozen more men from Birchfield, Galion, and Ashland dropped off, and girls leaning out the Casino window hurried to the dressing room to powder again.

Hermann Bauer nodded to a group passing the window. Upstairs the feet went slip a-slip a-slip to a waltz, on the stool opposite him Hulda crocheted a daisy over a waltz foundation.

The Salvation Army stood in front of Hermann's, they fixed their eyes on his motionless face while they sang shrilly and mechanically to the dreary jangle of a tambourine. Bill Delaney's place was silent, a little light gleamed in the attic above the Bon Ton Hat Shop, the Bon Ton itself was dark. Now the life of Lamptown had concentrated two floors above Bauer's Chop House.

Dance Number Three, a Robber's Two-step.

In front of Bauer's a long low roadster stopped. Hunt Russell's. Hunt, by some freak of inheritance, certainly due to no fault of his languid self, owned the Works, owned Lamptown, you might say. Now his tall lean person swung out of the car, followed by the equally lean figure of Dode O'Connell, the factory forewoman—a proud hard face she had beneath masses of red hair. She was Hunt Russell's woman. No matter whom she had belonged to before, now she was Hunt's. They went up the steps to the Casino. Dance Number Four.

Quietly Hulda Bauer laid down her crocheting, nodded to her husband, and waddled up to bed. It had been quite an outing for her.

⸙

"Tonight I am going to demonstrate to you," said Mr. Fischer, "the dance I created for the United Dancing Masters of the World last summer at our convention in Atlantic City. This dance, ladies and gentlemen, is now taking New York by storm. It is called the Duck Slide. If you please, Mr. Sanderson."

One and two and a three and dip. One and a two and a three and turn. One and a two and a dip and turn and two-step right and two-step left—thank you, Mr. Sanderson.

Elsinore Abbott usually danced first with Mr. Klein the gas man. He was too old for the factory girls and besides he admired a woman who had spunk enough to run a business, always looked trim, always a lady. In the midst of the factory girls' gay colors her dark blue taffeta and black satin pumps seemed wistfully chic, her pale clear-cut face beneath the heavy brown hair gave no hint of naïve pleasure in the dance, her cool gray eyes revealed no vulgar excitement over crowds and music. Over Klein's honest shoulder she watched Fischer, immaculate in evening dress, demonstrating the next movement of the next dance. Fischer had broader shoulders than any man in the room. It was curious that his great muscular body should yield so exquisitely to a dance for it belonged to mighty masculine deeds. He had thick sleek black hair, hard black eyes, a strong-boned heavy face. In a bathing suit at Atlantic City the muscles of his back must have shown powerful and rippling, muscles must have bulged from his shoulders, arms, and legs, his throat must have looked thick and strong like an animal's, like a prizefighter's. Elsinore followed Mr. Klein's painstaking lead through the second movement.

"In a little while we will pass him standing there," she thought. "In a little while . . . there's no hurry."

When they passed she did not look at him.

In the center of the floor Hunt Russell and Dode O'Connell, cheek to cheek, danced beautifully, silently, as couples do who are certain of other contacts. Hunt Russell, worth a quarter of a million, with a background of Boston Russells and Carolina Blairs, owner of Lamptown, preferred a factory forewoman to a woman of quality, chose Harry Fischer, small-town dancing master as his boon companion, lounged in Bill Delaney's saloon, a billiard cue in one hand, instead of in country clubs, drove his expensive cars down dingy Lamptown streets instead of on foreign boulevards. There were men who would not dare be like that, but no one slapped Hunt on the back, few women dared solicit too frankly the inquiry of his cold amused eyes. And because for two years she had been Hunt's woman Dode O'Connell's head was always high, her proud red mouth flaunted the exclusiveness of her kisses.

After Mr. Klein there were the uncertain young men who had gone to last winter's dancing class with Elsinore, who knew that her own lack of skill would make her less critical of their mistakes. They would learn with her, thought Elsinore without resentment, but after they became expert they would choose younger women as their partners. One of these men, in a waltz, brushed her past Fischer. He stood in a corner talking in a low voice to Hunt while Dode whirled by with one of the train dispatchers.

"You'll have to wait till about one," Fischer said looking at his watch. "Then I'm good for all night. But what about Red?"

"I'll fix that," Hunt tossed a cigarette in a palm bucket. He was not over thirty but his temples were already gray.

Fischer laughed.

"Better look out—she'd kill you for less than that. . . ." and then he clapped his hands. "All right, people . . . one moment, Mr. Sanderson. I want to announce the date of the tango contest to be held in Akron two weeks from tomorrow night. The rules for the contestants, ladies and gentlemen, are as follows . . ."

He stood almost at Elsinore's elbow, no more conscious of her than of the palm on the other side of him. Elsinore did not mind. She wanted nothing from him, after all, only the rare privilege of being allowed to think about him, as she had thought of him for over a year. Nights after the Bon Ton was closed she had lain in bed wondering where Fischer was now. In Birchfield Mondays, Columbus Tuesdays, Delaware Wednesdays, Marion Fridays. Tonight I am going to demonstrate to you, ladies and gentlemen, the Duck Slide. . . . She saw the young girls of Marion, Birchfield, Delaware looking at him, and saw him selecting this or that eighteen year old for an exhibition dance. With these petal-cheeked young girls surrounding him, why should he remember that once he had singled out Elsinore Abbott for a schottische demonstration? Yet she had been eighteen once as these girls would one day be thirty-six. And he was even older than that. But why should he remember her—why indeed should he trouble her mind, Elsinore sometimes wondered, his ways, his manner, littered her memory as confusingly as a man's clothes in a woman's bedroom. She tried to recall what she had thought of before she saw him, but it was as difficult as trying to decide what she wanted of him now that she did think of him. She was married to Charles. He was married to someone in Columbus. What else could there be?

In the doorway of the Casino two new men appeared, and Elsinore, thinking of her husband at the very moment, saw him invoked before her eyes. The natty checked suit, the flawless necktie, the perfect fedora, the cigar—it was indeed Charles Abbott. His roving blue eyes had found her at once, and quietly she left her partner and went up to him.

"I didn't expect you for another three weeks, Charles," she said following him into the hall.

"No?" Charles looked at her with faintly mocking suspicion. "Since when have you been going to factory girl dances?"

Elsinore flushed.

"You knew I had taken it up," she said in a low voice. "I told you I was taking the course last winter. I go out very little, Charles. You know that. This—I like."

Charles watched the dancers with a fixed smile, tapping his cigar against the railing by the door. He nodded to a dancer now and then whom he knew either as a patron of his wife's shop or as a fellow patron of Bill Delaney's place.

Elsinore's partner looked at her questioningly and she shook her head in the negative.

"Close the shop, do you, to come over here?" inquired Charles with seeming affability.

"I never neglect the shop, Charles, you ought to know that," said Elsinore. The color had not left her face. She turned to him abruptly. "Let's go now. Things are almost over. We can talk."

"No hurry," Charles said. He waved his cigar nonchalantly to Hunt Russell. Elsinore went to the dressing room for her coat. She passed Fischer again, standing with arms folded beside the palms. He bowed to her, his face a smooth ruddy mask of courtesy.

"Goodnight, Mrs. Abbott," he said.

Elsinore lowered her head.

"All right, Mr. Sanderson, the next dance will be a Circle Two-step. A Circle Two-step, ladies and gentlemen."

> Come sweetheart mine,
> Don't sit and pine,
> Tell me of the cares that make you oh so blue—

Hunt Russell leaned against the exit door and sang the words softly. Charles followed Elsinore with the suggestion of a swagger, an air of being made to leave a gay occasion against his will. Elsinore did not look back. The music, the laughter, had ceased to be once she turned her back upon them. Abruptly she locked away her thoughts of Fischer for these were precious matters not to be dwelt upon with strangers like Charles nearby.

"The good old Bon Ton," Charles observed lightly as Elsinore fitted her key into the lock of the shop door. Elsinore did not answer.

Long afterward Morry was awakened by the dance music stopping. He heard voices in the street and stumbled sleepily to the window. The Casino windows were dark—only one light burned in Bauer's Chop House. Before the restaurant Hunt Russell's car stood, and beside it were Hunt and Dode O'Connell facing each other.

"You cur," Dode was saying in a cold hard voice, "You dirty double-crossing cur."

Morry yawned and went back to bed.

☙

Trains whirred through the air, their whistles shrieking a red line through the sky behind them, they landed on Jen's bed without weight, vanished, and other trains, pop-eyed, roared toward her. Trains slid noiselessly across her eyelids, long transcontinental trains with diners, clubcars, observation cars. The people on these trains leaned out of their windows and held out their hands to Jen.

"California, Hawaii, Denver, Quebec, Miami," they chanted, "oh you dear child, New Orleans, Chicago, Boston, Rocky Mountains, New York City."

Then two dark porters made a London bridge and caught her, they said, "Which would you rather have, a diamond palace or a solid gold piano?"

Old Mrs. Delaney finally put on her carpet slippers and opened Jen's door.

"Well, what's the matter with you now?" she wanted to know. "Waking folks up this hour with your yelling?"

She was irritable, for Bill had been hiding in a closet ever since he came upstairs. He'd been drinking too much and after the big Akron wreck when he'd been the faulty engineer he had spells when every engine chugging by sent him sobbing to some hiding place. There was nothing you could do with him but sometimes his mother, her withered old face grim and dark, her gnarled hands clenched, sat waiting all night for him to quit moaning and come to his senses again.

"No—no, I've changed my mind," Jen cried. "Not the piano—the other—the diamond palace."

"That'll be about enough out of you tonight," said Mrs. Delaney. Jen opened her eyes and blinked at the old woman in the feeble dawn light.

"There won't be any diamonds for you, young lady," grumbled Mrs. Delaney. She pulled the cover over Jen, jerked a pillow into place. "Diamond palace my eye."

"All right," murmured Jen as her foster parent slipped out of the room, "I'll take the gold piano."

"Aren't you afraid of the old woman?" Morry Abbott asked one night when they sat out on the steps above the saloon.

Jen shook her head.

"I'm not afraid of her," she said. "That's just the way old women are. I'm not afraid of anybody. I feel sorry for them, coming to me someday begging me to forgive 'em because they didn't realize I was going to turn out so rich and famous."

"You kid yourself a lot, don't you?" Morry said curiously. He heard voices in the saloon back room of older boys about town and he instinctively drew up his cap down over his eyes. His own place at seventeen was in the saloon downstairs, instead of hanging around kids like Jen. He was old enough to be getting over that queer sickness the saloon smell gave to him, about time he stopped coughing over whiskey, listening frankly awe-stricken to tales of amorous adventures. He would go down in a little while for the only way to learn anything was to get used to it.

"What did the Delaneys take you out of the Home for?" he wanted to know.

Jen looked at him suspiciously and then brushed back a lock of black hair, stuck it behind her ear.

"What's the matter with me—why shouldn't they pick me?" she demanded.

Morry blushed, at her attack.

"Well, people usually adopt those little yellow-haired blue-eyed dolls—you know—you're all right only—"

"The hell they do," said Jen and Morry was conscious of the same sick feeling the saloon smell gave to him. "They always pick somebody that looks like a good worker. Once in a while some woman that's had her pet cat run over picks out one of those pretty ones. There aren't many of them."

"You don't have to say hell," said Morry. It annoyed him that words which stuck in his own throat should flow so easily from a young girl's lips.

Jen wriggled and sucked her thumb sulkily.

"Well, anyway Lil's like that—she looks like a little wax doll," she went on. "Everybody that visits the Home always wants to hold her . . . but nobody's adopted her. I told the matron not to let anybody because I'm the one to take care of Lil. She's so little—she can't stand it without me. I've got to look after her. Gee!"

She suddenly brushed her sleeve over her eyes. Morry was fired with an aim in life.

"You leave Lil to me," he said. "What about me adopting her myself?"

Jen seized his arm. She was radiant.

"Will you—Morry—will you do that?"

And then Morry remembered the truths that his father mockingly and Nettie Farrell bitterly had so often flung at him. Worthless, overgrown cub, no good to anybody, in everybody's way. If he was going to amount to anything in the world, why was he hanging around talking big instead of hunting a job, why didn't he study one of those correspondence courses at night instead of reading romantic trash till way after midnight? Fellows no older than he was were making money out selling or working in garages or factories and if they could do it he supposed he could stand it. But here Morry shuddered. He couldn't see himself in overalls, he dared not picture himself an agonized applicant for an office job. Somehow he always saw himself a sort of Hunt Russell, a success without calluses and without the embarrassment of however honest sweat. But even Morry could see that this wasn't the way a young man ought to enter the struggle—gasping at the very start. He was miserable remembering the dooms forecast for him by Nettie and his father. Still—Jen St. Clair didn't know all these things about him. On the contrary she seemed to think he could manage anything he promised to do.

"We'll take care of Lil all right," he repeated with slightly less emphasis this time.

"That's fixed, I guess," sighed Jen. "I'll write Lil and tell her. I didn't want to write until I could promise something."

"Does the old woman make you work?" Morry asked, relieved to have the subject of Lil's rescue safely out of the way. "I mean if that's what they got you for—"

Jen looked over her shoulder to make sure Mrs. Delaney was out of earshot.

"I guess they made a mistake," she whispered. "I look bright but I can't seem to pick up anything. The covers stay in little bumps when I make the beds."

She looked gloomy.

"The bottoms of the dishes get egg all over as fast as they're washed," she went on, "even when we haven't had eggs, they do that, no matter how hard I scrub. And when I made popovers yesterday they didn't come out popovers at all. Sort of like pancakes . . . You'd think popovers would be easy, wouldn't you, Morry?"

Jen sunk her chin in her hands.

"It makes it pretty hard for the old woman," she said regretfully. "It was Bill's idea adopting somebody and now they've picked me they've got to keep me."

Morry got up. He thought he might as well go down and get the saloon over with. Jen's black brows contracted. Tomorrow or the next day she would see him again and yet it was a lamp going out each time he went away. She wished for some marvelous surprise to detain him with—a diamond palace or a solid gold piano. "Wait," she would cry and he would come back. She would open the door. "Look," and there would be the palace, its towers glittering, a sapphire light glowing in each window. And so he would have to take off his hat and stay.

Jen didn't answer when he said goodbye. She stood with one hand on the wall and the other on the railing and scuffed the toe of her shoe on the top step.

"Wait," she said when he was halfway down, but when he turned expectantly, she said lifelessly, "Oh nothing."

Diamonds, my eye!

꙳

"One beer," Morry said standing at the bar with Hogan, fireman on Number Eleven, and a couple of brakemen from the short line.

The boys of Morry's age usually played pool in the front room and only occasionally joined the older men in the barroom, but now the front room was empty and so Morry went back to the bar. Here Bill Delaney, short, blonde, serious, stood leaning over the back of a chair at one of the card tables talking to three men from the freight yards.

"You've got no kick," he was saying. "You pull down your hundred and fifty smackers every month, you're all right. I'm tellin' you you fellows got it pretty goddam soft."

"You tell all that to the pope," Hogan advised over his shoulder.

"Your dad was here yesterday, Morry," Shorty said wiping up the counter. "Some sport, Charlie Abbott, let me tell you. Some sport even for a traveling man."

"Yeah?" said Morry, whose one aim in life was to keep out of his father's way, or at least out of range of his father's ironic eye.

"You goin' sellin' on the road like your dad?" Shorty asked.

"No," Morry said and then explained, "I'm sort of looking around."

"How about brakin'?" said the brown young man in blue overalls on the other side of Hogan. "You get good pay."

"Don't do no railroadin', buddy," Hogan advised. "We're a tough old bunch, listen to me. You've got to know how to handle your liquor and your women."

"Leave that to Charlie Abbott's boy all right," chuckled Shorty.

"Jesus, when Buck here and me had that seven-hour run out of Pittsburgh—" Hogan drained his glass, banged it on the counter, raised one finger significantly to Shorty.

"Seems to me I get more on the local," Buck said. "Girls in these little towns around here ain't so damned aristocratic."

"He ain't goin' railroadin'," Shorty dismissed the whole business. "He looks all right but he's just a kid. How's the game there, Skin?"

"These fellas don't want to play poker they want to crab about life," Bill Delaney shrugged and came back to the bar. "Enough guys come in here hollerin' for jobs you ought to be glad you're workin'."

"That's a lot of baloney from Father Tooey," growled one of the three shuffling the cards again. "You damn micks let him run this whole town."

"Leave Father Tooey out of it, see," Bill retorted. He poured himself a seltzer. "You fellas make me tired always sore about somethin', always crabbin'. You don't have to work, you know. You could get a room in the poorhouse."

"Aw, a guy wants to see something ahead of him, Bill, that's all," the youngest of the three men cut the pack, the oldest silently dealt a round. "Hell, we don't want to be stuck in this god-forsaken dump all our lives at the same stinkin' little jobs."

"Have another?" Bill asked Morry but Morry shook his head.

Hogan leaned back, his elbows on the bar.

"I would rather have been a French peasant and wear wooden shoes. I would rather have lived in a hut with a vine growing over the door and the grapes growing purple in the kisses of the autumn sun," he said in a sing-song voice, his eyes closed. "I would rather have been that poor peasant with my loving wife by my side with my children on my knees, I would rather have been that man and gone down to the tongueless silence of the dream-less dust than to have been that imperial impersonation of force and murder known as Napoleon the Great."

He looked at Morry with bright blue eyes.

"That's old Bob Ingersoll, the greatest man that ever lived, bar none. Have a drink."

But Morry dropped two dimes on the counter and with a quick nod to the others, went out the front door. Even two beers made him feel dizzy. He almost collided with his father coming in, hat jauntily at an angle, cigar in his mouth.

"Well, well, so you've made the club," Charles Abbott said, his eyes mockingly on his son's red face. "Isn't that splendid! Isn't that just splendid! . . . Go on home, there, and see if there isn't something else you can do to worry your mother."

"I'm going," said Morry.

He dodged the Bon Ton's front door where Nettie stood and went in the alley entrance.

"I would rather have been a French peasant and gone down to the tongueless silence of the dreamless dust," he mused going upstairs. "That's Bob Ingersoll, the greatest man who ever lived, bar none."

⁂

Elsinore knew that Charles Abbott was a weak, blustering man, but after the day he first kissed her these matters receded, a cur-tain dropped definitely between her and his faults. She had worked in a millinery shop when he was a candy salesman from a Chicago wholesale dealer, she had gone on working until now the shop was hers, and he still traveled. Every three or four months he was home for a fortnight. He was a spendthrift, a gambler, a sport, people said, but on the other hand, as Nettie Farrell frequently pointed out to gossips, he was a jealous husband and that always proved something.

When he was home Morry went out early in the morning and hung closely to his room at night for his father held him in complete scorn. Charles slept all morning, drank whiskey quietly and steadily all afternoon, and aware of being drunk, stood silent around the Bon Ton showroom, his hat on the side of his head, always smoking a cigar. He flicked ashes over the workroom table, left his cigar stubs on the showcases, but Elsinore said no word of reproach. Sometimes he dropped into Bill Delaney's for a card game but he drank mostly at home. In Elsinore's plain little bedroom he lay evenings reading the Columbus newspapers, dropping his cigar ashes over the white bedspread, hanging his heavy suits over her slight woman's things, keeping his whiskey bottle on the dressing table between her lilac water and her talcum.

In the cities of Charles Abbott's world there were painted little blonde girls who kept his picture on their dressers, there were women who made engagements with him for three months ahead, and all these were gay party women with whom a man liked to be seen. But even now, nineteen years married, there was still for him something curiously chic in Elsinore's manner and dress, something haunting in her white cold face, her isolation made her desirable.

When she closed the shop and came up to bed the night after the dance, and for many nights after that, Morry in the next room was kept awake by their low voices.

"See here, there's something in this dance business, Elsinore. . . . Some guy there you go to meet."

Elsinore's voice then, cool and tired.

"Don't be silly, Charles, you know there's no one else."

"That's all right, you're not taking up this dance idea all of a sudden for no reason at all. It's some man. Somebody's got you running at last."

"You know how I am, Charles," Elsinore would say wearily.

"I do know—cold as hell, but I always knew if you ever snapped out of it there wouldn't be any limit for you. . . . I know you. . . . Who is the fellow, anyway? Come on, now, let's hear it."

Elsinore would turn out the lights, go to the window in her white nightdress to draw up the shades, stand for a moment to look at the pale far-off moon. She got into bed quietly.

"I tell you, Elsinore. I don't like this business of you starting to run around," Charles's voice in the dark, bereft of his mocking eyes, his jaunty cigar, was weak and querulous. "It's not like you. It means something and I don't like it. I've got to find out, damn it."

Elsinore drew the sheets over her. A freight train rumbling by hushed him for a little while. And then—

"Who is it, Elsinore—come on. Is it Russell? Is it one of those railroad bastards? . . . Elsinore, for the love of Christ. . . ."

"Go to sleep, Charles. . . . I've told you there never was anyone else."

Grumbling still he fell asleep and she put her arm across her eyes.

Where was Fischer tonight—what young girl's light body was bent to his in a dance, what town was rocking to his one and two and one and two?

❧

When you stepped out of the back door into the alley at night you stomped your feet to scare away the rats. For a moment you heard them rushing over the rotten boards of back porches, scuttling over the ash cans, over the cistern bucket, and into weeds.

And then you could proceed in safety to the pump or to the store-house shed where old frames were packed away in trunks, where from a shelf there leered antique window heads with hay-colored pompadours drooping over one eye, or with black bangs madly frizzed and stiff enough to balance any hat three inches above the head.

Nettie came back from this shed with a stack of wire frames on one arm, a flashlight in the other hand.

Morry, about to go out, ducked back in the hall.

"Going to the saloon, I suppose," said Nettie, a little out of breath. "Going over there and drink, you're just a good-for-nothing, Morry Abbott, you ought to be ashamed."

"Well, what are you going to do about it?" Morry retorted sulkily. "What do you want me to do, stick around here and trim hats?"

"Better than hanging around saloon trash and girls out of foundling homes," Nettie flashed back in a low tense voice. "Better than sitting up nights reading books by atheists."

"What were you doing in my room?" Morry demanded, amazed and angry.

Nettie tossed her head defiantly.

"I have a right to go where I please, Morry Abbott, in this house. If you're reading things you're ashamed of I'd advise you to hide them, before your father sees them. I've heard about that Ingersoll man. . . . The idea!"

Morry opened the workroom door for her, angry at his own inability to be devastatingly rude to her. His mother saw him.

"Don't go out, Morry," she said quietly. "Your father's over at Delaney's and he wouldn't want to see you there."

"All right," said Morry.

He heard Jen's voice—"Hoo-oo!" softly calling from outside. He would go upstairs and wait awhile, then go over for a minute to sit on the steps. In the hat shop he heard the voice of Mrs. Pepper, the corsetiere, and in some alarm he hurried upstairs. But was even his room safe from feminine intrusion, he wondered bitterly, since Nettie's admission of having snooped around? Very likely the next time Mrs. Pepper arrived in town she would use his room for fitting. If only he didn't mind the smell of saloons so much, he thought, he would spend his days and nights all in that safely male retreat.

"Just something to confine the hips, that's all," he heard Mrs. Pepper say, "but darling, if you don't mind my saying so—you really do need that—"

And then Morry hurriedly banged his door shut, while downstairs the female figure came into its own. Every fortnight Mrs. Pepper called in Lamptown and with her headquarters at the Bon Ton fitted the factory girls and shopkeepers' wives who could afford it with marvelous devices in pink and orchid satin-covered steel. She was a short, laughing, fat little woman, with a delicate charm and effect of feminine frailty conveyed by a tinkling laugh, tiny plump hands, jeweled, fluttering in perpetual astonishment to her heavy brassiered bosom.

"Oooh—why Mrs. Abbott!" she would gurgle breathlessly, "Why—why!" and then her tinkling silver little laugh.

A woman's figure was to her a serious matter, and her blue eyes would widen thoughtfully over any dilemma of too big hips, flat chest, or protruding stomach.

"I had a lady—Mrs. Forest in Canton—you know A. Z. Forest, the lawyer, and she was big here the way you are and then thin right through here the same as you. You know Mrs. Forest, don't you, Nettie? Nettie remembers her. She came here for a hat once. I gave her the Nympholette Number 43 and everyone says, 'Why, Mrs. Forest, why you look so *stunning!*'"

Mrs. Pepper made everyone lie down to be fitted for that was the only way she could get their real lines. For this purpose Elsinore had a screened couch in the alcove between salesroom and workroom.

"Now just relax," Mrs. Pepper would say. "Put down 38, Nettie. And 46 for the hips."

Mrs. Pepper sometimes went to the Casino but only to watch for she had never learned dancing. It was only because Mr. Fischer was such an old friend—they had the same territory, the same towns to cover.

When Mrs. Pepper's round baby face was bent over her order books Elsinore sometimes stole a look at her. Fischer never talked to Mrs. Pepper, except in the formal way he did to every lady in his hall. Yet someone said once they were seen together in the back seat of Hunt Russell's automobile long after midnight, and that those foursomes with Hunt and Dode occurred other times. Was this the woman, then, that Fischer cared for—or had once cared for? Elsinore wondered again and again about it, for Mrs. Pepper with her lace-frilled daintily powdered throat, her little white hands, her tiny silken ankles swelling to heavy thighs, her delicate sacheted underthings, had the air of being desired by men. Yet Mrs. Pepper was a lady, ridiculously refined.

Once Elsinore, driven by her wonder, deliberately mentioned Fischer's name to her but Mrs. Pepper's childish blue eyes never blinked.

"Mr. Fischer is such a gentleman, isn't he," she said. "He must be a lovely husband. Mrs. Fischer is a lucky woman, I'm sure."

"He must see a great many pretty women in his work," Elsinore, faintly coloring at her own tenacity, went on, "A dancing teacher like that."

"And he is so handsome," sighed Mrs. Pepper. "Such a strong man, too, don't you think? Such a big strong man."

And that was all Elsinore could get out of her.

The Bon Ton was in a state of all day excitement when Mrs. Pepper was there. It must keep open until after eleven to accommodate the working girls. Their outer garments hung over customer's chairs while they tried on samples, and Nettie, with both hats and corsets on her mind, fussed about like a hen with chicks. Charles lounged in Elsinore's room upstairs or in the poolroom and ate at Bauer's.

Elsinore alone remained serene as she would if her business suddenly included all of Ohio and two thousand Netties fussed about in the workrooms.

Morry kept upstairs this evening for a little while until a confusion of feminine voices below assured him that he would not be noticed. Then he tiptoed downstairs. The workroom door was open and lying on the table, a pillow under her head, was a girl naked except for a gauze undershirt. Nettie, frowning, was measuring her waist with a tape, which meant that Mrs. Pepper was so besieged with customers that the hat business had been temporarily pushed aside. Morry tried to tiptoe past but the girl sat up and squealed.

"Oh, Nettie—there's a man!" She clutched, rather futilely, a cluster of velvet roses and held them before her protectively. She was Grace Terris, the Bauers' waitress. Before Nettie could answer Morry shot out the back door, quite pale, his ears burning furiously.

⚬

The people around her grave were satisfied with their hides because of course they were used to them now, though Jen, in this dream, wondered how they could feel so content when the skins complete were passed out by the public bath house with no regard for individual expression.

These dream people held their handkerchiefs before their unknown faces and wept; their black taffeta dresses and their black swallow-tail coats and their black cotton gloves holding tall black hats almost hid the white wreaths, and the mothball smell of their clothes covered the sweet sick smell of funeral flowers. Mrs.

Hulda Bauer in vast black dabbed a crocheted medallion at her eyes, but the other people, Jen knew, were hired funeral people who came with the rented coaches.

Morry Abbott, wandering past the cemetery, came in and saw the name done in red carnations on a white rose wreath "Jennia St. Clair." But he did not cry.

More people in black arrived with faces for funerals handed out to them at the gate, all Lamptown and all the Children's Home came, and their shoulders shook silently, rhythmically beside the grave, but Morry Abbott only looked on, smoking a cigarette, no more than half interested as he always was. Presently, although the singing was about to begin, he pulled his cap down over his eyes and went away.

"Come back, come back," Jen called to him faintly, but even in dreams she could not keep him from leaving, there was nothing she could do alive or dead to make him stay beside her. There was nothing you could do about Morry Abbott. So Jen threw away the graveyard scene and if he wouldn't care, then he wouldn't care.

But sitting on the stairs with him the next evening, Jen remembered her dream and that he wouldn't cry at her funeral, and was very snappish with him. She thought, resentfully, "Someday I'll make him have feelings, I will."

Old Mrs. Delaney was in. She came out and saw them sitting on the stoop, she stood in the doorway, bent and old and fierce, looking at them.

"You'd better get in here, young woman," she said. "Get your socks darned and your towels mended or you'll get what's coming to you."

"When I get ready," Jen answered serenely, and Morry, who was afraid to talk back to even Nettie, cringed. The old woman didn't mind Jen's back talk, she muttered something and went back in the house.

"I'm going to get out of this town," Morry said somberly. "A young fella hasn't got a chance except to go on the railroad or out selling like my dad, or go in the Works, and stick all his life. I'm thinking about doing things, getting somewhere."

"Working?"

"Sure, working. 'The hand that holds Aladdin's lamp must be the hand of toil'—that's Robert Green Ingersoll," said Morry. "He was a great man. I got the book."

"Going to do something in Lamptown?" Jen asked, worshiping.

"Not a chance. I'm going somewhere where there's something doing," bragged Morry. "This town's run by a bunch of micks from Shantyville."

"I guess they're better than rich loafers like Hunt Russell," Jen retorted. "The micks work, but what'd Hunt ever do for his money?"

"Hunt's all right," said Morry. "He's a gentleman and that's enough. He could be a barkeep or a fireman but he'd always be Mr. Russell. I'm going to be like that."

Jen dug her chin in her hands.

"Well, what about Aladdin's lamp and the hand of toil? Why don't he do something with his money? Why couldn't he get Lil out of the Home, he could without bothering. I hate him and people like him."

"Will you hush up, you young ones?" Mrs. Delaney's voice complained from inside. "People hear you for miles around with your big talk."

Jen stood up when the door banged shut again and held her finger to her lips.

"Let's go somewhere," she whispered.

They tiptoed down the stairs and then across the tracks to the dark factory road.

"His house cost about a million dollars, Bill said," Jen said. "It's got real marble for steps and it's got solid crystal doorknobs.

But *he* never earned it. Hunt Russell never really earned a nickel, and it's not fair."

Hunt Russell's house was no such palace, Morry knew, but he wouldn't have cared if it was. He wanted Hunt to have things and to be a king because in his own mind he, Morry Abbott, was Hunt. Now that he and Jen seemed to be on the way to the Lamptown showplace, Morry was as anxious for Jen's awed admiration as if the estate were his own. He took Jen's hand and they ran part of the way down the silent dark road.

By day Hunt's home was to the passerby a mile of high iron fence backed by a thick hedge and broken by an arched stone gateway through which one glimpsed a leafy winding drive. At the end of the drive was a huge old brick house spreading out in white-pillared porches and glass-roofed sun parlors. A flagstone terrace sloped into rosebushes and flowerbeds and overgrown grass. An iron deer lifted its antlered head in perpetual fright in the middle of the great shaded lawn, and near the driveway a pair of stone Cupids gazed into a cracked stone fountain bowl and saw that their noses were broken off.

By night the place was a dozen black acres of complete stillness for Hunt lived here now all alone with the caretaker's family. It was far beyond the factory houses, past block after block of empty lots, past an abandoned pickle works and the charred foundations of an old farm.

Jen and Morry clung to the iron fence and peered into the darkness.

"Gee, that's a big house," said Jen and then added indignantly, "Why it's bigger than the Home! He's got no business living there as if he was a king. He's got no right."

"Sh!" Morry squirmed uncomfortably at her resentment because if she belonged to Lamptown's laboring class, he, for his part, was with the aristocrats. He looked on luxury without envy but breathed deep with pride in it.

"You got to give Hunt credit for staying in Lamptown, at least," he argued. "He could have been a big bug in Chicago or New York if he wanted."

Jen, climbing up higher on the iron grilling, was not impressed.

"Well, why doesn't he go there, then," she wanted to know, "instead of hanging around this town aggravating people that have to work for their money. . . . Come on, I'm going on up to the house."

"No—he might see us," Morry protested, but Jen was over the fence and he had to follow. They crept up across the thick grass until they were right by the house. It was dark but for a light in the kitchen and another light in an upstairs room. Jen picked up a pebble and tossed it lightly against the house, and then she and Morry stood looking at each other, paralyzed, for the stone crashed right through one of the dark French windows.

"Gee!"

A light flashed on in the room and before they could move Hunt stepped quietly out of the window. He was in white flannels and Morry could never forget him standing on the porch looking at them, not saying a word, just tapping his pipe on the porch railing. Then—

"Well," he said looking from one to the other, "Are you just out breaking windows or are you up to some other damage, too?"

Morry's tongue would not move. Jen nudged him and then it angered her that anyone should have the power to frighten Morry—Morry, of all people.

"Aw, you can buy more windows," she answered defiantly.

Hunt lit a match and peered down at her.

"'You're not big enough to talk that way, young lady. I might take it in my head to spank you."

"Try and do it!" urged Jen. "I'm not sorry I smashed your window. Go buy stained glass next time, why don't you?"

Hunt whistled. Morry, who had been sick at Jen's outburst, now found himself angry at Hunt for lighting a match again to coolly examine Jen. His gray eyes traveled from her black hair to her checked gingham dress and then to her flashing blue eyes.

"Come on, Jen," Morry's voice came back, hard and cold. "We'll fix up the window, Hunt. It was just an accident."

"I don't know about that. I'm not so sure it was an accident," Hunt said slowly. "What were you doing here, anyway, you two?"

Morry was amazed to find words again in his mouth—smooth, convincing words.

"I was coming in to ask you about a job at the Works, and we—we were walking by and I thought I'd come in."

Hunt gave a short laugh.

"A business call, I see. Not social. I thought when the window crashed it was just a friend. . . . All right, Abbott, I believe you. Come down to the factory next week if you want a job—don't go around crashing my windows. And you—young lady—"

"Don't worry about me," Jen snapped, "I'd like to break every window of your rotten old house."

Again Morry was furious at Hunt's roar of laughter—it was laughter he wanted to carry Jen away from. He seized Jen's arm to leave but Jen twisted around to shake her fist at Hunt.

"I'll do it, too," she threatened and Hunt laughed again. He said something—it sounded like an invitation to call again, but Morry did not hear. They heard the sound of a woman's voice and when they looked back from the gateway they could see two figures in the lighted doorway, one of them a woman with red hair.

"You—you workin' for him!" stormed Jen, "I won't stand for it. You're worth ten of him, but you'll have to run errands for him. It's no fair, I tell you."

"It's the way things are," Morry said, "You don't need to start crying about it."

But Jen would cry anyway. They stood outside the big iron gate, Morry sullen and uncomfortable, while Jen cried against his unwilling arm.

"It's no fair, that's what I'm crying about," she insisted. "He lives there like a king—he owns the town, he owns you now, too. He's got everything, all we get is little bits he doesn't want. I'm glad we broke his old window, that's what I am."

Jen hung on to his arm, fuming, all the way home, but Morry wasn't conscious of her. He felt sick and afraid but a little excited, too. For now he had a job. His "future" had begun and it was no gay golden door swinging open, either, but a heavy iron factory door with a time clock beside it. For a second he was scared, wondering what came after that.

⁂

"Ten dollars a week—fancy!" Charles Abbott smiled charmingly at his son and pushed aside his plate as tactful reminder of the fabulous dinners to which he was accustomed elsewhere. "Next it will be twelve dollars and by the time you're fifty, my boy, you'll be earning sixteen or eighteen dollars a week. Elsinore, I congratulate you on your son."

"That's all right," said Elsinore absently.

When they did not snatch their meals at Bauer's Chop House, they ate in a corner of the workroom. A gas plate and sink were behind a curtain and usually it was Nettie who fixed the meal— canned beans, soup, and sandwiches, with one of Mrs. Bauer's pies for dessert. Then Nettie pulled out the ironing board and with this as a dining table the meal became a sort of family picnic. Eating together in this way was so intimate that Morry always had to fight against the tenderness he suddenly felt for his family, as if they were like some other family. He wanted to tell about his job, to tell everything that happened from eight in the morning till six at night, what the foreman said, what Hunt Russell said. . . . But you couldn't say these things before your father or Nettie, you had to act as if the whole business was of no consequence to you. If you talked to your mother she listened patiently but never lifted her eyes from her plate, or if she did, made some abstracted reply. It was very hard and Morry ate fast to get out the quicker. After all, when you stopped to think of it, it was sissy for a young man to be eating on an ironing board in a millinery shop.

"I'm surprised he can earn ten dollars," said Nettie. "I'm surprised he could get a job at all, Mr. Abbott, I really am."

Charles broke a sardine sandwich carefully and disdainfully so that, Morry thought, each sardine must apologize for not being an anchovy or a shrimp.

"Oh you're perfectly right, Nettie, Morry isn't the factory type. More of the artist, don't you think? . . . Ten dollars a week. See that you give eight of it to your mother, young man."

"I'm sure he'll give what he can, Charles, stop nagging him," Elsinore said impatiently. She did not see fit to remind Charles that eight dollars a week was more than she had ever had from him and that this solicitude for her, was as a matter of fact exquisitely ironic.

"He ought to give every cent and let Mrs. Abbott give him money when he asks," said Nettie.

Charles nodded approval of this suggestion and Nettie shot a complacent glance in Morry's direction.

"See here," said Charles, "since you're grown up enough to work why don't you take care of your mother—a great lummox like you sitting up there reading all winter while your poor mother has to go out to dances alone. You ought to be ashamed."

"Charles—I—" began Elsinore.

Charles waved her aside.

"It won't hurt him to take you to and from places when I'm away," he went on virtuously. "I don't like you coming home alone at midnight from the Casino dances."

"But—Mr. Abbott—just across the street!" Nettie was incredulous at such beautiful concern. Elsinore kept her eyes on her plate.

"All very well but my wife can't come three steps alone like some common woman. I won't have it. No sir. I never liked to see a woman alone at night. Morry, that won't hurt you, understand, you're to see your mother to and from these dances."

Morry suppressed a groan.

"I can't dance."

"It's time you learned," said Charles sternly. "Seventeen years old and not able to take a woman to a dance!"

"He might as well learn, I suppose," Elsinore said, weary of the wrangling. "He really ought to know how to dance."

The horror of exposing his deficiencies in grace made Morry choke with misery. It was enough getting up early every morning, trying to be as good as hundreds of inferior factory people, wasn't it, without letting himself be the joke of the factory girls and boys at Lamptown public dances. . . .

"Unless, of course, you'd rather go alone, dear," Charles added gently to his wife, his eyes on her face. "If you'd like to have your fun privately of course—"

"Morry will come with me, I'm sure," Elsinore answered evenly.

Morry, dejected, nodded his head.

"Oh, sure," he murmured.

Suddenly Nettie got up and flounced over to the sink, and banged her plate and cup into the dishpan.

"Why shouldn't I take lessons, then—I ought to learn dancing as much as Morry ought," she snapped. "But I suppose I'm to take care of your old shop while Mrs. Abbott and Morry are over at the Casino having a good time."

Elsinore looked up in amazement.

"I thought you liked the shop, Nettie."

"Oh, I like the shop all right," Nettie sulkily answered. "But Morry needn't act so smart with his ten dollars a week and dancing class. I'm sure I could go to Mr. Fischer myself and he'd be glad to give me special private lessons."

"No! That's too ridiculous, Nettie!" Elsinore's voice was harsh.

Something hot surged in her veins, a swift desire to slap Nettie's young impudent mouth for speaking a sacred name so lightly—the thought of Nettie smirking through a dancing lesson alone with Fischer angered her.

"Don't worry, I wouldn't go near the Casino," retorted Nettie. She washed her dishes under the faucet, rattling them against each other. "I don't go out with those factory girls, thank you."

The consciousness of having earned two weeks' salary emboldened Morry.

"What about the factory girls? What's so different about them?" he challenged. "They're as good as you are."

Nettie stared at him with horrified eyes.

"Oh you would say that, Morry Abbott—you would! You'd even go out with them, I suppose—that's just your level. Delaney's back room and factory girls!"

Morry's courage, under his father's contemptuous amusement, faded. He choked down the last of a sandwich and made a dive for the door.

"Don't forget you're taking your mother out next Thursday night," called out his father commandingly, as he slid out.

"I think he's just too terrible, Mrs. Abbott!" declared Nettie. "He's getting coarse, that's what he is."

She helped Elsinore fold up the ironing board while Charles, leaning against the sink, lit a cigarette.

"What do you think of having him as a bodyguard from now on, Else?" he asked, tossing the lighted match into the sink. He did not dare look at her.

"A good idea, Charles," said Elsinore gravely. "Very good, I think."

❧

"Morry's going to be a swell dancer, you know," said Grace Terris, beaming at Morry through her glasses. "Mr. Fischer said he had rhythm. This young man has rhythm, he said the other night."

Jen and Mrs. Bauer both looked at Morry critically to see if this odd quality showed, but apparently it only came out on Thursday nights for he looked just as he always looked. Mrs. Bauer resumed her crocheting and Grace and Jen went on polishing silver.

Jen did not really have to help in the Bauers' kitchen, nor for that matter did Morry have to lounge there late at night this way, but Mrs. Bauer liked to have Jen around and somehow Morry drifted in there too, particularly now that the cold weather made Delaney's stairs unappealing.

"I don't care for a dancing man," pronounced Mrs. Bauer. She twisted her chair to get a view through the dining room of Hermann at the cash register. "Dancing men don't make good husbands."

Grace giggled and looked coyly at Morry. Jen laid down a knife and cleaning rag and stared at her indignantly, then at Morry. Morry was smoking calmly. He didn't even know when someone was flirting with him, Jen thought with disgust.

"Hermann is such a good husband," went on Mrs. Bauer. "I've never had a care. When we were first married it was the same. What, doing the supper dishes when you're so tired, he'd say! No, no, Hulda, he'd say, I won't have you worn out like that. You wait and do them in the morning, he'd say."

Morry yawned. Jen and Grace scoured knives silently and diligently. Grace stole a beguiling glance now and then at Morry, and Jen, puzzled, stared from one to the other.

"I'll never forget one day he called me stupid," Hulda's fat moonface became ruddy with sentiment, her fingers dawdled with the crochet hook, "I was hurt—you know how a young bride is—and then lo and behold! That afternoon a wagon came to the door with a present from Hermann to make it up to me. Two bushels of the finest peaches you ever laid your eyes on. As big as your head, Jen."

"But what could you do with two bushels of peaches?" Jen inquired.

"Can them, dear. Hermann always loved preserved peaches. I put cloves in them and English walnuts. I was up till long after midnight putting them up." Mrs. Bauer smiled wistfully at the glimpse through the doorway of Hermann's bald head. "He was a good husband. Always. If he had to go away on a trip he always said, 'Enjoy yourself, Hulda. Let things go. You can do them all when I get back.' That's your good husband, let me tell you, girls."

"I'm not going to marry anyone in the restaurant business," said Grace. "Believe me."

"I guess you'll marry a railroad man," prophesied Jen. "They're always around."

"Don't pick a dancing man, girls, they're no good," warned Mrs. Bauer. "You never find them in a nice business of their own later on in life."

"I don't see why all a man's for is to be a good husband," Morry objected, "Is that all he's made for?"

"Yes," answered Mrs. Bauer placidly, "that's all."

"Morry dances too well, then," Grace giggled. Not even Cleopatra could have had Grace's complacent assurance of mastery over men. Jen glared at her jealously, and Morry squirmed, uncertain of the cause of the curious tension. "You know the class gets to stay over to the regular dance next week, Morry. Won't it be exciting?"

Morry thought of all the older girls sitting in a row waiting to be asked to dance, and he thought of his own inability to control their motions or to synchronize his own with theirs. He mumbled an evasive agreement with Grace's enthusiasm.

"You and I will have to stick to each other," laughed Grace.

At this point Jen got abruptly to her feet. She wasn't going to be left out of things—she'd get out of her own accord.

"Where you goin', Jen?" Mrs. Bauer demanded in surprise. "I thought you was going to help Grace finish."

"Oh, let her boyfriend help her," Jen retorted haughtily. "I'm going home."

Morry was embarrassed and reached for his cap.

"You're not going home now, are you Morry?" Grace's pale blue eyes conveyed a coquettish challenge but Morry didn't want to understand it. He couldn't help thinking of Grace's thin white thighs as she lay on the table being fitted for a corset by Mrs. Pepper. He grew red at the mere memory.

"Gotta get up early," he explained and started to follow Jen out.

"See you Thursday night at the dance," Grace called.

"Sure," said Morry and reached the door just as Jen let it bang good and hard in his face. Grace laughed shrilly as Morry pulled the door open again.

"A temper, that Jen," said Mrs. Bauer, and counted four stitches under her breath.

⁂

"One, two, three, FOUR, one, two, three, FOUR, one, two, three, FOUR," chanted Mr. Fischer, walking backwards, and the line of thirty wooden figures advanced toward him, one, two, three, steps, then kicked out a stiff left foot on the fourth count.

"Right foot first, one, two, three—hold it please. Miss Barry is out of step. One, two, three—now, ladies and gentlemen, we'll try it with music. Mr. Sanderson, please."

> Will someone kindly tell me
> Will someone answer why

To me it is a riddle
And will be till I die—

In a long even row they followed Mr. Fischer across the floor.

"Dance with the lady on your left!" roared Mr. Fischer.

Stiff country boys placed arms around factory girls' hard little bodies, damp hand clutched damp hand, iron foot matched iron foot, and each dancer kept count under his breath. Mr. Fischer clapped his hands and the music stopped.

"The class is getting on magnificently," he said, "I'm sure you will have no trouble at the regular dance tonight. All you need is confidence. I want each and every one of you to dance every dance on the program. Now we'll try it again. Mr. Sanderson, please."

So Mr. Sanderson's thick hands came down on the keys again and young men danced with the ladies on their left. Morry placed a rigid arm around Grace with a one two three kick, and a one two three kick. He thought if he could lose Grace somewhere he might learn but if you danced you had to have a partner as a lawful handicap. No matter how beautifully you waltzed, you'd never have a chance to waltz alone because it wasn't done.

Grace paid no attention to the commands. She tipped her head to one side and smiled perpetually. When she lost count she said, "Oh, I'm just terrible." Then Mr. Fischer would correct her posture.

"Not quite so close, Miss Terris—the arm should not go all the way round the young man's neck."

Solemnly then the fifteen couples stepped around the room behind Fischer, and since they were afraid to lose step by turning around on the corners, the dance became nothing more than a march with odd little jerks on the fourth count.

"Fine!" said Mr. Fischer and clapped his hands twice. "The class for this evening is now over. You will please remain for the regular Ball."

And then the rope at the door was let down and the line of people waiting outside were allowed to present their tickets and enter. The drummer arrived and experimented with his instrument, gravely aided by Mr. Sanderson. Crowds of giggling girls, with chiffon scarfs over their curled hair, hurried from the door to the dressing room, and their vivid perfumes mixed intoxicatingly in the air. Mr. Fischer stood by the ticket man at the door, shaking hands with this or that one, greeting everyone with formal politeness, while his black eyes shot appraisingly from time to time toward the cashbox. Then he tweaked the ends of his white bow tie and whirled around toward the dance floor.

"Dance Number One!" he shouted above the excited chattering. "Dance Number One!"

The music began again and men slid from the doorway to the women's dressing room across the floor to select their partners as they emerged. Morry Abbott stood beside the solitary palm tree, first on one foot and then the other. His breath came fast and he had to struggle with a feeling that he, too, could sway and whirl with marvelous ease. This assured feeling must be checked, he thought, before he impulsively invited someone to dance and then woke to his inadequacy with a load of responsibility in his arms. So he went into the smoking room and sat down by one of the brakemen he'd seen in Bill Delaney's often. The young man, dressed up in a much too blue suit and a green tie, was looking through a magazine of photographs. On the paper cover was painted a cream-white blonde in a very decollete spangled silver dress. The man rapped the picture with his pipe and looked up at Morry.

"There she is," he said proudly. "That's her. Lillian Russell. A looker, eh?"

Morry squinted at it judicially.

"All right," he granted. But she was beautiful as no woman could ever be, at least, he thought, no woman in Lamptown. Underneath was printed, "America's Most Beautiful Actress."

"You bet she's all right," insisted his friend. "I'd marry her like a shot, I would."

He picked up the magazine and stuffed it into his pocket.

"Like to cut these out to paste up in my room," he explained, as he started out. "So long."

Through the door Morry could see Grace dancing with one of the engineers who ate at Bauer's, and he was amazed that she seemed no different in action than the other girls on the floor. He had rather expected everyone to stop dancing and point the finger of shame at her. Since they didn't seem to notice her errors, he felt encouraged to go out on the floor again, and when the music stopped he boldly asked Grace for the next.

"Isn't it swell, Morry?" gurgled Grace. "I'm having a lot of fun, aren't you?"

Now that the dance had started it was all easy, easier than the lesson, for in this crowd your feet were not observed. Then in his arms Grace changed curiously. She was not the Bauers' waitress at all, a thin blonde with glasses, but a stranger, a stranger who belonged mysteriously to dancehalls and to music and perfume.

"Like Lillian Russell," Morry thought and if he just kept looking at Grace's curious blue eyes it almost seemed that she had on a silver dress. When the dance was over Grace kept her hand on his arm, but Morry thought, "I wouldn't dare ask her for another dance just yet."

He went back to the smoking room to wait the proper length of time for he did not dare ask any other girl. The boys his age who hung around Bill Delaney's saloon did not dance, they stood in a little group outside the hall door smoking and sometimes jeering at friends inside. Before this night Morry thought he would have died at their ragging, but when they called teasingly to him two or three times he was not afraid to answer back with certain pride. After all he was the one on the inside.

Elsinore was there. Morry caught a glimpse of her slender black-gowned figure without knowing who she was for a few seconds, and then he wondered at the flare of pride he had in her. He tried to puzzle out just why she stood out among the others. Was it because the factory girls were all powdered and painted and wore loud colors, was it because she was his mother, or was it that she looked startlingly out of place without a background of hats and trimmings? She looked over her partner's shoulder from across the room and smiled faintly at her son. Suddenly Morry wanted to do something wonderful for his mother, something to make her glad of him; but what could one do?

"It's almost over, Morry," Grace said, standing beside him. "We ought not to miss this one."

Morry obediently started dancing with her. She pressed against him with a sigh.

"You seem a lot older somehow than some of the railroad fellas," she said. "I don't know why, but you do. More like somebody that's been around, know what I mean?"

Morry wished she wouldn't talk. It made him lose count and it made the picture of the woman in the silver dress fade further away. Couples were dancing very close and very quietly now. Grace kept her head demurely on his shoulder. He wasn't quite sure what was expected of him but knew something was.

"Do you want to stay for the other dance?" he found himself asking her. "It's the Home Waltz."

Grace looked at him thoughtfully.

"We could go now," she said. "If we go down the backstairs no one will notice us. My room is right at the back—just above the kitchen."

They danced around again. Morry's head was swimming. He saw his mother, he saw Hunt with Dode and Mr. Fischer, and he wondered if they knew about this spinning in the head, a sort of premonition of disaster, yet you couldn't exactly call it disaster.

"You go first—I'll follow," he whispered, and Grace dropped out of his arms with a sweet smile. Presently he saw her, with her wrap over her arm, going out and he got his hat and followed, after a few minutes. He went along the dirty outside hallway to the back where a staircase went down to the Bauers' rooms on the second floor. Morry fumbled his way down the pitch-dark stairs. On the second floor there was another dark old hallway with a gas jet dimly flickering in the far end. No one was in sight, but Morry's heart stopped at the creaking of the old floor beneath his feet. He passed dark doors with tin numbers tacked on—"27"—"29"—"31"—and the sweat came out on his forehead wondering what would happen if one of these doors should suddenly open. It wasn't likely though, for a lodger didn't come to Bauer's more than four or five times a year. . . .

At the end of the hall water leaked slowly from the ceiling above and made a dirty puddle beneath the gas jet. Morry wanted to drop the whole business and run. He thought with a shock of horror that he was to have taken his mother home, that indeed had been the sole purpose of his dancing lessons. . . . It was too late now—or was it? . . . Then he saw Grace motioning to him from the farthest doorway. She held her finger to her lips warningly. Oh, yes, it was too late now. . . .

Morry, with sinking heart, tiptoed toward her. She reached out a thin bare arm and pulled him coquettishly in, and the door swung swiftly shut behind him.

❧

Old Mrs. Delaney stood inside the Bon Ton's workroom door. She had on her black bonnet and black mitts and a market basket on her arm. It was barely breakfast time, and Nettie had only a moment before unlocked the shop door. Elsinore was washing the coffee cups at the sink.

"What is it?" she wanted to know in some surprise.

"I want to tell you this much, Mrs. Abbott," said the old woman. "It's got to stop or I speak to your husband. That's all I came to say."

Nettie sat down quickly to her sewing so that she would have an excuse to hear all. Elsinore stood looking at her caller, puzzled and alarmed.

"But what is it? What are you talking about? Is it about Morry?"

"Who else would it be about?" snapped the old woman. "It's about that boy of yours all right. Things have got to stop, that's what I'm telling you."

Nettie tried to keep on sewing casually but she had to look up every now and then, first to the old woman and then to the hall doorway, because she had heard Morry's footsteps outside. He was out there now listening, she thought, listening and afraid to pass the door lest he be called in.

"But Morry's a good boy," Elsinore protested. "I can't see what he's done to worry you, Mrs. Delaney."

"He's going on eighteen, ain't he?" retorted Mrs. Delaney. "Old enough to be getting girls in trouble. I speak out that way, Mrs. Abbott, because an adopted girl's a big responsibility. I'm telling you he's got to stay away from my Jen."

Nettie sewed furiously and kept an eye furtively on Elsinore. But Elsinore just stood there looking quietly at the old woman. Mrs. Delaney sat down on one of the work stools.

"I don't mean to worry you, Mrs. Abbott—I don't mean you're not a lady," she muttered in a gruff attempt at apology. "Only when you've taken a girl from the Home and she's got old ideas and an older boy keeps hanging around her—well, she's got bad blood in her, that Jen. . . . You can't trust bad blood, you know."

"Morry has never cared about girls," Elsinore said. "He'd never dream of bothering your Jen."

Mrs. Delaney's gnarled fingers tightened over the market basket.

"I'm telling you he does, Mrs. Abbott," she said somberly. "He carries on with the Bauers' waitress—Hulda Bauer told me that. And don't I hear him and Jen out on the steps night after night whispering and talking? Don't I hear her out there cryin' and snifflin' when he don't show up? That's what I'm telling you."

"Oh! Oh!" came from Nettie Farrell's mouth, and Elsinore looked at her, rather surprised.

"That's bad when girls cry over someone," Nettie said hurriedly. "I'm sure Morry isn't as good as you think because you're his mother and you don't see anything. Things right under your nose, too. But he's always going over to that saloon—I could tell you that much—and when you ask men in there about him they say they haven't seen him. He goes upstairs to see that girl, that's all."

"That's right," confirmed Mrs. Delaney.

"But what harm is there in it?" Elsinore argued gently. "A child like that—barely fourteen—"

"Pooh!" sniffed Nettie. "That kind learn young."

"She's got old ideas," insisted Mrs. Delaney. "Old ideas and wild blood in her and outside of that I trust no young girl. They're all alike, crazy to get into trouble, always stuck on the boys. I've had 'em go wrong with me before and I won't have it this time."

"But Morry's so safe," Elsinore said incredulously.

"I don't trust him neither," the old woman flashed back. "What's his father, I ask? A hard drinker and a fast man. I don't mind coming out with truths once in a while when it's necessary. That boy's old enough to know what he's about and you've got to keep him away from my Jen. Hear me?"

Elsinore could only nod weakly. Mrs. Delaney got up, panting a little. She drew her black shawl over her humped old back, jerked her bonnet down over her ears.

"I said I'd come and I did," she grumbled. "I said I'd put a stop to it and I did. I won't have any more girls in my house going wrong. Won't have it."

She went out the door banging it angrily behind her. Nettie held her needle transfixed in the air and her mouth wide open. Elsinore stood still and thoughtful for a moment, then sat down and picked up a ribbon she was to shir. Suddenly Nettie threw her sewing down and her shears.

"That boy!" she exclaimed. "You can see it's all true—he's running after that girl just because she's wild and now he's working in the factory and dancing he thinks he can do whatever he pleases. What are you going to say to him, Mrs. Abbott? Or will you tell his father?"

"Oh no, I wouldn't ever tell Charles," Elsinore murmured. "And after all, Nettie, Mrs. Delaney's so old she gets funny ideas. Morry isn't a bad boy at all."

"But he's grown up, nearly, and you can't tell what he'd do if girls started getting after him," Nettie rushed on. "He thinks he's so smart, not paying attention to them. He just acts that way to show off. Then he goes and picks some little foundling over a saloon! He would!"

Elsinore went to the drawer for a cluster of satin ribbons. There was a creaking of boards in the hall outside. Nettie jerked her head significantly.

"I knew he was out there!" she whispered. "He heard every word! He was afraid to let on he was out there."

The cloud on Elsinore's horizon lifted with dazzling speed.

"He really heard, do you think?"

Nettie nodded impatiently.

"Of course he did. Shall I go call him in for you to talk to?"

"Not now, Nettie," Elsinore said and Nettie's face fell.

Her full red lips pursed into a sullen line. Mrs. Abbott was afraid to talk about things to Morry, it was silly how shy she was with her own son that way. She'd rather let him run wild than speak up to him. It angered Nettie. She got up and walked determinedly to the hall door. She opened it swiftly and was in time to see Morry sliding out on tiptoe, his dark face burning red. Nettie whirled back.

"He did hear! He stood there listening!" she was triumphant. "Serve him right, too. And now's the time for the whistle to blow and he's late to work besides. Oh, you must talk to him, Mrs. Abbott."

"If he heard us, then he knows all there is for me to say," Elsinore said tranquilly. "I needn't go into it any further."

She never even looked up to say this. Nettie stabbed her needle into her straw braid and muttered something quite savage under her breath.

※

Lamptown hummed from dawn to dusk with that mysterious humming of the Works, the monotonous switching of engines and coupling of cars at the Yard. The freight cars rumbled back and forth across the heart of town. They slid out past the factory windows and brakemen swinging lanterns on top the cars would shout to whatever girls they saw working at the windows. Later, in the factory washroom one girl might whisper to another, "Kelly's in the Yard today. Said be sure and be at Fischer's Thursday night."

"Who was firing?" the other would ask, mindful of a beau of her own.

"Fritz was in the cab but I couldn't see who was firing. Looked like that Swede of Ella's used to be on Number 10."

The humming of this town was jagged from time to time by the shriek of an engine whistle or the bellow of a factory siren or the clang-clang of a red street car on its way from one village to the next. The car jangled through the town flapping doors open

and shut, admitting and discharging old ladies on their way to a
D.A.R. picnic in Norwalk, section workers or linesmen in overalls, giggling girls on their way to the Street Carnival in Chicago
Junction. As if hunting for something very important the car rattled past the long row of Lamptown's factory boarding houses,
past the Lots, then on into long stretches of low, level hay fields
where farm girls pitched hay, stopping to wave their huge straw
hats at the gay world passing by in a street car.

There was gray train smoke over the town most days, it
smelled of travel, of transcontinental trains about to flash by, of
important things about to happen. The train smell sounded the
"A" for Lamptown and then a treble chord of frying hamburger
and onions and boiling coffee was struck by Hermann Bauer's
kitchen, with a sostenuto of stale beer from Delaney's back door.
These were all busy smells and seemed a six to six smell, a working town's smell, to be exchanged at the last factory whistle for the
festival night odors of popcorn, Spearmint chewing gum, barber-
shop pomades, and the faint smell of far-off damp cloverfields.
Mornings the cloverfields retreated when the first Columbus local
roared through the town. Bauer's coffee pot boiled over again,
and the factory's night watchmen filed into Delaney's for their
morning beer.

It was always the last minute when Morry left his house for
work and on this morning he had been trapped into eavesdrop-
ping on Mrs. Delaney and his mother. If he only could have gotten out of the house before she said those dreadful things. He
slipped out of the alleyway, his hands jammed into his pockets, his
cap slouched over his eyes, and he burned with shame thinking of
what the old lady had said to his mother. He'd never look at Jen
again without remembering—never! Of course it wasn't Jen's
fault but he was angry with her, too. She was the one who called
him to come over, wasn't she? He only went because the kid was
lonesome, never saw anybody else hardly, didn't seem to make

friends in school. Now he was afraid of her. Next time she called he wouldn't hear her.

Along Market Street the shopkeepers were out lowering their awnings, shouting their morning greetings across the street to each other, or peering from behind their show windows at rival window displays. Old Tom, Lamptown's street cleaner, sat on the curbstone in front of the saloon in dirty white painter's overalls, broom in hand, and held a sort of welcoming reception for all passersby.

"Morning, Mr. Robinson. Morning, Miss Burnet. Howdy, Morry, how's your old lady? Late today, ain't you? I just see the last of the girls going in."

Morry crossed the street before he remembered Grace, and there she was in the Bauers' window smiling at him significantly. Morry jerked his head into a sort of nod of greeting and went on. He was ashamed of his winter's affair with Grace. In the saloon the trainmen talked about her. "God's gift to the Big Four," they called her. Morry hated her. She always acted as if he was hers, always beaming at him when he went by and lifting her eyebrows so knowingly. He was eighteen now. He wasn't going to work in the factory all his life, was he, and run with waitresses. . . . Maybe he'd better get a job on the train. You saw cities that way and in the right one you could drop off and start doing things. But do what? Something, this much he knew, that would make his mother very proud of him, because now he felt overwhelmingly grateful to her. He knew she wouldn't say a word to him about Mrs. Delaney's visit and about Jen—as far back as he could remember she had never said anything to reproach him. She could easily have called him after the old woman left and scolded him, but how could they ever have looked at each other saying such intimate things? . . .

He knew. He'd get out of this town, that's what he'd do. He'd study—but what did you study? Fellows went to college but that cost money and nobody in Lamptown went to college, except a guy now and then who went to Case Engineering School in Cleveland. Fellows in Lamptown went into the Works or into their fathers' stores or on the railroad. If they got on the railroad, they stuck there. It was like the Navy, they said, you had a hard time working into a regular job after you got out. . . . All right then, he'd stick to the factory. He'd work until he owned the Factory, that's what he'd do. He'd work—hell, he hated to work. He hated plugging away at lamps and accessories. He wasn't adept like the girls and he felt perpetually ill at ease around them. They worked faster than he did and made more money, and they kidded him.

Morry could remember when he was only six he was so overgrown that the little girls were afraid of him. "He's so big!" they sobbed into the teacher's lap. "We don't want him to play in our games." Now even when the girls in the packing room smiled invitingly to him, he was sure they were making fun of him; he didn't know where to hide when they whispered, "Morry Abbott's a swell-looker now, ain't he? Look at them shoulders!"

He would always feel like the unwanted stranger with these factory girls. He wasn't like them—he wasn't like the fellows in the saloon, either. He'd be a big somebody someday, a big gun—but Morry didn't see himself grubbing away, getting there a little at a time. He saw himself already arrived, a Hunt Russell, a somebody who got there without plugging. Got where, though? . . . Morry saw himself on the decks of great liners, sitting on balconies in tropical cities, always at ease, always secure from Netties and fathers and Graces. He was the master of this fabulous orange grove, he was the manager of this beautiful actress, he was the owner of this estate on the Hudson, stocked with books, thousands of them, and pictures, and liquor, too, French wines and things that weren't so hard to drink as Delaney's Scotch. He'd— but here he was at the factory, twenty minutes late to punch the time clock.

"Docked again," jeered the office boy in a jubilant whisper. Morry sidled through Door 6 to his table in the packing room. His foreman came toward him scowling.

"With men out of work all over this country," he began sternly, "it seems a damn shame, Abbott, that a fellow with the luck to have a job can't get to it on time. Now, I'll tell you what's coming to you if this keeps up. . . ."

⁂

But really Lamptown was no place for a boy, Mrs. Pepper said.

Take Mansfield or Norwalk or Elyria—pretty little towns they were, every one of them, with nice homes on pleasant boulevards and lovely girls for a young man to marry. But Lamptown! All railroad tracks and factory warehouses and for a park nothing but the factory woods or the acres of Lots which were nothing but clover fields with big signs every few yards—

LOTS $40 an acre and up
See HUNT RUSSELL—

Rows of gray frame factory boarding houses on dusty roads in the east and to the west the narrow noisy Market Street—choose your home between these two sections.

"Really, Mrs. Abbott, actually you know," gravely said Mrs. Pepper, "it's not the place at all for a young man. Don't you know anyone in Columbus or Cleveland who would board him there—someplace where he would have opportunities?"

"If Morry went to the city he'd get a swelled head and never be anything," declared Nettie crossly. "I don't see what's the matter with Lamptown, if he's any good he can get on here. The trouble with Morry is he thinks he's too good for everybody here. He's too good for the girls, he stays upstairs and reads novels instead of acting like a regular fellow."

"I'd hate to have him go away," Elsinore murmured. "I wouldn't know what to do without Morry."

Nettie looked to Mrs. Pepper for sympathy.

"As if he ever talked to anyone or as if he was any company to you," she said sarcastically. "Why, Mrs. Abbott, you know you hardly ever talk to each other."

Elsinore put her hand to her forehead and smoothed it thoughtfully.

"I know, but you see that's just it. We don't need to talk to each other. We never have needed to talk to each other."

Mrs. Pepper tried to assume an understanding expression.

"I know," she sighed. "Indeed I know."

She went to the mirror and daintily replaced a straying lock of hair behind her ear. Nettie watched her with critical eyes.

"Pretty dress," she said.

Mrs. Pepper was pleased.

"I got it in Akron," she explained. She patted her hips and turned around to view the skin-tight perfection of the back. "Cute, isn't it?"

Nettie examined it and urged Elsinore to admire its lines. It was a tight silk dress bursting into irrepressible ruffles at the hem and at the wrist, and yoked with tiny lace ruffling deep on her bosom so that a garnet sunburst was coquettishly lost there. A circlet of tiny pearls followed a seductive line around her fat creamy throat and was matched by a pearl and opal ring on her fat little finger.

"I wonder," mused Mrs. Pepper leaning further toward the mirror, twisting her head a little to one side, "if perhaps my neck is a little too plump for pearls."

Over her pearls and the sunburst her dove-like little hands hovered ceaselessly. She sat down again and the wide silk bows on her tiny kid slippers flopped down like the ears of a sleepy dachshund. Sometimes when she was crossing the freight Yard a young fireman would stick his head out of the cab and yell, "Hello Fatty!" This would make Mrs. Pepper tighten her little red mouth to keep from smiling for after all there was something flatteringly endearing in the term "Fatty." But when she kept her lips so sternly from smiling three dimples popped out in her cheeks and the next bold fireman was likely to call out, "Hi there, Dimples." So Mrs. Pepper, after many such experiences had decided that men were always teases and there was no use being cross with them.

"Lamptown does make the young men rough, you know that," Mrs. Pepper pursued, now doing her nails carefully while Nettie stood in the doorway looking up and down Market Street for possible customers. "If you traveled from town to town the way I do you'd know. People say this is the toughest town on the Big Four."

"It doesn't have as many bad houses as other towns," Nettie said without turning around.

"Well, you see, there are all those factory girls," delicately innuendoed Mrs. Pepper with a blush. "Not that some of them aren't lovely girls, understand, and they do take the best care of their figures. Only last week I took orders from the girls for upwards of sixty dollars worth of corsets."

"This shop couldn't do without the girls," Elsinore reminded her. "We've got no kick, Mrs. Pepper, you and I."

"I know—I'm saying the girls give me my living," Mrs. Pepper hurried to explain, "but I only mean it's not a good town for a boy. I don't see how you ever raised him to be so decent in such a rough place."

"I did my best," said Elsinore and then she thought of Morry.

She thought of Morry consciously so seldom that she came to the subject with almost a shock. Morry—grown up! Morry—old enough to go away just as she'd gotten used to having a baby around the shop. Because even as a baby he'd been a stranger—oh yes, part of her in some curious way that made his presence always welcome, but nonetheless he was a stranger. She wondered if other mothers were perpetually astonished at their maternity and secretly a little skeptical of the miracle, more willing to believe in the cabbage patch or stork legend than in their own biological responsibility. She had moved over for Morry as you would move over for someone on a street car, certain that the intimacy is only for a few minutes, but now it was eighteen years and she thought why, Morry was hers, hers more than anything in the world was.

"Don't I know you did your best with that child?" exclaimed Mrs. Pepper. "She had a lonely time of it too, Nettie, let me tell you—Mrs. Abbott had no easy time."

Elsinore stared at Mrs. Pepper's shoe ribbon flapping on the floor, and for a second she ached for that lost baby with startling pain. The young man Morry they spoke of was hers only because he too could remember the baby. Upstairs in the front bedroom he had been born—with Charles away of course. Charles only came home twice a year then, but Elsinore never complained. Husbands were like that, and Morry and his mother understood.

Whenever Charles did come home Elsinore and the baby moved into the little room, now Morry's, because crying inspired Charles to frenzies of temper. Elsinore's calm protection of the baby annoyed Charles even more than the crying. Both Morry and his mother were relieved when Charles picked up his sample cases and went away. Once Morry, aged two, had gotten into the sample cases and found them full of candies. Usually just before he came home a printed business postcard arrived with the red-lettered tidings—

"The Candy Man will visit you on—"

Then the date was written in by Charles and after digesting this warning Elsinore let the baby have the postcard with its cartooned Candy Man. Charles beat the child after that invasion of his wares so that ever afterward the arrival of the Candy Man's card sent Morry under the bed or downstairs hiding in one of the hat drawers. Indeed Elsinore suspected that it was the beginning of his learning to read.

Elsinore, thinking of all this now, forgot to sew and the black ribbon in her lap that was to be a turban, unrolled on the floor.

"Do you remember when I used to keep Morry in his baby carriage all day in front of the shop?" she asked Mrs. Pepper.

Mrs. Pepper sighed.

"Oh dear yes. . . . He was such a big baby and you were so small to be taking care of him. . . . I only had one model to sell then, the Diana Girdle. Gracious, what a long time ago. Let's see—he was three or four when I started working . . . hm. . . . I was twenty. Just twenty. Imagine that."

"Think of it, you and Mrs. Abbott were making your own living then just the way I am now," Nettie said, coming back to the counter and leaning her elbows on it, "and you didn't think anything much of it, but all the same Mrs. Abbott thinks it would be too bad for Morry to get out on his own. And he's eighteen. Older than his mother was when she started this shop."

"I need a man here with me," Elsinore said, irritated. "There's no use your talking about it, Nettie, I need Morry. You don't understand these things at all."

"Some factory girl will marry him and that'll be the end of him," grumbled Nettie.

Mrs. Pepper, as always, strove to soothe everyone by switching their interest.

"There are so many of the girls, you can't blame them for going after the younger men," she said. "Nine hundred girls, all young and lively there at the Works with no men's factory around to give them beaux. Why Mr. Fischer tells me half the time they have to dance with each other at the Casino because there aren't enough men."

"There's never enough men. . . . A girl's got no chance in this town," Nettie complained. "There's twenty-five of us for every man. Every time a new man comes to town it's like dividing a mouse up for a hundred cats. If I was a boy in this town I'd almost be afraid to grow up, I would."

"No chance for a girl to marry," Elsinore said, as if marrying were still to her mind the ideal state for any woman.

"Sometimes the girls go away and marry," Mrs. Pepper said brightly. "Dode O'Connell told me they write their addresses on the crates that are shipped out from the factory and they get answers back sometimes from all over the world. That little Tucker girl they say went all the way to Australia to marry a man she'd never seen. He'd gotten her address from the shipment and they started writing each other."

"Yes, they'd all go to Australia at that factory if they got the same chance," said Nettie gloomily. "Those girls do anything to get a man. They hang around the high school freshmen even. They're wild for men. I've seen 'em calling up to Morry's window sometimes after he's gone upstairs, telling him to come out and take a walk."

Elsinore was puzzled and startled too. This was so new to her, considering her son as a potential husband for someone.

"But he doesn't go out," she said.

Nettie laughed sardonically.

"Oh no, only if she's real pretty and then maybe he goes out. Or if he's on his way to go over and see that Delaney kid, that Jen."

Elsinore stared at Nettie.

"But he doesn't go over there any more, Nettie, I'm quite sure."

"They sit on the top stairs still plenty of times," Nettie blurted out indignantly. "That's what they do. And if he isn't with her then he's in the saloon or probably with some little tart from the factory. That's the way Morry Abbott is and that's the way he's always going to be."

"But you said a little while ago that he thought he was too good for the Lamptown girls," protested Elsinore.

"Too good for good girls!" Nettie flared up. "That's what I meant."

Her nose quite red Nettie whirled into the back room and for several minutes Elsinore and Mrs. Pepper heard her banging drawers shut and whistling shrilly to indicate how well under control was her temper.

"How funny Nettie acts about things," Elsinore commented.

She bent frowning over her work once more and the little chamber of her mind marked "Morry—Private Thoughts"— swung slowly shut again. Mrs. Pepper picked up her orange stick again and coaxed an elegant half-moon on her rosy thumbnail.

సా

Mrs. Pepper thought the crying doll was simply sweet, but Nettie detested it because ever since Charles Abbott had sent it, the factory girls were constantly running into the shop to listen to it.

"Wind it up for Ethel, now," they would beg, and Nettie, with a scowl of resignation would take the doll out of the show window, reach under its red satin ruffles and wind it up again. A thin little tinkle of doll music wailed faintly through the shop, while the girls listened in rapt silence.

"This is a hat shop, not a doll store," she complained to Elsinore.

"Charles says in the city the best hat shops always have a doll in the window," said Elsinore. "He wouldn't like it if he came home and didn't see it there. After all he sent it for that purpose."

"Well, you don't have to wind it, but I do," muttered Nettie, not really meaning her employer to hear her mutiny, but always unable to keep her annoyance to herself.

Elsinore was used to Charles sending strange presents. He sent seaweed picture frames from Florida, enormous bottles of perfume from New York, knowing she never cared for scents; once he sent her a pair of chameleons which alarmed her so that Mrs. Pepper with many delighted squeals took them away. He never sent her money or any practical thing. Usually if Charles fancied an article he bought three, one for the blonde girl in Chicago, one for Elsinore, and one for the last hotel telephone operator he had entertained. If Elsinore suspected this she never said so. She kept his gifts carefully wrapped up, as a rule, and wrote him polite little letters of thanks.

"The doll must have cost twenty dollars," declared Mrs. Pepper. "What a thoughtful husband, Mrs. Abbott. You are lucky! And letters almost every day Nettie says. Did he always write you every day?"

"Oh no," said Elsinore, "only lately."

Charles's letters . . .

I suppose you think I don't know what you're doing while I'm gone. You think because I'm away you can get away with anything you like. Else, old girl, you'd better get that out of your head. I know you too well, and I can tell when things aren't right. Answer me this—why did you get two new silk dresses last fall if it wasn't to show some man? What made you start in powdering your face when you never used to do more than brush it off with a chamois? Think that over, Else, and you'll realize your husband's not so dumb as you think. . . .

Then a few days later from another town . . .

Well, while I'm lying here in this rotten little hotel with the grippe, I suppose you're having your good time, going to your dances and dancing with this guy whoever he is! I guess you didn't notice me watching you when you dressed for the dance last time I was home. I pretended to be reading the paper but out of the corner of my eye I saw you put perfume on your hair, the way a chorus girl does when she's got a date. You did up your hair and looked at yourself in the mirror and then took it all down again and did it over. I said to you, why did you do that, and you said, oh it makes me look so old the other way.

Yes, I went to the Casino and I stood out in the smoking room watching you as I guess you knew because you were too smart for me and knew better than to give yourself away that night. If you've fallen for one of those train men you're a damn fool, Else, and I'll lick the man if I ever see him, I swear I will.

Elsinore wrote her usual brief letter in reply, ignoring all of Charles's suspicions, but this made him write even more insistently. Sometimes she opened a letter, came to an accusing paragraph, and tore up the letter, not angrily, but quite coolly, because what she read might stay in her mind, so she had to protect herself from all disturbing thoughts.

You said in your letter two weeks ago you were either going to Cleveland or Columbus for some velvets in a few days. Then yesterday in your letter you never said anything about the trip. It's easy to see that you made that trip all right and just don't want to tell about it. It wasn't on any millinery business either but to meet someone. I can just see you going to some hotel there thinking your husband is far away up in Minnesota and won't know what you're up to, but I got enough brains to read women and I can read between the lines, don't forget it.

If Elsinore herself could read between the lines she would have seen the erasure marks on the crying doll package when it arrived. She might have detected another woman's address written in pencil and then rubbed out and she would have concluded that the crying doll had been originally purchased for someone else, someone with a taste for such novelties. And then inexplicably Charles had decided that his wife should have it, instead. She might, too, have thought from his letters, "No one but a person who has been guilty himself could read guilt in others so well."

But Elsinore would not allow such thoughts to become important. If she permitted Charles's slowly developing jealousy to worry her, then it might creep in her mind when she was dreaming of really vital things, of Fischer, for instance. There had never been a moment that Charles existed in her imagination. Charles—well Charles *was*. He was not real. His letters—his jealousy—these things *were,* and things that *were* could not enter Elsinore's mind except it gave her pleasure. She wondered if Fischer himself were as real as her thoughts of him.

When she sat fashioning a hat silently, there was no room in her for fretting over an absent husband's suspicion; there was room only to listen to the mechanical rhythm of Mr. Sanderson's piano thumping, there was room only to see Fischer at the Casino, or in the Palace, in Marion, or Akron, or Cleveland, demonstrating a pirouette with his shining patent-leather feet. . . . She had no time to wonder over Charles's wanderings, for she was wondering what fresh-cheeked young girl was at this minute being selected as Fischer's partner. Did this fortunate one have blue eyes and yellow hair? Unconsciously Elsinore discarded the red ribbon for the hat under her hand and selected a blue strip more suitable to this blonde image. Did the new love have a baby face or did she have, in spite of her youth and fairness, a strong handsome nose like Nettie's with the same full lips . . . with this new image Elsinore tore the blue strip off of the frame and from the deep drawer beside her drew out a wider model, more becoming to long noses. With thoughtful eyes she tried the blue velvet strip across the front and underneath the brim.

Nettie watched this changing design, bewildered.

"Will you please tell me, Mrs. Abbott, why you threw away the poke for that big milan?"

Elsinore's reply left her assistant completely baffled.

"Because a girl with a nose like that shouldn't wear a poke. You know that well enough, Nettie."

"Like what? What are you talking about?" asked Nettie, still staring, and Elsinore, conscious of Nettie's scrutiny, turned her head away ever so slightly, as if Nettie might read there a whole catalogue of hat designs for Fischer's probable women.

"I was thinking of something else, Nettie," she said. "I was thinking that next week we must make an entire new outfit for the crying doll—something in rose-colored velvet, I think. . . . And remind me to write Charles and thank him."

She wished Nettie wouldn't ask things—she wished people wouldn't always intrude.

☙

Charles came home late in the summer. He was thinner and without a new line in his face or a single new gray hair he managed to seem ten years older. He walked into the Bon Ton one Saturday afternoon with no greeting but a "Pretty as ever I see, Nettie" for Nettie, an ironic "Well, Mrs. Abbott" for Elsinore and then seeing Morry in the workroom eating a sandwich he scowled.

"Still hanging around your mother's skirts, I see."

Morry never answered. If he lived to be eighty his father's mockery would still make him curl up with hopeless shame and mortification. A mere glance from his father would always be enough to remind him that he was a huge clumsy fellow—with no

more business in a house, least of all a woman's millinery store—
than some prize steer. He was taller than his father by at least six
inches, but this could only give him a feeling of inferiority. With
his father home there was less than ever a place for him here.
While Charles took his bags upstairs, Morry quietly dove out the
back alley. Where would he go? He didn't think Delaney's was
safe because it was a hangout of his father's. Bauer's Chop House
had been out of the question for some time, because Morry shuddered at the mere sight of Grace now. She was apt to say whenever
she saw him, "When am I going to see you again, Morry? What's
the matter—are you afraid of me?"

Morry stood out in the alleyway, lighting a cigarette, looking
up and down the street. He wondered if old Mrs. Delaney was
in—if it was safe to run up Jen's stairs. But he didn't really want
to see Jen. He was vaguely annoyed with her now. The kid was
always tagging after him and the old woman glared at him like
some old witch every time he had the bad luck to run into her.
The only thing—and this Morry would scarcely admit even to
himself—was that nobody believed so firmly in Morry's importance as Jen did. She thought he was somebody. Away from her
he remembered the old lady's warning, Nettie's taunts, and the
factory girls' kidding. But with Jen he fell under the sweet spell
of her worship, her reverent, adoring eyes, her perfect conviction
that he was incredibly superior to anyone in the world. While
Morry stood in the alley weighing these matters he heard Nettie's
voice inside answering some inquiry of his father's.

"No, he's gone out, Mr. Abbott. He's probably up on the
Delaney's backstairs with that girl of theirs. He always is there."

This decided him. He threw away his cigarette quickly and
hurried through the courtyard to the saloon back door.

"Kid Abbott!" roared Hogan as Morry sauntered up to the
bar. "Don't he look like a prizefighter though? Say, wait till he
gets mad once! Look at the chest on him, will you, Delaney? Got

that delivering bonnets for his ma. Look at them shoulders. Say, there's muscle for you. Kid, you're all right. Understand? You're OK and I like you. Delaney, another beer for the Lamptown heavyweight."

"What about the factory laying off men, Abbott, anything in it?" Bill leaned across the bar toward Morry but Morry, as usual, had heard none of the inside rumors.

Three men sitting at a card table started grumbling.

"Yeah, Russell would lay off the men before he would the women. That redhead of his would see to that. . . ."

"I seen in the *Dispatch* that Lamptown Works was cutting out the accessories. Next the Works will go," Hogan said. "You fellows will be out in less than six months, the factory will be closed up unless the girls keep it open for their own private business, eh, Bill?"

"Russell's all right, he's got enough dough," one of the men at the table said. "If the Works gets shaky he can put money back into it. I ain't worried so long as my thirty-two fifty comes in every payday."

"Yeah, and what if Russell ain't all right," Hogan argued, his nose now a bright pink. "Who's going to pick up the pieces of this town, then? As I see it the whole damned town goes round to Russell's tune and if he stops the town stops. What's he ever done but inherit the money that lets things skid along on their own wheels while he sits there on his twaloo or runs around with cookies."

"Say, Hogan, you don't know it all, just because you live in Bucyrus and shook hands once with Bishop Brown. What the hell do you know about Lamptown? You run down the tracks here once or twice on a three-wheeler and you think you saw everything. Who's you, squintin' into beer steins and spoutin' Colonel R. G. Ingersoll?" The overalled mechanic from the Works spat toward the cuspidor and missed. "Let me tell you this guy Hunt Russell's got brains, he don't have to break his back learning things. He's got the brains of this town as well as the kale."

Hogan went over to the table and planted both hands on it. A couple of chips rolled under the table and were stopped by a big rubber boot.

"All right, he's got brains, has he? Listen, if he had brains, do you think he'd let his town—the town his old man made—be the state honeydump? Do you think he'd sit up there on his pink plush carpets eating his little bonbons while the town around him stood rotting? He's the guy here with the power and he's got the money. Why, if he had any brains he'd wipe out your Market Street there and build a row of office buildings down to Extension Avenue, he'd tear out that street of old boarding houses and build a big swell hotel, he'd get himself made mayor and throw out all these Irish politicians from Shantyville, he'd have all the sayso and by Judas he'd say something, he'd build chateaux on his lots, yonder, chateaux with gardens around them. He'd make this little mudhole the gardenspot of Ohio, he'd make playgrounds for his employees. But does he do it? Hell, no."

The cardplayers were impressed, and Hogan leaned back and folded his arms across his blue shirt.

"Why, boys, you don't know things, that's all. You haven't read, you haven't seen. You let one guy run your whole town, a guy that don't give a hoot in hell for any of you."

"How are you going to do anything else?" Morry asked, excited as he always was, by Hogan's fantasies.

"You fellows ought to get your own hooks into that factory so you won't be wiped out when Russell lays down for his beauty nap, and the business blows up. . . . Oh, I don't say Shantyville will be wiped out—you'll always have your little flower bed, the priests will take care of that all right."

"What'll it be, Morry?" Bill picked up Morry's glass and Morry dropped another dime on the counter by way of answer. What about a Lamptown such as Hogan described? What about avenues of green surrounded "chateaux"? Shutting his eyes, Morry could see them now, rows of houses, all different, this one all gables and low-spreading, white, and the next one rough-stone like a little castle. He saw the picture postcards of these places stuck up on Bauer's cigar counter instead of the perpetual three-for-a-nickel—"The Yards, Lamptown," "The Works, Lamptown," "Bauer's Chop House, Lamptown." He saw one picture very clearly, a mansion looking like the State Capitol vaguely, and beneath the tinted photograph these printed words, "Home of Morris Abbott, Lamptown, Ohio."

Suddenly he thought he had lived over stores long enough, he wanted someplace to stretch his long limbs, someplace where he belonged, where he wasn't always ducking to keep out of peoples' way. Gardens, chateaux—Morry saw them laid out like spangled Christmas cards—vividly colored invitations to a fairy-tale world. He felt homesick for spacious houses set in spreading lawns fringed with great calm shade trees—he was homesick for things he had never known, for families he had only read about, he missed people—old friends that had lived only in the novels he had read. Homesick . . . for a Lamptown that Hogan had just created out of six beers. He wanted to do something fabulous, something incredible, that would bring this Lamptown nearer to reality. He'd do all those things Hogan thought Hunt Russell ought to do. . . . But then Hunt had the money, that's what mattered, what did he, Morry, have but two suits and forty dollars in the savings bank?

"Say, if I had Russell's bank account I'd tear up this damned town and go right back to where old man Russell started with it. I'd make it all over again, I would," Hogan leaned one elbow on the bar and became impressively oratorical again. "Why in no time at all I'd have this town a god-damned Utopia, I would. I'd have an opera house where the Paradise Picture Palace is now,

I'd have a business college where kids could learn how to make a living, I'm damned if I wouldn't."

"Say—say Hogan, how would you go about building those chateaux for instance?" Morry edged up closer to the oracle. "How's a fellow going to learn how to plan and build like that? I don't mean like those Extension Avenue frame houses but— well, you know, different houses like you see in the magazines."

"Thing for you to do is to get a job with a contractor," Bill Delaney told him. "Get in with Hogan's wife's old man. He's a builder, if that's the trade you want to learn."

The mechanic at the table scraped his chair around to face Hogan.

"Yeah, Hogan, that's what you'd do with money, is it? What'd you do with the two thousand your wife got from her old lady? Bought stock in a Mexican opal mine, that's what you did, Big Noise. An opal mine—Christ!"

Hogan wiped his mouth on his sleeve and patted his stomach fondly.

"Well, boys, I'm off. The old horse waits without."

"Hey, Hogan, what about it? How about that there opal mine?" yelled Delaney, and the others roared with laughter as Hogan vanished, grinning, through the swinging doors.

Four Italian section hands strayed in and began dropping nickels in the pianola. An air from "Il Trovatore" rattled out. The darkest, hairiest of the four leaped beside the piano to bellow the words, gesturing ardently to the painting of a fat nymph surrounded by dazzled doves. Morry dropped into one of the big chairs that lined the barroom walls. A copy of the *Cincinnati Enquirer* was in the next seat and he picked it up.

"Cut out the opery," yelled Delaney good-naturedly.

"Come on, Spaghett, give us 'Down Among the Sheltering Palms.'"

"So that was opera," mused Morry enviously. If you were a wop working on the railroad you knew a lot of things like that. What doors did you open to find out these things, where were these doors anyway? Restlessly Morry started reading. A familiar cough at his side startled him. There in the seat next to him was his father, his gray fedora pulled over one eye, a cigar held between two fingers, a faint smile on his lips.

"This is a surprise," said Charles, "and a pleasure. Stand up! Or no, you needn't. I can see already that you're built for big things . . . moving pianos, say, or pitching hay."

"Great kidder, your dad," Bill Delaney, wiping off the table, said. "How's Frisco, Charlie?"

Morry didn't feel that he disliked his father—he only wanted to keep away from him. He didn't remember ever having thought of his father one way or the other. His only thought had been to keep out of reach, and therefore free from this scalding sense of shame that a look from his father could bring to him.

It was after suppertime and the Saturday night crowd had begun to filter in . . . a few farmers, but mostly factory men or loafers from Shantyville whose wives did Lamptown's washing. Charles motioned Morry to come to a corner table with him, and trying not to show his reluctance, Morry followed. Charles ordered a highball and Morry was about to take a beer, when Charles called Shorty, Bill's helper, back.

"Two highballs, Shorty," he said. "No beer drinkers in this family."

"Now, isn't this a picture," he chuckled sardonically. "Father and son on a happy holiday."

He tipped his glass expertly into his mouth, set it down, and studied Morry's less finished drinking.

"And now you're a man, what about it?" he said. "Do you plan to spend the rest of your life in a little tank town or is it possible you have ambitions?"

"I was just thinking about planning houses," Morry blurted out, although it was agony for such a secret thought to form in words for a stranger's ears. "I thought I might get in old Fowler's office someday—he's Hogan's father-in-law, and if I was in there I might learn the business."

Charles Abbott bent his head with such an exageration of rapt attention that Morry became mute and ashamed again.

"Go on," urged his father kindly. "I am delighted to see that you have such a sense of humor. I had no idea. I hope these houses are to sit a decent distance from the family residence. Fancy such pretty little ideas in such a great big head. Did you tell your mother?"

"No." Morry shook his head.

His father motioned Shorty to bring another pair of highballs, and Morry's throat burned at the mere mention. Charles shook his cigar ashes on the floor with an elegant air of doing the floor a service by this decoration. Then he looked at his son and laughed softly.

"Such pretty little ideas for a young man that looks like a prize bull. A bull with a taste for perfume. A prize bull with a lace handkerchief. Why, if you had any good in that six feet of muscle you'd be supporting your mother by this time."

"I do intend to," mumbled Morry. The bar was filling up and he yearned to bolt outside. A drunken tenor from Shantyville was singing at the bar, Bill's voice got louder and shriller in an effort at discipline. "What about her, then?" his father's voice was low and insistent. "You've been around your mother, you've been taking her to these dances. Well?"

Morry didn't know what the other was driving at. He blinked at him stupidly.

"Don't try to look innocent. You know who she meets, you know damn well what she does. Well, who is it? Who's the guy?" Charles rapped on the table with his glass. A kind of horror seeped in to Morry's brain. He unconsciously shoved his chair back from the table.

"Who's her man, I'm asking you?" Charles repeated threateningly. "Don't think I can't get it out of you. You know damned well what I want to know and by God you're going to tell me. Who's she chasing?"

"What?" The question wasn't out loud because something seemed to stick in his throat and no noise would come out of his mouth. Morry wet his lips.

"I'm asking you who's her lover, damn you, that's what I'm asking!" Charles banged the table with a clenched white hand. Morry noted the onyx and diamond ring on his white flesh.

Now he hated his father, hated the false gentility of his voice, the nice perfection of his collar and pearl stickpin, he loathed the smooth-shaven bluish face with its small correct nose, its even small white teeth, he loathed the scarcely perceptible odor of lilac hair tonic, he hated him, and even with his eyes shut Morry knew every slight thing about his father that he hated. Helpless always in words with him, Morry could think of only one thing to do and that was to get away. The door of the bar to the front poolroom was blocked by a crowd of shouting Italian railroad workers, and there was only the back door into the court. It was toward this that Morry dived, but the minute his two feet were on the stones of the courtyard he realized that his father was there with him, his hand was on the back of his neck in a steely grip.

"Are you going to tell me what she's up to, or aren't you?"

Words finally burst through Morry's chattering teeth.

"I'm damned if I will."

The next thing he knew was a stabbing blow under the chin. Morry, in a flood of rage, swung out on his father, but as soon as his huge fist struck he was ashamed, for his father was such a slight, soft little man. It was like hitting some kid. . . . Morry took a step back in the pitch dark of the courtyard with the headlights of an oncoming engine in his eyes, and the second's hesitation gave the other his chance. His fist tore into Morry's face and then it seemed to Morry that the engine had left its wonted track beside the saloon and had come roaring into the courtyard. Then the roaring suddenly stopped.

The saloon back door opened and Shorty came running out.

"What the hell...."

Charles Abbott was yanking his collar into place. The shoulder seam of his right sleeve was torn, the barkeep noted, and he breathed heavily even while he smiled. The younger Abbott was crumpled up on the stone pavement.

"Give us a light there, Bill," Shorty called back and the back door opened wider. Someone was singing to the pianola's tinny accompaniment.

> Down among the sheltering palms,
> Oh honey, wait for me, oh honey, wait for me....

Shorty knelt down.

"Hey ... hey, Morry, what the hell...." Steve lit a match and looked from the bloody cheek on the pavement rather curiously at Charlie. "What's the idea here, Charlie?"

"Just teaching," Charles panted, as he dusted off his hands, "the boy ... how ... to fight."

"Well," said Shorty, "they ain't much fight in him now."

꒰꒱

Charles left for the road early the next morning. He said he'd be gone several months this time through the Southwestern territory, and he seemed so much quieter and saner than he had before, that his wife felt relieved.

As for Morry he took good care to keep out of sight as long as possible and when he finally did try to sneak through the back hall, Nettie saw him.

"He's been fighting. Look, Mrs. Abbott!" she cried out, pointing to Morry's face. "Look at those marks on his eye. It's a good thing his father's gone or he'd catch it good from him."

"Why, Morry!" Elsinore's clear gray eyes were wide with astonishment. "Your face is all bruised. What ever happened to you?"

"That's why he's been eating at Bauer's these last two days, and keeping out of the shop," declared Nettie triumphantly. "Didn't I tell you there was some reason for it? Didn't I tell you he was up to something? And Dode was in last night and said he wasn't at work all day yesterday."

"But you worked today," said Elsinore, her eyes still fixed on the scarred forehead. "What happened?"

Nettie's black eyes glowed with satisfaction as Morry sullenly stared at the floor.

"See, it was a fight! He got into a brawl over at Delaney's Saturday night, he can't deny it. That's why he didn't get up all day Sunday, don't you remember, and that's why he hasn't let us see him. I knew there was something behind all that!"

Elsinore waited for Morry to answer. But he wouldn't open his mouth, just stood there getting red in the face.

"Was it or wasn't it a fight?" challenged Nettie. "Just ask him. Go on and ask him."

Morry scowled furiously at her.

"All right then, it was," he retorted, "and what do you think you're going to do about it?"

Nettie backed away, pouting. She smoothed her sleek black hair and marched haughtily into the front showroom swaying her hips with each step. Elsinore and her son stood looking at each other. Elsinore knew there was something she must do, something she must say, because this was her son and there was some word you said to sons so that they didn't brawl in saloons. She thought of the saloon smell, of the old tipplers whose obscenities echoed to her bedroom window on Saturday nights, she thought of the hard-eyed young men that hung around the poolroom, whispering of things mysterious and horrible—and suddenly she shivered.

"Morry," she began, in a funny little voice as if she were called upon to make a speech at a great banquet and her knees shook a little. "Morry!"

Morry looked away. Then because he knew how bothered she was he turned around and rushed upstairs, and his mother breathed a tremendous sigh of relief.

Nettie kept harping on Morry's bruised eye, though, for days. She thought it had something to do with some girl—it was a fight over a factory girl or maybe over Jen St. Clair. Morry let her talk and kept out of the Bon Ton as much as he could. He didn't see much of Jen anymore, but he knew Nettie wouldn't believe that. After what the old woman had said he felt queer and sick every time he thought of Jen. He'd stay away all right, he'd leave her alone, but every day after work he missed her, at dusk when they used to sit on the steps talking. He knew she watched him from the Delaney's upstairs window whenever he passed, and once when he walked home from the factory with two of the girls he worked with, someone threw a pebble down at him from up there, but he walked on without looking up. But at nights, when he'd be reading in bed sometimes he'd stare at a page half an hour or so worrying about the whole business, about what the old woman had said to his mother, and he felt lost without Jen to talk to.

One Saturday afternoon when his mother sent him in the backyard for boxes from the store-shed he looked over toward Jen's stairs. Someone was sitting, out, sitting so primly that he had to look twice to make sure it was Jen. She had on a hat. Nobody ever wore a hat in Lamptown unless it was Sunday or else they were going away. It struck Morry with a shock that maybe she was going away, leaving Lamptown for good.

He glanced quickly over his shoulder to make sure the Bon Ton was not on watch, and then sauntered boldly over to the stairs. If she was going away, the old lady certainly couldn't kick about his coming over to bid a civil good-bye. He said hello tentatively but Jen only nodded indifferently to him without smiling. He came up the steps with growing curiosity. A blue lace hat sat awkwardly on Jen's head and in her arm was a stiff popeyed china doll in a pink satin costume.

"What's the idea?"

"My mother's come to see me," Jen explained drearily. "She went to the Home for me and they sent her here."

"Is she taking you away?"

"I don't know."

"I guess I'd better go," he said hastily, but dying to see what Jen's folks were really like. He looked through the screen door and just inside the parlor he caught sight of the visitor. She looked like one of those actresses, Morry thought, only fatter. She had a voluminous white veil over her stiff straw hat, and a tight-fitting soiled green suit, and white shoes and stockings. She sat on the edge of her chair and talked to old Mrs. Delaney hunched in her little chair on the other side of the room. Morry sat down cautiously out of line with the old woman's eye.

"She's been talking now for an hour," Jen murmured in his ear. "I guess it's pretty nice to have your mother come and visit you, especially if you never saw her before. She gave me this hat. Look. She gave me this doll. I'd like it if it cried like your mother's doll does."

Morry wanted to laugh at the hat. He'd never seen Jen in a hat and it sat up on top of her head as if it was meant for the doll instead. This was because Jen's mother had no memory for dates and had a vague impression that her daughter was barely eight. As for the dolls, he couldn't imagine Jen ever playing with dolls.

"What'd she come for, then, if she isn't taking you with her?" he wanted to know, but Jen refused to talk. She sat glumly clutching her doll and looking straight ahead while her mother's voice chattered on and on.

Finally Jen whispered, "She said she wanted to see if I was in a good home. She said she couldn't be easy until she'd seen if I was with the right people. That's what she said."

Morry glanced carefully through the screen door. There was old Mrs. Delaney sitting with her shoulders bunched up, her arms folded over her shrunken calico bosom, her thin lips clamped together, rocking, rocking while Mrs. St. Clair went on and on talking, as if she was selling soap.

"I used to be a beauty. I give you my word, Mrs. Delaney, when I was married my waist was no bigger than that. As it is, it's only my hips that are big, and most men like big hips, that's what I say. People say I lace to make my waist look so small. I give you my word, Mrs. Delaney, you could put your hand inside my corset this minute and see how much room there is. I don't have to lace, I tell them. . . . I had beautiful hair as a girl—thick like Jennia's out there, but that Titian red, you know. My friends say, oh yes, she dyes it. I give you my word people don't think it's real. They think I dye it, and you know how many women my age do have to color their hair, because do what you will, the gray will come out if it's there. But dye my hair? Ha! I said to this friend of mine, 'Look here, I want you to come to my room and I'll just show you the stuff I wash it in.' I showed her. 'Absolutely no dye,' it said on the bottle, 'merely restoring the hair to its natural brilliancy.' Well, that time the laugh was on her. . . . I'm glad to see Jennia in this beautiful home, Mrs. Delaney. I can see you're a good influence."

Now Mrs. Delaney opened her mouth.

"Well, then, who was the girl's father?" she croaked. "If she had one."

"Mr. St. Clair was a gentleman," said Jen's mother. "We had

words but I don't deny he was a gentleman. Such hands, Mrs.
Delaney! No wonder, he'd never done a lick of work in his life,
but I will say they were beautiful hands. He went to Africa. I
think he had interests there."

"Africa? Was he black?" exclaimed Mrs. Delaney, and even
Morry jumped then, so that Jen put her finger to her lips warningly.

Mrs. St. Clair threw up her gloved hands.

"Mrs. Delaney! God forbid! My husband black!" She shuddered. "That was uncalled for, Mrs. Delaney, that really was. Do
you know, Mrs. Delaney, that my husband was considered the
handsomest man in our company? The best-looking man in the
'Laughing Girls' company? Not only that but the smartest as
well. He had a big future on the stage, but as I say he had interests
in Africa, and when Lil was born—that's my youngest, we were
staying at a hotel in Youngstown then, the company had broken
up—why Bert just walked out on me with a note. I waited till Lil
was a month old, then left her on the Children's Home doorstep
right where baby Jennia had been put, the year before. I tell you I
cried my eyes out, Mrs. Delaney, because there's nothing like a
mother's heart."

Tears now came to Mrs. St. Clair's eyes and she plucked them
out carefully as one whose tears had too often had to cope with
mascara.

"Oh, I've not had an easy time of it, Mrs. Delaney. When
Jennia was born—that was when we were playing in Toledo, so I
left her there with a very fine family—my friend said aha, it's
only a six months' baby. My own friends said that, mind you. But
I could show you the book where I wrote down the dates of my
wedding and when Jen was born, and I could prove that everything was just as innocent as I sit here now. I was brought up refined, Mrs. Delaney, I had my education. I was every bit as good
as Bertie was but he never would believe it. My people were from
Virginia. My mother was an O'Brien."

Mrs. Delaney's thin mouth snapped open again.

"When did you get Jen back from that Toledo family you left her with?"

Jen's mother leaned forward confidentially.

"Mrs. Delaney, you wouldn't believe people would be like that, but when I got back to Toledo that family had put her in the Orphanage in Libertyville. I never would have put her there, and the only reason I left Lily there was as kinda company for her sister, you know. I never saw either of my babies from the time I left them till now when I'm looking them up again. When Lily was born I spent every penny I had to get her to the very same orphanage because I wanted my little girls to be together. You're a mother yourself, Mrs. Delaney. You know a mother's heart."

"Do you want to get Jen back now?" challenged Mrs. Delaney. "Is that what you're after?"

"Do I—oh dear, no,—oh no, not now. Does she sing or dance? Let me hear her sing once. Jennia—oh Jennia, sing me a song, dearie. I want to see if you've got your father's voice."

Jen shifted her doll to the other arm, stood up and with her nose pressed against the screen door in order to face her audience, sang. She sang at the top of her voice and very fast so as to get it over with.

> Will someone kindly tell me,
> Will someone answer why—
> To me it is a riddle
> And will be till I die—
> A million peaches round me,
> Yet I would like to know,
> Why I picked a lemon in the garden of love
> Where I thought only peaches grow.

Mrs. St. Clair gave a little flattering cry of pleasure. "You know really that's not bad, Mrs. Delaney, not bad at all. When I was her age I was getting four and five dollars a week singing in my papa's café in Newark. Customers would throw the money at me. I had my training all right before I ever stepped on the real stage. Nowadays of course a child performer gets even more than a grown-up—and a curly-haired little girl. . . ." Mrs. St. Clair studied Jen appraisingly through the screen. "Her legs are good, too, that's a blessing."

Jen mechanically pulled her apron down over her knees, and her mother laughed fondly.

"Never mind hiding them, dear. . . . Now, do you know what I've a mind to do? . . . Hmm mm. . . . Yes sir, I've a good mind to take her along with me to Cleveland. I have my little room there, and we'd manage. Yes sir, I think that's what I'll do, especially since the Home won't let me take Lily. . . . Stand up, dearie, I want to see if you can travel half-fare. She's pretty tall, isn't she?"

Mrs. Delaney got up suddenly and limped over to where her guest sat. She put her arms akimbo.

"You don't get her, missy, do you see?" she spat out her words. "You'd like to put her in a café or on the stage and let her make a living for you but you can't do it while old Susan Delaney's alive and I'll tell you that right now. She's here to help me, that's what. You don't get a chance to make of her what you made of yourself, now, take that, and I'll tell you right to your face that I don't like your looks and I'm sorry you came."

Mrs. St. Clair's mouth fell open. Red spots came into her cheeks and her hands clutched the arms of her chair tightly. Outside, Morry decided he'd better leave but Jen clutched him tightly. When he tried to pull away she took both hands and held on to his coat, and the doll clattered down the steps.

"See!" hissed Morry. "You've broken it now. Say, I want to get out of this, hear me?"

"I know you—I know you as well as if I'd borne you myself," went on the old woman shrilly, "you can get away from here and stay away. I got enough to do keeping that wild 'un straight without her ma breaking in."

Words came to Mrs. St. Clair.

"Oh, what an old bitch," she choked. "To think I spend my good money coming all the way from Cleveland just to be kicked out of my child's home. What a rotten old bitch you are! Got no more sympathy for a mother than a snake."

Mrs. Delaney pointed a gnarled finger toward the door and lowering her white veil the other woman whirled around to go. Morry and Jen backed out of the way.

"Here, Jen, give her her hat and her doll," commanded the old woman.

"Oh, can't I keep the hat?" Jen implored.

"Give them back!" thundered the old woman, and Jen hastily took off the hat and picked up the doll to hand to her mother. Mrs. St. Clair gathered her green skirts about her and ran down the steps.

"You'll be sorry for this," she shouted from the bottom of the steps. "I'll get Lily and I'll get Jennia, too, they'll stick by their mother. I only came here for a motherly visit and you—"

"You came here to stay and live off me if you could, don't deny it!" quavered the old woman fiercely. "I tell you I know you like I'd know my own daughter, and you can get out and stay out."

She panted back into the house, stopping to glare at Morry.

"And you, too. You clear out of here, too."

She banged the door shut.

Jen, bereft of doll and hat, hung over the bannister.

"Oh, mother! Goodbye, mother—come see me again—"

But Mrs. St. Clair was storming angrily up the street to the Big Four depot, a pink satin doll under one arm and a child's blue hat crushed under the other.

Jen turned to Morry.

"Now I'll never see her again," she said despondently.

"What do you care? She wouldn't do you any good," Morry consoled her.

"I know, but it's my mother, Morry, it's my folks," Jen said, troubled.

Morry heard the door rattling ominously.

"I'm going to beat it," he said, "the old lady's on the warpath."

Jen didn't try to stop him. The barkeeper stuck his head out of the saloon back door as Morry dashed down the alley. He stepped out and stared upstairs at Jen, shading his eyes with his hand.

"Who was that up there doing all the singing for God's sake?" he demanded.

"Aw, shut up," grumbled Jen. "I gotta right to sing, I guess."

※

Jen went to the parochial school in the Irish end of Lamptown, the part they called Shantyville. She played hookey half the time, and lost her books in the woods hunting mushrooms, and fought with the boys in the school yard. Every few days a black-robed sister would climb the steps above the saloon to old Mrs. Delaney's quarters and during this interview Jen usually disappeared, well aware that the visit had to do with her own waywardness.

Sometimes when she knew beforehand that the sister was to make a call, she'd stay away from home till nine or ten at night, coming in bedraggled and muddy-booted, with a lapful of muddy wildflowers and burrs sticking to all of her clothes. She never quite understood Mrs. Delaney's rage over these night wanderings, nor could she see why they were proof that she'd never grow up into a decent woman. Once it was eleven when she got in and old Mrs. Delaney sat humped up by the kitchen stove waiting for her. Bill was eating a cold supper on the oilcloth table.

"Well!" said the old woman.

"I been picking flowers out in the Lots," Jen said. "Here."

She laid a clump of sweet Williams and Johnny-jump-ups on the table.

"Who you been with—that Morry Abbott?"

"I went by myself," said Jen.

"That's likely. Eat supper?"

"I found some green apples. I'm not hungry."

"Look here, Sister Catherine says you throw your books at the boys and that Peter McCarthy had to be sent home today because you bit his hand so hard. She says you swore at Myrtle Dietz."

Jen looked sulkily at her flowers. Bill jerked his chair around.

"Speak up! Tell the old lady what's the idea. We give you a home and then you stay out half the night. We send you to a good school so you can grow up to be somebody that is somebody and you raise hell all over the place. Speak up, kid."

Jen chewed her fingernails silently.

"What's the big idea throwing books at the boys? What's the idea scratching up this McCarthy boy?"

"I'm not gonna be mauled by any of those smarties," Jen said defiantly. "And I was just getting even with Pete McCarthy. I had a reason."

The old woman pricked up her ears alertly. Bill's fork hung in midair. Both looked suspiciously at Jen.

"What happened? What'd he do to you? Speak up there, now, out with it."

"He chased after me coming down the tracks one noon and—"

"I knew it would happen," moaned the old woman, "I said it would happen. Every girl I ever had under my roof, the same every one of them. Out with it, then, what'd he do?"

"Kissed me, that's what!" Jen said indignantly.

Bill and his mother exchanged an unbelieving look.

"And that's all? Now, no lying!" the old woman insisted. "You're sure that was all?"

"I guess that's enough," Jen mumbled, feeling embarrassed that the outrage should be taken so lightly. "I got even with him for it, all right."

"And you beat him up just for kissing you!" marveled the old woman. "I've a mind to give you a good tanning for it. . . ."

"Leave her be, ma," Bill said. He fished more pickled pigsfeet out of the jar, and stuffed his mouth.

"Wash up those dishes, then, and get to bed," urged his mother. "Wandering around the Lots this hour the night. One of those fresh fellows at the Yard get after you once and then where'd you be?"

"She'd scratch his eyes out, don't you fear," promised Bill. "She won't have anybody around her but maybe Morry Abbott and he don't bother her much, now he's working and going after real meat."

Jen tied on an apron.

"He'd better not show up here any more after I told him not to," said Mrs. Delaney. "No use your sitting out waiting for him, either, because I told his ma I wouldn't have it. And no use your thinking you can meet him nights outside because if I find out I'll give you a hiding."

"I don't care," Jen retorted, banging the dishpan into the sink. "I can get along without people, I guess. I guess I'm old enough to get along by my own self."

"You bet you're old enough! Next you'll be hanging around dance halls, the Casino and the like—"

Jen clapped her hands.

"Aw, Bill, let me learn to dance, will you? Look, I can two-step already."

She two-stepped around the kitchen, waving the dish-mop in the air. Bill whistled a tune for her.

"Say, what do you know about that? Look at that, ma. . . . Now, wait a minute, and tell you what I'll do, I'll show you the schottische."

He got up and took Jen's hand stiffly in his own fat red hand. He held his foot poised in the air in the third position and Jen raised a muddy shoe to the same angle.

"Now when I say 'Down!' you sachet to your right, and watch now. Down!"

> Don't you see my
> Don't you see my
> Don't you see my new shoe?
> Don't you see my
> Don't you see my
> Don't you see my new shoe?

"They don't dance that way any more, I've seen 'em," objected his mother. "Things are different now."

"Never mind, she's a fine dancer. What do you say I take her over to Fischer's some night? I'd like to go over some night myself, especially if I had someone to dance with."

Jen caught hold of his arm.

"You wouldn't really, would you, Bill? Take me to the Casino?"

Bill began to regret his offer, but he didn't dare take it back.

"Get to those dishes, will you?" snapped Mrs. Delaney. "You got to do better with Sister Catherine before you go out nights, young lady, yes sir, even with Bill."

"I'll wear my hair up!" Jen was jubilant again. "Like Nettie Farrell does. Give me a dime for hairpins, will you, Bill?"

Jen couldn't wait to go to the Casino. She could see herself dancing around amazing Morry Abbott and Grace Terris and the men from downstairs. She saw Lil there, too, because Lil was always a part of her ideal dream pictures. She could see herself grown up, taking Lil across the Casino floor and people crowding around her because Lil was like a little yellow-haired wax angel. And Lil would be dazzled by all this glamour, too. Whenever she remembered Lil, back in the Home, Jen felt guilty. Lil, back there in dark blue calico, always too skimpy, swinging on the iron carriage gate, while here was Jen having all this fun in Lamptown, with her own room, and a pair of silk stockings and a box of talcum powder. . . . Soon the Home would send her out to work because she was fourteen now, Lil was. Jen'd have to do something about her, quick, too . . . then Jen skipped all that and was back again in the Casino with Lil, both in pink silk dresses, dancing, with Morry watching. . . . Jen turned a handspring joyously across the kitchen floor.

"See, now you've started her," Mrs. Delaney said morosely to Bill. "Dancing and then what? Mind you, one crooked move, and out she goes."

Nevertheless the next week Jen started going to the Casino dances.

⅜

On a rainy Saturday night Dode O'Connell strode into the Bon Ton Hat Shop. Mrs. Pepper was sewing garters on a Stylish Stout model in pink brocade. Elsinore and Nettie sat on the green wicker sofa watching the rain and waiting for customers. The rain zigzagged across the show window in torrents and black gleaming umbrellas with frantic legs beneath were blown past. Market Street lamps were wet golden blobs dripping futile little puddles of light that made no difference to the black, wet night, and the lightning that cracked the sky showed up Lamptown as such a shabby, lost little corner of the earth—it was nothing, just nothing at all for that dazzling second.

Dode's tall person was wrapped in a man's topcoat, and a Roman-striped muffler was wound round her red hair. Nettie, closing the door behind her, saw Hunt's car just beyond, in front of Delaney's, its curtains buttoned up.

Dode shook off the damp coat and patted up her hair in front of the gilt mirror.

"I want that big hat that was in the window last week—the one over the doll," she said, and Nettie and Elsinore bustled around with this hat and another like it in blue, because Dode spent good money and besides she usually got her clothes in Cleveland, so that this visit must be quite a compliment.

Mrs. Pepper, sewing on her corset, grew crimson when Dode nodded to her, and she moved a little away as if to avoid any personal contact with this customer. Dode, tilting a hat over one eyebrow, looked over at the corsetiere rather cynically.

"What's the matter, Pepper, you mad at me for that Cedar Point business?"

Mrs. Pepper looked up, confused.

"I—oh no, Dode, I—"

"You and Fischer sore?"

"No—I—"

Now Elsinore's blood began to tingle ominously, in a minute she was going to overhear something she almost knew but didn't ever want to hear spoken out loud. She saw Mrs. Pepper look helplessly from Dode to Nettie. Nettie was busy stretching a hat and pretending not to listen. But Dode paid no attention to the two milliners.

"Well, then, what was the trouble up at Sandusky—did you miss the boat? We waited over at the Point for three hours for you."

Mrs. Pepper puckered up her rosebud mouth very firmly.

"I was too busy. I had a great many customers in Sandusky—"

"Whereabouts—at the Soldiers' Home?" Dode laughed.

"He needn't think I can drop everything and run just because he says so," Mrs. Pepper said tartly. "Besides you know how he is when he's had too much."

Dode's eyebrows went up scornfully.

"Say, that's good coming from you."

Mrs. Pepper tossed her head and jerked her chair around. Dode took the hand mirror Elsinore gave her and studied the back view of her hat.

"The plumes are five dollars apiece," Elsinore said hesitatingly, but after all plumes did cost. "That makes it eighteen."

"Put another plume over on the other side, will you?" Dode requested. She lifted up her skirt and pulled a roll of bills out of her stocking. Her black silk stockings came all the way up her long shapely thighs, and there were dozens of tiny ruffles on her white silk drawers.

"I'll come in and get it Tuesday."

She started winding the muffler around her head again. Nettie shook out the topcoat and held it for her.

"Say, Pepper."

Mrs. Pepper looked around unwillingly.

"Get into your clothes and come out. We're going to drive over to Marion and pick him up. Come on."

"I might—and I might not," said Mrs. Pepper huffily.

"Hurry up," ordered Dode.

"In all this storm?" Elsinore said because now she knew it was true about Fischer and Mrs. Pepper, and she couldn't bear to have her go out to meet him. She'd known about this and known it was true, she thought, ever since she first heard the rumor, but it never struck her full in the face until tonight.

Mrs. Pepper, sputtering angrily, got into her coat and hat.

"I wouldn't go over there for a minute if it wasn't that I have to see a certain party in Marion."

Dode laughed.

"That's the stuff, Pepper. Don't let 'em know when you're sunk."

The lightning slashed the black sky again as they ran out into the street. Nettie shut the door and in another minute Hunt's car rolled through the flooded gutters down the street.

"In all this rain, too!" Nettie said slowly, and then her face wrinkled up and she began to cry and dab at her eyes with her tiny sewing apron.

Elsinore looked at her, irritated more than surprised. For one thing, Nettie or anybody else crying was nothing really in her life. The only real thing was the terrible certainty that Fischer belonged to Mrs. Pepper, just as people had always said, and that they met often, and it was all secret which made it mean so much more.

"I don't care," Elsinore thought, and in her mind she didn't, it was only that something sharp like lightning quivered through her chest, and made her want to scream.

Nettie went on sniffling into her apron.

"I get so lonesome sometimes," she whimpered. "People going out on dates in all this storm—those factory girls always have dates, not that I'd be seen with any man in this town, but when I think of a fat old thing like Mrs. Pepper going out riding . . . while I stay here and work all the time. I never get out, and anyway I'm afraid of lightning. It makes me—so—nervous!"

"Shut up!" Elsinore cried so harshly that Nettie was frightened into awed obedience. Elsinore rubbed her forehead, dazed, as if she had shrieked out some secret in her sleep. Nettie blinked at her, and Elsinore began to be sorry for her, as she was sorry for herself. She was glad when the hall door banged as Morry came in.

"I can't stand people crying," she explained to Nettie. "I never cry myself. If you're so anxious to go out, though, in this storm, why don't you ask Morry to take you to the Paradise to the picture? It's only nine o'clock. There won't be any more customers here on a night like this."

"I'd never ask Morry to do anything for me!" Nettie dried her tears.

Morry stuck his head in the door. He'd been over to Delaney's place and he smelled of smoke and beer.

"Did you call me?"

"Morry, get my umbrella and your old coat and take Nettie to the Paradise tonight. She doesn't feel very good."

Morry and Nettie looked at each other antagonistically. Nettie knew, if his mother did not, how significant it was for a couple to go to the Paradise together. Nobody ever went to movies together in town but engaged couples. Girls went alone and fellows hung around the drugstore outside to take them home afterwards, but to go in together. . . . How he detested her for her smooth, tear-streaked face, her woeful mouth, all the signs of her feminine helplessness, all the appeals for sympathy. . . . What would she care if all the fellows stared at them and snickered when they came in together? That's just what women always liked.

"Well?" challenged Nettie. "See Mrs. Abbott, he won't take me, he'd rather go with the factory girls."

"You'll take Nettie, won't you, Morry?" Elsinore asked him again. "You can wrap yourself up good. It's the first Saturday night she's ever had a chance to get out. Go on and put your things on, Nettie."

Morry scowled down at his wet shoes while Nettie joyously ran into the back room to get ready. He hated the Paradise—only sissies went to the movies, he was disappointed in his mother, and he wished somebody would give Nettie's smug, smiling face a good slap.

"In just a minute, Morry," Nettie called out.

Elsinore caught sight of the pink corset Mrs. Pepper had left on her chair. She picked it up and threw it across the hall into the workroom, and banged a drawer shut. Morry's jaw dropped. He'd never seen his mother in a temper before.

"Leaving her trash all over the place!" Elsinore fumed. "I won't have it. I've stood it long enough! I won't let her come here again ever!"

Nettie ran out, popeyed, pulling on her hat.

"What is it? What happened?"

"Out she goes the next time she comes to Lamptown!" went on Elsinore. "I've got no place here for her or anybody else like her!"

Morry, for some obscure reason, felt the need to protect his mother from Nettie's curiosity.

"Come on, let's get out of here if we're going," he ordered brusquely, and shoved Nettie out the front door into the rain.

Nettie raised her umbrella, not at all disturbed by his surliness. Small rivers of rain ran off the shop awning, and two girls, bent on getting their Saturday night dates somehow, ran squealing by with newspapers over their heads. Market Street blurred uncertainly before them.

"Here!" Nettie handed Morry the umbrella, and clinging very close to his unfriendly arm, she tiptoed carefully along beside him.

৯৯

Morry could never forget that walk in the rain with Nettie Farrell. To be huddled under an umbrella with a woman he hated, to smell her violet talcum, her scented hair, to feel her warm, plump hand squeezing his elbow, her body pressing against his, so that not for an instant could he forget that it was Nettie, Nettie Farrell, and that he detested her. He said nothing to her, tramped straight through all the puddles leaving her to scamper along beside him with tight, prim little steps.

He was glad of the umbrella when they passed the drugstore, because the fellows inside couldn't recognize him then. He pulled his cap down over his eyes at the gilded ticket window of the Paradise, and pushed Nettie ahead of him into the theatre. The storm had kept people away and for a glad moment or two he thought there was no one he knew in the little scattered audience. He wished Nettie wouldn't make so much fuss getting into her seat so that everybody turned around to stare. Then he saw directly across the aisle the small pointed face of Jen St. Clair. She was with Grace Terris and Grace was nudging her and giggling, but Jen only stared at him as if she'd never seen him before and then, with her chin in the air, turned her attention to pictures.

Morry had spoken to her and now he wished he hadn't. Every time he ever saw Jen he wished she wouldn't show everyone so plainly her worship of him, but now that the worship seemed to be gone he was simply furious with her. He watched the shadowy adventures of Clara Kimball Young and thought of all he'd done for Jen St. Clair, promising to help get her sister and all that, and now she tried to make him feel like a fool by not speaking to him right before Nettie Farrell and the whole Paradise audience. He glowered at the picture, but out of the corner of his eye he could see Grace peeking over at him now and then, and whispering and giggling with Jen.

Nettie kept wriggling in her seat and turning around to speak to people—not to Grace or Jen—but to Bon Ton customers here and there. Morry slid down in his seat a little—it was no use, though, because everyone knew those big shoulders and the coal black wavy hair belonged to Morry Abbott and to nobody else in town. . . .

It was amazing about girls, how lofty and complacent they became when they got out in public with a man—any man—while a fellow shrank and felt ridiculous and prayed for the ordeal to end. It was amazing about women, anyway, Grace over there, snickering behind her hand and Jen, stony-faced, remote, and Nettie, bending over his knees to pick up a handkerchief, fussing around in her seat, brushing her ankles against his and then hastily drawing them back, pressing her plump arms against him, then moving primly away. . . . God, how he hated the whole lot of them, Morry thought, the way they knew how to make a man squirm from old Mrs. Delaney on down to the littlest girl. It was their function in life, making men feel clumsy and dumb, that was all they ever wanted to accomplish. . . . He remembered the little girls in big pink hair ribbons at parties years ago, looking scornfully at him, twice their size, until he wished for sweet death to swoop down on him. Now, in the Paradise, with the thunder growling over the roof, and surrounded by Nettie, Grace, and Jen, he thought of those smart little curled girls of ten and twelve years ago and wanted fiercely to be revenged on them. Nettie's hand touched his carelessly and he boiled with rage and jerked his own hand away. . . . But what revenge would fit these enemies . . . of course he might leave town forever and go to Pittsburgh, no sir, New York City, and show them up as cheap little village hicks while he was a polished city man. This was a soothing thought, as soothing as if it were already accomplished—he even saw himself now on the screen before him, that natty young man in the opera hat emerging from the café door, lighting a cigarette from a silver case while music played.

He saw Hogan dressed up going down the aisle, and wondered what Hogan was doing here. Then he remembered Milly, the piano player and a professional lady of joy. That explained everything. He wished Hogan would tell his pianist girlfriend not to stop dead in the middle of a picture so that you forget what you were thinking of.

Grace and Jen got up—Morry saw them and was determined not to look when they passed but Grace said "hello" and he had to look up and meet Jen's cold, accusing eyes. She glanced away again and went out, pulling on her coat.

"I wonder who those two are going to meet," Nettie whispered to him and Morry gritted his teeth. Those two! As if Jen was like Grace Terris! Those two! His vague anger settled definitely on Nettie now.

Hogan ambled to the back of the theatre nodding to Morry with an innocently casual air as if no one would ever guess he was there to date up the town's light woman, the talented Milly. Cynically the audience watched the pianist, a few minutes later, get up from her bench, close the piano in the very middle of the heroine's death-bed scene, powder her nose leisurely before the piano mirror, set a large plumed hat reverently over her magnificent pompadour; she jangled bracelets up her fat arms and drew on long gloves; she made an intimate adjustment in her stayed velvet gown; gazing with calm insolence over the audience she finally swept majestically up the aisle. Unwillingly the audience gave up Clara Kimball Young's death-bed scene to watch Milly's exit, reluctantly they conceded the dramatic value of her performance, heads turned to watch her pause at the back of the house to look patronizingly at the picture, exchange a laughing word with the usher, and then a cold draught blew in as the exit door swung open and shut for her departure, leaving the audience to the lesser reality of the screen.

Everyone always knew that of course Milly was joining some man or other outside, and this local passion was more exciting than the filmed one. Some ladies thought Milly's private profession should disqualify her as the Paradise pianist, still the cold facts were that no one else in Lamptown could play the piano that well and you had to have music with your pictures, no matter where it came from.

With the pianist gone the picture seemed dull and people wandered out into the rain again. Morry was impatient to go. He was perfectly conscious of Nettie's bosom rising and falling with each breath so that her lace frill quivered gently. A gold locket on a frail gold chain had a way of sliding down beneath the frill every time she moved forward and Nettie, with a little shocked exclamation, would reach down her blouse and fish it out again. A faint whiff of violet sachet followed this maneuver, but Morry pretended not to notice anything.

"Everyone's going," Nettie whispered. "Come on, let's go."

They went out and stood for a minute in the lobby while Nettie fussed with her rubbers. The storm was over so that now there was no excuse for the umbrella. Morry could see men peering out at him from the drugstore window and wished there was some way of dropping Nettie then and there.

"Going back to the shop?" he asked her.

"No," said Nettie primly. "You'll have to take me out to my place, Morry."

There was no getting out of it. They'd have to walk through all the mud of Extension Avenue to the house where Nettie boarded. The maple trees dripped down on them and the pods crackled underfoot. They passed the factory boarding houses with the girls giggling in the doorways or hanging out the windows. A gramophone squeaked out some ragtime to shatter the black gloom outside, and it kept tinkling through Morry's head. Once an automobile slushed through the mud and spattered Nettie's skirt and she went on about that but Morry stalked silently along, his hands in his pockets, his wet shoes weighing a ton. Now they reached the darkest end of the road. Nettie's house was dark—the Murphys were downtown.

"Bye," Morry said gruffly at the doorstep.

"I suppose if you wanted to," said Nettie, unfastening a glove carefully, "you could come in and get dry. I'm sure I don't care. Only you'll have to take off those filthy boots because I won't have you tramping up Mrs. Murphy's new rug the way you do your mother's rugs."

Once more Nettie became all of the smug little starched girls sent into the world to make mankind feel loutish and immeasurably inferior, and once more Morry was stung with the desire to be revenged on all of them. He followed her into the house. She lit the hall gas lamp, from its brass elbow a string of gilded buckeyes dangled. She took off her wraps and hung them on a golden oak hall rack and arranged her hair in the diamond-shaped mirror above. Then she saw Morry standing behind her and stamped her foot.

"Look at you, Morry Abbott! Look at you making tracks all over that new rug with your great big shoes! I could kill you for being so clumsy! Look what you're doing!"

Suddenly Morry seized her two wrists and twisted them until Nettie squealed with pain. He held them tightly with one hand, and with the other pulled her into an iron embrace. Nettie's eyes were terror-stricken, her mouth wide open, the pulse in her white throat throbbed frantically.

"I hate you, Morry Abbott! Don't you dare to touch me. See, you're tearing my dress. . . ."

Morry lifted her up and carried her with her heels kicking, to the green satin settee at the foot of the staircase. He had no desire for Nettie, only a fierce antagonism that amounted to a physical necessity. He would like to have taken her by the neck and shook her like a dog would shake a hen, but all he could do was to sink his teeth into her round shoulder and bite as hard as he could. Nettie stopped kicking him and began to whimper childishly. She put up her hands to fix her hair again and to pull her torn blouse back into place. She wouldn't lift her face to look at him, just made funny whimpering noises like a frightened puppy. When she wriggled away from his knees Morry jumped after her and the settee tipped backwards and upset a blue and yellow jardiniere of ferns.

"Mrs. Murphy'll come in any minute," Nettie wailed, fixing the jar on its mahogany pedestal again. Morry might have left her then but she started to dash past him upstairs. He tore after her and caught up with her on the top landing and got one foot inside the bedroom door before she could close it. His fists were clenched as if for a battle.

The upstairs hall lamp shone into the bedroom through the transom after Morry had shut the door tight. The room smelled of violet talcum and scented soap. Nettie was perfectly quiet, he had to fumble toward the bed where she sat, leaning back on her arms, challenging him. He grasped her shoulders and she drooped limply against him, not saying a word, and the familiar detestable perfume of her hair made him grit his teeth again.

A door opened downstairs.

"Now do be quiet about it," Nettie whispered warningly, and didn't even bother to put up her hands in protest when he started tearing her blouse again.

He was astonished and even chagrined at the ease, almost skill, with which she yielded. Somehow he felt it was she who had conquered and not he, after all. Tiptoeing down the stairs sometime afterward he thought cynically, "I'll bet that's the way they all are. Easy, every one of 'em!"

It made him very angry.

⁂

Morry was out in the court pretending to fix the lock on the storehouse door but hoping Jen would call him. He could see her dimly through the dusk sitting on the top stairs. She hadn't called to him since the night he'd gone out with Nettie. It might be on the old lady's account but he doubted if Jen was really afraid of her. Secretly he was worried about her—he didn't especially want to see her but he liked to feel sure she was around and lately he'd heard Bill say something about "shipping the kid to some farm where she'd learn to work—no damn good to the old lady as she was, always getting kicked out of school, always breaking something."

He lay awake nights trying to figure some way out because it would be terrible for Jen to have to go to some farm. He almost thought of asking his mother to let her work in the Bon Ton the way Nettie had started in, then that made him think of Nettie and he thought probably Jen would be better on a farm. If she was taller she could say she was sixteen and get a job at the Works. Then he remembered the way Hunt had laughed the night he and Jen went there and he thought probably Jen would do better out of Hunt Russell's reach, too.

He looked toward the stairs again—she couldn't help but see him, still she made no beckoning gesture. Ungrateful, he thought, just as if he had already done all those things for her that he had planned. Then reluctantly he started over. He stopped at the foot of the stairs. He wasn't afraid of Bill's old woman any more—or anybody else for that matter.

"Want me to come up, Jen?"

"Sure, come on." She seemed to have gotten grown-up since she'd come to Lamptown, still nothing but a kid, Morry thought, with her eyes always wild and frightened as if she expected somebody to hit her any minute. Now with Morry sitting beside her, she was happy again, but she knew by this time that if she let him see it he would go away at once, because that's the way he was. If she could only keep from speaking to him he'd always hang around her, because silence seemed to mystify him. . . . Or, she reflected, if she could only stay angry with him for all the times he'd hurt her, but when he was here, right here beside her like this, she forgot all the times he'd made her cry all night . . .

"I thought you'd be out with Nettie," she said. "Like two weeks ago Saturday."

Morry sniffed.

"She can't get me to go out with her anymore," he said. This wasn't quite true. Nettie still treated him like dirt under her feet in the daytime and this so puzzled Morry that he had to reassure himself at other times that he was really the conqueror. He hated Nettie, though, he never would forget that he hated her.

"Say—say Jen, what are you going to do about Lil? Has she been adopted yet?"

Talking about Lil always pacified Jen . . .

"I wrote her to run away if they started adopting her," Jen said. "I could look after her. I sent her my birthday dollar."

Morry remembered his own brave promises about Lil—he was the one that was going to rescue Lil, he was.

"I've got a job, too," said Jen. "Anytime I want to, I can get three dollars a week waiting table at Bauer's. Grace gets six and her keep but I have to go to school part time."

"Next year you can get into the factory, too," said Morry, "You'll get ten there—maybe twelve."

"I'm not going to work in any factory," Jen told him casually. "I guess I'll go on the stage or be a dancer, maybe. If you'd been to the Casino lately you'd a seen me. Mr. Fischer says I'm a born dancer. So that's what I'll be doing."

Morry was silenced and awed. He saw Jen in a ballet skirt puffed out all around, her picture in some magazine, and at first he was proud, proud because she was his invention, then he was jealous of all the men who would be looking at a ballet girl's picture. He wanted to be glad of this glamorous future for her and he wanted to be fair, but he couldn't help warning her that it was pretty hard to get on the stage, and besides the Delaneys wouldn't let her, and what's more, who'd look after Lil?

Jen refused to be discouraged.

"I guess I'll do what I please when I'm earning regular money over at Bauer's," she said. "They can't stop me. I could look after Lil, and you said you'd help."

"Sure," said Morry. It was a promise.

The Chicago train thundered by with a fleeting glimpse of white-jacketed porters and lit-up dining cars. Morry and Jen watched it hungrily, they were on that train whizzing through Lamptown on their way to someplace, someplace wonderful, and looking a little pityingly out of their car window at a boy and girl sitting on the backsteps over a saloon. The train went ripping through further silence leaving only a humming in the air and a smoky message painted on the sky.

Morry and Jen looked quickly at each other—this was the thing that always bound them—trains hunting out unknown cities, convincing proof of adventure far off, of destiny somewhere waiting, of things beyond Lamptown. It was like that first time they sat here....

"I'd never go away, Morry," Jen finally said, not looking at him, "not unless you went first."

Morry didn't know what to answer. Windows in the court were slowly lighting up, downstairs the player piano jangled out "Under the Double Eagle." The kitchen light of the Delaneys' apartment went on—the old lady might come out any minute and chase him off. . . . No, it was different from the first night they sat here because now they were grown up, Jen was old enough to go to the Casino dances.

"Say, Jen, who do you dance with over there?"

He didn't think anyone would ever ask her to dance. "I dance with Bill and with Sweeney and the men from downstairs," Jen answered. "And last time I danced with Hunt Russell twice."

Morry blinked at that. Hunt was an old rounder. If he got after Jen . . . Well, after all, someone would sooner or later, wouldn't they? Now he looked at her with Hunt Russell's eyes and saw that she was different from anyone at Lamptown dances, she was—yes, you might say pretty, but strange-looking, maybe it was her eyes or something stiff and proud in the way she held herself, yes, there was something here worth hunting down, a man would think....

"It's funny dancing with Hunt," Jen said. "You think he's made different from other people—all solid gold clinking in him instead of lungs and a liver—and it's like his skin was more expensive than other people's, all heavy silk, the very best. It's like dancing with a prince."

"Who—that loafer?" Morry laughed scornfully.

"I used to think so," said Jen, "but you told me how wonderful he was, don't you remember, and I guess I was wrong."

"I don't know about that," said Morry uncomfortably. "Anyway he's not so different as you think from other people."

From far off came the train whistle, an invitation to mystery, to limitless adventure. A few stars showed up faintly. He could see Jen's face on that magazine cover, in a filmy white ballet skirt . . . it was all very far-off, some place where trains went . . . Hunt Russell, there, too, smiling quietly. . . .

Morry's arms went around Jen's shoulder, he kissed her hard on the mouth and received as reward a stinging slap in the face. He sat up straight, rubbing his face indignantly. Jen jumped up.

"You leave me alone, Morry! Don't you suppose I know about you and Nettie Farrell? Don't you suppose Grace and I followed you down to the Murphys that night, don't you think I got any sense? So leave me alone, now, will you?"

"Say—oh now say, Jen."

Morry was crushed by this unexpected attack.

"Go on and kiss Nettie if you've got to be kissing somebody," Jen flung at him. "Don't think I want to have Nettie Farrell's old beaux, I'll get my own, thank you."

She fled indoors leaving the screen to shut in his face.

Morry's face burned at this attack. He was through with Jen St. Clair, that was certain. Nobody was going to slap his face, no tough little kid could tell him anything. With his hands jammed in his pockets he slouched across the alley to his home, angrier at every step with Jen, with Grace for following him that night, with everybody. Inside the hall doorway he bumped into Nettie who was standing there, her finger to her lips.

"I've been waiting for you," she whispered. "The Murphys are out tonight. I'm going to be alone."

It was the last straw.

"Isn't that too bad?" he snorted mockingly. "Now, isn't that a goddamned shame?"

He pushed past her upstairs and banged his door loudly shut. Nettie stamped her foot furiously and went back into the shop.

৵

Mrs. Pepper cried telling Nettie about how Mrs. Abbott had changed, and Nettie answered that it was very funny for Mrs. Abbott to act that way after the years they'd known each other. They stood in front of Robbins' Jewelry Store discussing it.

"I'd hardly got inside the door, Nettie," said Mrs. Pepper tremulously. "I'd just set my grip down when she came out of the workroom, white as a sheet, and she said to me, 'Mrs. Pepper, you've been coming here a long time, too long, in fact, and I just wanted to tell you that it's going to stop right now. I got no place,' she says, 'for your corsets and trash in my shop, and it'll suit me if you take your stuff somewheres else.' . . . Well, Nettie, you know how I am, tenderhearted, and always a good friend to everyone. I didn't know what in the world to say. I said, what is it, whatever happened? . . . And she said, tight-mouthed, the way she is, 'It's my place, Mrs. Pepper, I think I have the right to have or not have people here just as I like.' . . . I said who's been talking behind my back, just tell me their names and I'll make them answer for it."

"What'd she say to that?" Nettie asked, thinking over the slurring remarks she herself had often made about the corsetiere, and feeling rather guilty. "Did she say anyone had talked about you?"

"That's just it," answered Mrs. Pepper. "She looked funny and said, oh, so you know there's talk, do you, but she wouldn't say anything else, so I packed up my few little things and went right across the street to the Bauers', and Mrs. Bauer's letting me have a room upstairs for fittings. But, Nettie, what could anyone have said about me? You know I've always tried to be a lady, I've never done anything a lady wouldn't, you know that, Nettie."

Nettie kept her eyes fixed on a gilt clock in Robbins' window.

"Well, she might have heard about you and Mr. Fischer," she said gently. "After all, you know he is a married man."

Mrs. Pepper's little red mouth made an O of astonishment.

"The very idea! If that isn't like a little town. Just because Mr. Fischer and I both travel from place to place and are old friends, people get to talking! So that's what she heard, you think . . . Nettie, that does make me feel badly! . . . But I'm glad you told me. I never thought people would be so wicked saying things, when I've tried always to be a lady in spite of being alone in the world. Goodness, Mr. Fischer would be so upset to know anyone in Lamptown talked like that!"

Nettie said no more. They started back up the street and Mrs. Pepper forlornly left Nettie at the Bauers' front door. Bauers' rooms were so dark and musty and gloomy. The Bon Ton had seemed gay with girls chattering in and out all the time over hats, telling who was going with who, and laughing. . . . But Hermann Bauer never smiled and Hulda Bauer had stopped thinking and settled into a contented jellyfish the day she married Hermann. It was not a jolly place at all for a sun-loving soul, and Mrs. Pepper, lacing a customer into a lavender satin brocade model in her dingy bedroom, dropped a few unexpected tears down the girl's back.

"Mrs. Bauer is good to me, of course," she choked bravely, "and Mr. Bauer is such a fine man that I'd be the last one to complain—but I think dark places like this ought to be torn down, I do, really. It would be a blessing if it burned, it's so gloomy, and when you're in trouble with your dearest friend, too—honey, are you sure this doesn't pinch your tummy?"

Nettie tried to find out why Elsinore had taken such a serious step but Elsinore gave her no details. She seemed silent and preoccupied, and all she said was that Mrs. Pepper was a hypocrite and besides the Bon Ton had no place for all those corset boxes and trash. Nettie was glad the extra work was out of the way, she was especially glad because now she was to go with Elsinore, it seemed, on buying expeditions to Cleveland or Columbus. Before, Nettie had kept shop while Elsinore and Mrs. Pepper went off together, all dressed up for a day in the city. Elsinore said this time they would close the shop and take an early train, so Nettie sat up half the night sewing a new frill on her black suit and washing out white silk gloves. She'd been to Cleveland a few times but this was most exciting because now she was going as a business woman, a woman of affairs.

They sat in the chair car going in the next morning. Elsinore, with dark hollows under her eyes from thinking so desperately of the plan she had for the day, and Nettie, dressed up and well-pleased with herself, her gloved hands folded over her new gold mesh purse, a blue veil drooping from her little hat, lace open-work on her black silk stockings. This was her real sphere, Nettie thought, going to cities and wearing little veils and white gloves and perfume, being a woman of the world and she thought it was funny her living in Lamptown when anyone could tell she was more of a city type . . . She was twenty now and she certainly was doing more with her life than other girls her age were. She was bound she'd be a success, this year she'd join the Eastern Stars, she thought, and she'd read *Laddie* and *The Little Shepherd of Kingdom Come;* she'd get baptized, too, join a church, and whenever she met anyone from out of town she'd always correspond with them so that she'd be getting letters from Cincinnati and Birmingham and St. Louis all at one time. She'd take dancing lessons, too, only she didn't see how she'd ever have the nerve to practice in public with all the younger people. She'd have a hat shop of her own, someday, she'd call it the Paris Shop, or maybe The Elite, Nettie Farrell, prop.

Nettie glanced guiltily at Elsinore to see if this disloyal thought had somehow been overheard, but Elsinore was drumming nervously on the windowsill, watching fields and villages slide past the window.

They went to different stores in the morning buying silks and trimmings and they were to meet in the Taylor Arcade for lunch but Nettie got mixed up the way she always did in Cleveland and waited in the Colonial Arcade instead. She stood at the entrance watching for Elsinore till half past one when a dark Jewish man smoking a cigar spoke to her. Nettie stared him down so haughtily that he rushed contritely into a little cigar store to peer at her over the inner curtains. Nettie, after a minute or two, walked slowly past the cigar store and somehow dropped her purse so he came out to pick it up. This time Nettie thanked him very distantly and when he went on asking her if she was just in town for the day she answered him rather loftily so he could see she was not an ordinary pickup.

When Elsinore finally decided to look for Nettie in the other Arcade she saw her through the glass window of a little tearoom at a table with some stranger. The man was talking and Nettie was sedately holding a teacup, little finger flying. Elsinore went in and Nettie said, "This is Mr. Schwarz, Mrs. Abbott. He used to travel for the same company Mr. Abbott did, isn't that funny, but now he's in the woolen business and he lives at the Gilsey. We're going to the Hippodrome this afternoon while you're seeing wholesalers."

Elsinore had been wondering how she would get rid of Nettie for the afternoon so she was much more agreeable over tea and cinnamon buns than she usually was with strangers, and Mr. Schwarz, at first wary, began to warm up to the idea of a little party for four. He said he'd call up the hotel and get hold of a friend of his named Wohlman, who also was in woolen, and tonight they'd all go to the Ratskellar and afterwards to a show the Hermits were giving. The idea alarmed Elsinore and she got away as fast as she could.

"Five thirty, then, in the Hollenden lobby," said Nettie gaily, being a woman of the world.

Elsinore took a Woodland Avenue car out to East 55th Street. She didn't dare think of what she was about to do or she might lose courage. She thought of Mrs. Pepper and after three weeks of hating her, even the mental image of the woman was distorted into a fat, lewd beast that deserved annihilation. Elsinore wasn't sorry she'd sent her out of the Bon Ton, she wasn't sorry when Mrs. Pepper's blue eyes welled with tears over this broken friendship; she wished she had it in her to be even crueler; she would like to have hurt her as much as she had been hurt herself. . . .

All these years, then, the town whisper about Fischer and Mrs. Pepper had been well-founded. Elsinore felt as betrayed as if Fischer had really been her own husband, she wanted fiercely to be revenged, not on him, but on the woman. Nor was the desire for revenge a spasmodic thought that died out after the first shock of suspicions proved true; she thought of it night and day ever since the rainy night Mrs. Pepper had gone out with Dode to meet him somewhere; she thought of them on Thursday nights at the Casino watching his heavy masklike face. . . . She had wondered often about his wife and now she felt somehow identified with her, as if Mrs. Pepper had deliberately wronged them both. What kept her curious indignation at fever pitch was the thought of how long Mrs. Pepper had fooled everyone with her wide innocent blue eyes, her baby face, her dainty ladylike ways, her sweet detachment in mentioning his name. Worse than a vampire, Elsinore grimly decided, worse than the commonest factory girl, because she pretended so much, because she fooled people.

At the other end of the streetcar, two girls in white flannel suits giggled over yesterday's moonlight ride on the Steamer

Eastland, and the conductor asked them if they were going to the big brewers' picnic next Sunday at Put-in-Bay. Elsinore listened to them intently because she wanted to know things that people around Fischer knew, she wanted to hear and see the same things he did, she could almost be him, she could half close her eyes and admire women and young girls the way he did. This was what he saw on his way to and from his house, and now that they were close to 55th Street, that must be the church over yonder where he sent his children to Sunday school, this must be the market where his wife did her trading, this was his stop. . . .

Elsinore's knees were shaky getting off the car. If she could only keep in mind how Mrs. Pepper had fooled her and Mrs. Fischer, she'd be able to go ahead with her plan, but she kept forgetting and having stage fright over being so near his place and so near to coming face to face with his wife. She asked a street cleaner where this number was and he pointed out an old house set far back from the street with a sign in the window in black and white—

HARRY FISCHER
Ballroom Dancing

Oh, she'd never have the courage to walk down that pathway with someone probably peeking at her from behind the lace curtains, and perhaps someone following her, too. . . . This frightened her, she looked over her shoulder, now she had a distinct feeling of being followed. If Nettie had taken it into her head to follow her, what would she say?

"I came to arrange private dancing lessons for both of us," she'd tell Nettie if it came to that, and she'd say it was always impossible to get a private word with Fischer about it in Lamptown so she'd just dropped in. . . .

If it was Fischer himself behind her, though, or Mrs. Pepper, or Charles, or someone from Lamptown. . . . Still, there wasn't a chance of any such thing, why should she feel guilty when she was only doing a friendly duty? . . . She walked quickly up to the gray gingerbread porch. She wondered if he owned this house, if he had a dance hall in it the way Mrs. Pepper had once said, and it made her ache to think of all the things in his life that she could never guess thinking about him in the Bon Ton. . . . She was on the porch, in a minute she'd turn around and run for her life . . . no, she was ringing the doorbell and her black gloved hand was quite steady. She couldn't run now, even if Fischer himself should confront her, her legs were numb, she doubted if she could even speak. She heard steps inside, the sound of a slap, and a child screeching and then the door opened.

"Well?"

Two towheaded children on a red scooter stared at her with bold black eyes, their mother tried to push them out of the way of the door, she was a large ash-blonde woman with heavy breasts and her voice was deep like a singer's with a vaguely Scandinavian accent. His wife. . . . Yes, she was Mrs. Fischer. The lady wanted to know about dancing lessons? Friday and Saturday were his Cleveland days, if she wanted to sign up for the course and leave a five dollar deposit. . . .

"It's not about dancing," Elsinore said, "It's about him that I wanted to see you."

Her throat felt swollen and tight, talking was like trying to scream in your sleep, driving your voice through your shut mouth with all your might and having it come out only a hoarse whisper.

"There's a woman that wants to make trouble for you and I thought someone ought to tell you so you could stop it."

Fischer's wife just stared stupidly at her. The largest towheaded child with a little yelp turned his toy car around and scooted down the hall, its bell going tingalingaling, and the littlest one remembered that his mother had slapped him and resumed his wailing, burying his face in his mother's skirts.

Mrs. Fischer pushed open the screen door.

"Do you want to come inside and tell me what you're talking about, missus?" she said, studying Elsinore from head to foot with a puzzled and not at all friendly eye. "What's this about my husband and who are you, anyway, that's what I want to know?"

Elsinore could feel her face reddening, she must be careful now, or Fischer might guess who had told.

"It doesn't matter who I am," she said hurriedly, "but I thought you ought to know—as one woman to another, understand—that there's someone your husband goes with out of town, there's a woman crazy about him, trying to break up your home."

She'd said it now, but Mrs. Fischer's thick pasty face took on an ugly expression. Her pale blue eyes narrowed, under the heavy colorless brows.

"I suppose you don't want to make trouble, too, hey? I suppose I'm to believe a party coming in out of the blue sky and not saying who she is, just bringing tattle tales to see what harm she can do—"

Elsinore backed away from the door, alarmed at the woman's tone. Mrs. Fischer came out on the porch after her.

"See here, what right have you got, coming to my home making trouble for me? If my husband's doings don't suit you, then you don't need to watch 'em, just mind your own step, that's all. Who are you, coming here with your tattle? Where you from, anyway? Who told you I wanted to hear tales about Harry?"

"I didn't want you to be fooled, that was all," gasped Elsinore, and backed down the porch steps with Mrs. Fischer coming right after her, her hands on her hips. "You had a right to know."

"Well, who said you were the one with a right to tell," Mrs. Fischer asked contemptuously. "I've got enough trouble without strangers trying to cook up more. I'd thank you to clear out, and I'll tell you here and now if anybody's got the right to spy on Harry, it's me, and nobody else, understand? So!"

Elsinore, faint with shame, rushed toward the street. Both children now were crying loudly and the toy car bell dingled raucously in her ears. She knew people were watching her, someone was following her again, that much was certain, she felt their distrustful eyes boring through her back, the footsteps behind her were ominous, but when she dared to look back it was only a mailman and further off two women wheeling go-carts, she could not find those watchful eyes. Foghorns croaked on the lake and made her head buzz, the city noises seemed more than she could bear. She climbed aboard the first street car that came along, it was pure luck that it was going in the right direction. Her face would never stop burning, she was so shamed, yet she was glad in a way because she'd had to do just that thing, she'd simply had to, nothing could have stopped her, and now it was over with, that was all. . . . What would she say to Nettie, she wondered, what could she tell her? . . . She sat next to a big colored woman who asked her where the May Company was, where you got off for the Interurban Station, how you got out to Gates Mills? She didn't know, she kept mumbling in reply, and planned what to say to Nettie.

"I went to Halle's for that taffeta, then I walked over to the Square and sat down for a while, then I went to the braid place, then I went into De Klyn's for a sundae and cocoa—no, for a cup of tea, then—then—"

She went into the hotel lobby where she was to meet Nettie. She was dizzy and faint, for she wasn't used to crowds and streetcars. Suspicious eyes continued to bore through her, she was certain someone had followed her all day, she was certain someone was reading her guilty thoughts.

It was long after six when Nettie came. Mr. Schwarz, perhaps a little self-conscious, was not with her, but Nettie talked about him a great deal on the way to the depot, because she'd never been out with an older man, a man of the world, before. . . . Elsinore did not breathe easily until she was finally on the train for Lamptown. No one had seen her. No one had followed her. No one knew.

"So then we went down to the Ratskellar," Nettie chattered on excitedly, "and Mr. Schwarz asked me what I'd have since I hated beer so much. So I took a Clover Club cocktail because Mr. Schwarz said that in Cleveland they were absolutely all the go."

⁂

Elsinore didn't dare go to the dance on Thursday night, she was afraid to face the dancing teacher for a little while. She closed the shop and sat in the dark watching the Casino windows, seeing couples whirl past and hearing Fischer's big voice boom out the commands. She leaned forward on the wicker settee and wrung her hands each time the music started for a new dance. If there was a circle two-step tonight she might have gotten him for a partner for a minute or two, but now she'd ruined the chances of that. She wouldn't dare go up again, he'd ask what right she had going to his wife. . . . At least Mrs. Pepper hadn't gone to the Casino either, because Nettie had seen her get on the streetcar going upstate earlier in the day.

The Bauers were in their window peering out at the passing girls, and she reflected bitterly that she might as well be Hulda Bauer now, nothing but a spectator. She saw Grace come out in front of the restaurant and hoo-oo, then the Delaneys' girl, Jen, came running across the street to join her, and they went up the Casino steps together. She saw her own son standing in front of her darkened shop, smoking, waiting for the right moment to go over. When Jen and Grace went up he turned around and stared idly at the dimly outlined hats in the Bon Ton window. Then Elsinore realized that in spite of the darkness, the lights reflected from the street made her faintly visible because Morry frowned and suddenly pressed his face against the pane, staring inside, as if he was seeing a ghost. She stood very still but after all her face probably showed up white and shadowy for Morry shivered and backed away, she saw him toss his cigarette into the gutter and hurry across the street, stopping at the foot of the Casino stairs for a puzzled backward glance at the Bon Ton.

There would be next Thursday night and the next and the next. . . . Elsinore grew dizzy thinking of all the torture in store for her, for how could she ever look at Fischer again after her Cleveland visit. . . . His wife must have told him everything and he had told Mrs. Pepper and probably Mrs. Pepper had put two and two together. . . . Elsinore dragged her feet slowly up the stairs to bed, but she wouldn't sleep tonight, she'd lie there listening to the music and the applause, and think. . . . It was no use, she knew that no matter what the risk she'd go next Thursday night. After all, she hadn't told Fischer's wife her name or even that she was from Lamptown, so how could anyone possibly guess?

She drew a rocking chair up to her bedroom window and huddled there in her nightdress.

"Dance Number Three."

Today some factory girls trying on hats had talked about the chance Fischer had to have a studio in Chicago only he'd refused to give up his Cleveland headquarters. It had been a great chance, they said, and he might change his mind, of course. Elsinore thought of dark, silent Thursday nights going on forever, for the rest of her life, and a Lamptown slackening into a dull shuffle with no Fischer to count out the rhythm. . . . Well, there was always a chance for a new millinery store in a big city like Chicago, she could get on there, she could always manage her business, Chicago wouldn't be any harder than Lamptown. Now it seemed a question of the Bon Ton moving to Chicago, and she'd forgotten why.

It must be a good dance tonight. Everyone sang softly with the orchestra, they blended into one gay humming voice that might be swelling out of the rickety old building itself though no one could believe it to look at the sleepy expressionless faces of Hermann and Hulda Bauer in the first floor window.

> Has anybody here seen Kelly—
> K-e- double l-y
> Anybody here seen Kelly—

Elsinore sat in the chair and wished she hadn't been such a coward as to stay away. She'd never stay home again, that was certain.

In the smoking room of the Casino Morry Abbott read a magazine with a red devil on the cover. If he went out on the floor Grace would smile at him waiting for him to dance with her, and he wasn't going to be trapped into anything again. If he looked up from the magazine he would see Jen whirling by with Sweeney, the telegraph operator, or with his own foreman; if she'd been sitting out by herself he might ask her for a dance but he wasn't going to compete with other men, he'd never do that. Let her have them, but he could tell by the way she flipped her skirts passing the smoking room that she wanted him to be jealous, and it annoyed him. He read on resolutely, all the stories ended in suicide, he wished he knew things so he could read the one story in French. He looked at it wistfully—"l'amour" was love, that much he did know. . . . Something made him lift his eyes and there was Jen dancing with Hunt. Morry threw down the book and went out. Some yellow-haired girl in a red flannel dress was sitting by the door chewing gum. He asked her to dance.

It was a pretty how-de-do, he thought, when people as fussy as old Mrs. Delaney let a kid go to dances and run with old rounders like Russell. He saw now that Jen wore Grace Terris's dress—Grace was wearing a new one—she had her hair fixed up like Grace's as near as she could make it, and she had on high-heeled shoes, surely Grace's, since if you looked closely you could tell they were too big for her, and she seemed unreasonably well-pleased with herself. Morry found himself burning with right-eous anger, partly because she seemed able to dance as well as anyone else without having had any lessons, and partly because she giggled too loud and tweaked Sweeney's necktie. He tried to ignore her but she always managed to get right in front of him and when he'd look somewhere else he'd encounter Grace's steady meaning gaze. All right, he'd go home, he wasn't going to stand around here like a fool, but when he put on his coat Hunt Russell was in the coatroom smoking and kidding the fat little hat-check girl. He beckoned Morry.

"Stick around, Abbott, we'll pick up a couple of women and drive Fischer over to Marion. . . . Got a date?"

It was the royal command and Morry obediently took off his coat. Dode wasn't around tonight and he knew Hunt would pick the two hardest-boiled girls in the hall but he didn't care. You had to do what Hunt asked you to—you wanted to, somehow. . . . He went back in the smoking room and read the red devil magazine again. Sweeney and his factory foreman came in and asked him to go over to Delaney's for a beer or two, and Morry said briefly:

"Can't. Going out with Hunt."

He was proud because Hunt didn't ask just anybody. He went with Hunt for ham sandwiches at Bauers' and a pint of rye at Delaney's at the end of the last dance. When they came out Hunt went on up to get Fischer and Morry strolled over to get in Hunt's car. The women were already in—one in front and one in back. Morry took a second glance and saw that the evening was already spoiled, for the girl in front was Jen, and the one in back, swathed in floating scarfs, was Grace.

"Oh, Jen, look, here's Morry!" gurgled Grace. "Won't we have a circus? Wouldn't Dode take our heads off if she knew? Wouldn't she, Morry?"

Morry gloomily got in beside Grace. Jen turned around to give him a triumphant smile. Morry was annoyed, because while he himself was dazzled by Hunt's glamorous position he thought it was ridiculous for a girl to be taken in by all that bunk.

"Thought you couldn't stand Hunt," he challenged her. "Thought you was just about going to burn up his house someday. I notice you've changed your mind."

"I never was in an automobile before," Jen resentfully explained. "I guess you'd go, too."

"Jen's never been anywhere," Grace laughed. "Why, when I was fifteen there was two fellas crazy over me and I had dates every night. I was more like a man's woman, I was. I certainly had a good time and I knew what was what, too."

Fischer and Hunt came down and Morry moved over to let Fischer in beside Grace. With a great roaring of the motor they started. Grace wanted Fischer to be affectionate and she kept leaning against him.

"Look at this, Jen," she'd call and playfully wrap her arms around him but Fischer firmly shook her off. He winked at Morry once and made a wry face, but Morry was only able to manage a half-hearted smile in turn. It was all easy enough to understand. Hunt was amused by Jen the way the men said he always was by every new kind of girl, he asked Morry because he'd gotten the idea she was Morry's girl, that was all. He really didn't give a damn who was in the back seat so long as he had what he wanted beside him in front there. It made his invitation not so flattering after all, and Morry blamed Jen for this disillusion.

Certainly the ride wasn't any fun with Grace on one hand making a fool of herself over Fischer and Jen in front with her hat off and the wind blowing her black hair all over, not talking, just watching Hunt as if he was some great wonder. She'd get it from the old lady when she got in, Morry thought, and if Dode O'Connell ever found out, she'd get it from her, too. It took two hours to drive to Marion—it would be at least four or five when they got back, and the Delaneys wouldn't stand for that. Jen ought to be more careful. Thinking of this Morry got angrier than ever with Grace for egging her into it, and he was angry with Hunt too. Hunt and Fischer drank the whiskey between them, though Grace, with much tittering took more than a few swigs from the bottle to show she was used to going out. Fischer didn't talk except to call something out to Hunt once in a while; he was sleepy, he said, and leaned back on the seat with his eyes closed most of the way.

It was three when they got to his hotel in Marion and then Hunt insisted that they all go over to the Quick Lunch for ham and eggs. Grace was eager for this because she'd only been a guest in a restaurant twice and she was anxious to be lordly with other waitresses.

"You'd better take those kids back to Lamptown, Hunt," Fischer advised. "You'll have Bill Delaney on your neck if you keep his girl out much longer."

"How'd you like to mind your own business?" Hunt inquired, lighting a cigarette. "This young lady's just about able to take care of herself."

Fischer got his handbag from under Morry's feet and banged the car door shut.

"I'm sure I hope so," he said calmly. "Well, goodnight."

"To hell with you," answered Hunt. He drove over to the Quick Lunch and they got out. Morry was sleepy, he'd never been out so late, and much as he wanted to be ranked as a sport like Hunt and Fischer, he only wished he was home in bed, and the thought of the long ride home sickened him, he didn't know why except that he knew Jen would get a good whaling when she got in and she was just a little fool and it was all her own fault. She was excited about being out with men in strange towns after midnight, but she was scared too, you could tell by her eyes, she was scared of what the old lady would say to her coming home in the morning.

"I knew Fischer wanted a date with me," Grace said over the white porcelain table. "He always is looking at me with those big black eyes sort of as if he'd like to say something to me but was afraid to speak out, I suppose on account of his wife. I kidded him tonight about being so bashful and he had to admit that he was, did you hear us kidding, Jen?"

Jen nodded and looked at the big white clock on the wall. It said four o'clock but Hunt wasn't in any hurry and Grace was having the time of her life. She got to talking about all the other swell restaurants she'd been in, and somehow her memory had blurred so that she seemed to have been the most valued patron in these resorts and not an employee at all. Nobody listened to her. Jen kept looking at the clock, more scared than ever now, but afraid to suggest going for fear they'd think she was young and not used to being out. Grace talked and Morry yawned over his coffee and squirmed restlessly when he saw Hunt stare lazily at Jen.

"Cold, Baby?" Hunt asked Jen when she shivered once. Then when they finally started back to the car Morry saw him put his arm over her shoulder.

"Good kid," he murmured and slid in behind the wheel. "Say, Abbott, anything left of that quart?"

"No," lied Morry, because he wasn't going to be killed tonight by wild driving. "I finished it up."

All the way back driving into the sunrise Hunt kept one arm flung over Jen's shoulders and Grace, after many coy attempts to engage Morry's attention, moved over to the edge of the seat and hummed softly to herself; sometimes she'd call Jen's attention to this house which was just like her Uncle File's, or that railroad depot which was only half as big as the one in Tiffin. Morry saw none of these things, he only saw Hunt's arm around Jen and he thought that it was just as Hogan said—Hunt Russell wasn't so damned much, people in Lamptown were taken in by him only because of the money his old man had made and Hunt was nothing but a sport and a waster with no more guts to him than a jelly bean. Dode O'Connell was the only woman that wanted him, he wasn't any matinee idol with his graying temples and his weak chin, what made him so complacently sure he could get Jen St. Clair if he so condescended?

Grace pointed toward Hunt's arm.

"Do you allow that, Morry?" she asked archly.

"Has he got anything to say about it?" Hunt called back, and slowed the car to lean over and kiss Jen. But she didn't slap him, Morry noted cynically, she didn't seem to mind at all, so Morry sullenly put his own arm around Grace for Jen to be sure and see.

It was six o'clock when they drew up in front of Bauer's. Grace rushed in, eager for Sweeney the telegraph operator to come in for breakfast so she could brag about the wild party. Morry and Jen crossed the street together. In the alley between their two homes they looked at each other.

"Well, you're going to catch it," Morry said. "It's Hunt's fault. He had no business asking you out, he knows how Bill is."

"I had a good time," answered Jen, but she looked a little doubtfully toward the saloon.

"See, you're afraid to go up," Morry challenged her. "Do you think she'd have the nerve to beat you up?"

"Pooh!" bragged Jen. "I'd like to see her try. I'd tell her right where to get off."

She was in no hurry, though. Morry wanted to do something big, in a casual, off-handed way to go over and pave the way for Jen, but he knew he was a lot more afraid of Bill's mother than even Jen was. Only the Hunt Russells knew how to have their way, how to get things, all anybody else could ever do was to wish and be afraid. He got his key out for his side door, and still

Jen hung back. She took his handkerchief and wiped her shoes off carefully, and straightened her hair.

"Wish I was Grace," she said. "I wouldn't be afraid of anybody then. I'd be on my own and nobody could say a word to me if I stayed out late."

"You're pretty stuck on Hunt, now, aren't you?" Morry said. "I noticed you kissed him and made no fuss about it, either."

Jen looked at him silently until Morry's own eyes dropped.

"I guess you know well enough who I like, Morry," she said. "Well. . . . I might as well go home and get it over with. They wouldn't dare lick me, you bet your life."

She winked at him and walked boldly across the court. Morry let himself indoors and climbed upstairs. His mother was in the doorway of his room, looking very pale and tired in the gray morning light, her brown braids hanging over her wrapper.

"I didn't mean to wake you—I was just out on a little ride," he stammered.

"That's all right, I wasn't sleeping anyway," she murmured. "I only looked in to see if you'd come in."

She didn't wait for an answer, just smiled and pulled her wrapper around her to go back to her room, her long braids swinging. Funny she didn't mind his being out all night. She hadn't even listened to his excuse. Morry was puzzled. Funny her not sleeping. . . . Morry for some reason remembered his father's insistent questioning that night behind the saloon, something hit him sickeningly in the pit of the stomach. His mother. What if . . . yes, there was some man. His mother. . . . Morry sat down on the bed and shut his eyes. He heard her moving about on the other side of the wall but suddenly he could see her face before him more distinctly than he ever had—the gray eyes now with faint lines at the corners, the fine hairs of her nostrils, the unsmiling straight mouth, the face of a stranger. . . . He was stiff, sitting there so rigidly, and his eyeballs ached for sleep, but he dared not close them because he had to think about this thing . . . his mother. . . .

On the Delaney back porch Jen rubbed her hand over her eyes to make sure of what she saw. But it was true, no doubt of it. There sat her yellow telescope, packed and strapped, with her hat and coat on top of it. The door was locked. Jen resolutely tugged at the screen door but even that was hooked tight. The old lady had fired her for staying out—that was all there was to it. She sat down on the steps, frightened. She fumbled with the hat—it was the round sailor she'd worn away from the orphanage and it was too little with a childish rubber band under the chin. She slipped it on. The coat was too tight, too, and the sleeves hardly came below the elbow. Gee, how she'd grown, she thought. . . . She picked up the telescope and went uncertainly down the stairs. She knew the old lady was somewhere behind a curtain grimly watching to see what she'd do. Well, there wasn't anything to do but go.

At the foot of the steps Jen shifted the bag to the other hand and looked toward Bauer's then over toward the Bon Ton. No use looking, nobody was going to look after you but your own self. She looked up toward the screen door again. Bill might come out and call her back. She waited but the door didn't open. She guessed she was pretty lucky the old lady hadn't given her a beating when it came right down to it. Her knees shaking Jen picked her way across the back lot to the railroad. There weren't any trains in sight. She might as well get going. . . . She looked over her shoulder at the Delaney kitchen window but nobody was leaning out there beckoning her to come back. . . . With both arms around the yellow telescope she started grimly walking down the track.

୬ୡ

She'd leave her telescope in the Tower with Sweeney, Jen thought; she'd walk east down the tracks and get a ride on a three-wheeler maybe to the next town. If she could get near Libertyville she'd go to the Home and get Lil. Then—then—well, she could get a job like Grace's in a restaurant, couldn't she? She was too ashamed ever to go back to Lamptown. People would know she'd been locked out because she stayed out all night and they'd say, just as old Mrs. Delaney had, that she'd turned out bad the way adopted girls always did. She'd get Lil herself now, so that Lil wouldn't ever be adopted and turn out bad.

It was a foggy morning. In the ditch beside the tracks burdocks and milkweed propped up dewy spider webs, fields were veiled in lavender, in the gray sky a hawk circled lower and lower so that birds were still. Jen hurried to reach the Tower before Sweeney got through because the day trick operators were stricter about visitors.

She was excited because she was going to do something big now, get Lil, and be on her own, but a faint sick feeling came over her when she thought she'd turned out bad the way Mrs. Delaney had always said, and that Lamptown with its dance music and Morry Abbott was behind her. The sun struggled through sooty pink clouds over the Big Four woods, lying under the trees were tramps sleeping with their hats over their faces and newspapers for covers. Two were kneeling by a little bonfire, skinning a rabbit. Jen was afraid of them because once a man was murdered here, they found his head rolling in the ditch and the stump of his cork leg. . . . She got off the track for a slow freight with cattle cars of whinnying western ponies and lambs bleating through their bars piteously. The brakeman waved his cap to her from the top of the caboose and Jen waved back. Names in big letters on the cars tantalized her—CLEVELAND, CINCINNATI & ST. LOUIS, MICHIGAN CENTRAL, PERE MARQUETTE, LAKE SHORE R. R., SANTA FE R. R., DELAWARE LACKAWANNA R. R.—Jen saw the brakeman far down the tracks still waving to her.

"Good-bye," she called to him and waved again.

She stumbled through the cinders on to the Yards. Everything was different, it was a new world today, a world to be measured and appraised with a view to possible conquest. As for Lamptown, it wasn't her Lamptown now, she saw it hungrily from the outside where she belonged. Behind the black fences all along here were the backyards of Shantyville, there was the spire of the Church of Our Lady. Shantyville backyards were different from the boarding house backyards where they sometimes had hollyhocks and grape arbors and swings for the girls. Here were only tumbled-down chicken houses with skinny pin-feathered chickens flapping around, washings always hanging out, gray sheds with dirty children on the roofs screaming and waving to the trains. . . . But even Shantyville was gay in its shiftless way and people were lucky to live there. . . . Jen wanted to reach the Tower before the factory men from this end of town started down the tracks on their way to work. They'd know she'd been locked out and they'd know it was because she'd stayed out all night.

It was funny about her feet walking along the ties as if they belonged to somebody else. She thought Bill might be following her to bring her back, indeed she was so sure that she didn't even turn around for fear of being disappointed. She stepped over rails and humming wires to the Tower stairs. Sweeney was in there alone with his fingers on the little black keys, the room ticked and throbbed with important messages.

"Hey, Sweeney, watch this bag till I come back, will you?"

Sweeney was mad because the day man was late this morning.

"You get the hell out of here before Tucker finds you!"

Jen shoved the bag inside and scurried downstairs again. The factory whistles were blowing for work and the men were coming down the track swinging their lunch pails. The old station agent hobbled over tracks swinging a bunch of keys and Jen saw him staring at her curiously as he unlocked the ticket office. She caught sight of one of the freight hands, a young Swede named Davey often in Bill's saloon, pumping a handcar down the track. He sometimes let her ride and today when she got on, his anguish over the English language saved her from any questions. On the handcar you ran off the tracks into cinderheaps every time you saw an engine ahead and you couldn't get very far that way. Davey was going to some section workers a few miles out, but only a few miles out made Lamptown seem far, far away, it seemed like a dream, last night in the restaurant hadn't happened, or the locked door—the real thing was the Children's Home where she belonged.

Near the water tank some Pullman cars were on siding, their names were spelled out in gold letters over their black sides—GRETCHEN—MINNEHAHA—NIGHTFALL—BLACK BEAUTY. Fortunate people looked out the windows yawning, and Jen saw a woman in a heavenly blue kimona smoking a cigarette. When would one ever get old, she wondered passionately, and know everything and have everything—if she could only be old like the woman in the blue kimona, and be looking back on all this, perfectly sure of herself, quite unafraid. . . .

The rotten planks on the handcar tore her dress, the old lady would scold her for that—but no—the old lady wouldn't scold her any more. The tracks went through low fields past an old quarry and here Davey pushed off and Jen said good-bye.

"You know where you're going?" stammered Davey, a little uneasily.

"Sure, I do."

She waded through muddy pastureland to the road. It was the road to the Orphanage at Libertyville, she could tell that, so she wasn't so far out of her way. She'd get Lil, then the two of them would get to Cleveland somehow and find their mother, that was the best thing to do. If her mother couldn't take care of them, why they could work, they were big enough. And nobody could stop you from going to your own mother. . . . She'd get in the back way somehow and find Lil, and even if she did run into the matron she wouldn't be afraid to tell her she'd come for her sister. . . . At least she didn't think she'd be afraid. But now that she was so near the Home the very trees had an air of inescapable authority, the woods, the fields, the houses all seemed busy and complete as if they were all there first and would forever be in command. Jen couldn't believe there had ever been moments when she'd thought herself free of them, when she'd actually planned to defy them and take Lil away. . . . She'd have to be at least ten or twenty years older, very rich, and with a bodyguard of powerful citizens before she'd dare venture inside the Home gates. . . . They'd treat her as if she'd just run away again, the way she used to do, and been caught; they wouldn't believe she'd ever been adopted and out of their hands. She'd never get away again, either, they'd hear from Mrs. Delaney about her and they'd put her to work for the rest of her life in the Laundry the way they did orphans that were too afraid to go out in the world when they got their liberty. . . . Jen began walking slower and slower. No sign of anything like Lamptown all around her, only yards of bushes and then a rain-rusted R. F. D box. She remembered these bushes for there were berry farms all along here. The orphans were let out to pick berries in the big season, they made six cents a quart and the one that made the most got a silver badge to wear, but all the pennies had to go to the Fund.

It was too late for strawberries but there were currants and gooseberries now, later on there would be potatoes to bug. Jen's heart dropped remembering when that was her world. She looked quickly over her shoulder—if someone from the Home saw her and recognized her she wouldn't stand a chance. They'd never let her get to her mother or to Lil either. She kept over to the edge of the road lingering in the tree shadows when anyone passed. If she was ninety years old, she thought resentfully, she'd never get over the fear of being clapped back in the Home again, made to say prayers out loud, sent out to pick berries. She'd been so certain she wasn't afraid of anything any more, but this one thing she'd always be afraid of.

There was a familiar sign tacked to a post here, "Red Clover Farm," and a muddy lane wound off the main road through a sparse woods. Far down this lane Jen saw someone coming, her hand over her eyes to stare longer and make sure. There was no doubt about it, it was a procession of children from the Home, all in blue calico and straw farm hats, berry pails clinking from their arms. In the lead was the Oldest Orphan, just as Jen had been once. Now it was a girl named Sadie whose folks were in the penitentiary so no one would ever take her. The Oldest Orphan carried the bun basket and behind her somewhere in this line must be Lil. Unconsciously Jen was backing into the bushes as she watched this oncoming procession, and thinking of how near she was to Lil her limbs began to shake. Suddenly she crashed through bushes and brambles for hiding—she forgot about everything but the fear of being caught again and made to go back. Hypnotized, she watched the line getting nearer, she saw the Oldest Orphan's brown sullen face, she could almost have whispered "Hoo-oo, Sadie!" but there was a woman in charge at the end. Then she saw Lil and it made her ache to see the sweet little dollface under the big straw hat; she wanted to rush out and say, "Here I am, Lil, see, come to take you away just like I promised." But they'd only make her fall in line and go back to the Home, too, that's all they'd ever do, she wasn't strong enough for them yet, she couldn't beat them.

The line went on up the road, they didn't laugh or talk, just marched along doing as they were told, and presently they went into the fields and Lil was lost. Jen came out onto the road again, weak and puzzled, too, that there could be something you were so sure you could do and when the chance came you were helpless. . . . So this was the way she was going to look after Lil, was it, always looking out for her own hide first, never able to do the wonderful things she'd planned. . . . Rage swept over her at being young, young and little, as if some evil fairy had put that spell on her. Why must you be locked up in this dreadful cage of childhood for twenty or a hundred years? Nothing in life was possible unless you were old and rich, until then you were only small and futile before your tormentors, desperately waiting for the release that only years could bring. You boldly threw down your challenges and then ran away in a childish panic when someone picked them up. . . . Jen stumbled along the road, glowering down at the dust, sick because she had failed Lil. She'd never get over being ashamed as long as she lived. Lil had been within two yards of her and she'd let her go, she was like all the visitors to the Home who'd promised her long ago they'd come back for her, and they never did, they never came back.

Coming to the Crossroads Jen sat down on a pile of fence rails. She wondered how far she was from Lamptown and she wanted to erase last night and go back. She thought of the pianola and the little gold chair from the World's Fair, and Morry. . . . She'd let Lamptown go and she'd let Lil go. She'd not been able to hold the things that meant the most to her. Maybe she never would. That was why she liked the tiny gold chair, you could close your hand tight over it and know it was always there.

She was hungry, it must be noon now, but that didn't seem to be the matter with her. The matter was that she'd failed. She was dizzy, too, trying to figure out where all these roads went. Cleveland? Akron? Columbus? She would like to be on a train named Nightfall going to some place where she'd be twenty-five years old.

An empty hay wagon came lumbering along and Jen hailed it.

"Give us a ride, mister."

"Going east?"

"Sure."

The driver was an old man with a Santa Claus beard, he had a face busy with a tobacco quid. He might have been asleep for all the heed he paid to his passenger. It was a relief to ride, and now if they should pass the Home by any chance, Jen decided she would hide under the burlap bags in the back. They jogged along, and looking about her the old aching years came back to her; going along shady country roads with the low branches flapping against her face. . . . She could remember being as tall as a wagon wheel, the caked putty mud on the wheel, stepping on the spokes and then on the muddy step into the wagon. She could remember being allowed to drive, the black leather reins slipping in her little hands, and her feet not halfway to the floor swinging back and forth, brown mud-caked boots with the buttons off except the first and last; she could see again the horse's black tail swishing back and forth at the flies. She had now the same scratches from brambles that she had then, and here were the same knotty trees that Johnny Appleseed had planted.

Along the road were neat little white and green-trimmed farmhouses with thin scrawny women outside watering rusty geraniums or pansy beds. They were the same women as before, Jen thought, women that would slap you with the backs of their hands so that the wedding ring cut your cheek, if you dared to touch the conch shell on the parlor mantel, or if you smelled the glass flowers in the vase; those women would make you get up before daylight to help wash, and you wouldn't get any breakfast till the washing was done, either. . . .

Digging postholes along the road were men in overalls, jolly-seeming sun-bronzed men, but they weren't jolly at all, they'd call up the Orphanage any time to say, "This is R. MacDonald on the Ellery Road. I saw a couple of the orphans out by here and thought they might be running away. If you want me to, I'll pick them up and bring them right over." This was because people liked the idea of other people being locked up.

She would never smell hay or blackberries or honeysuckle without that gone feeling of being trapped, Jen realized, while pianola music, saloon smells, engines shrieking, and the delicious smell of hot soapy dishwater from restaurant kitchens—these would always be gay symbols of escape.

They were at the pike road now, there was a streetcar track crossing it and a big sign reading "Turnpike Dairy."

"Here's where I go, girlie," said the driver. "Somebody else'll give you a lift now, I guess."

Jen got down. She didn't move till the wagon was far out of sight. Then she started limping down the car tracks. Her feet were sore and her eyes were full of dust and sleep. She came to a wide shallow brook and tiptoed over the trestle high above it. If a streetcar should unexpectedly come along she'd have to let herself down and dangle between the trestle ties, hanging by her fingertips, she planned. . . . She was so tired now she could go on forever without seeing or feeling anything. But this wasn't quite true, for before her was a banner across the road. It said—

WELCOME TO LAMPTOWN

Jen stopped dead. Lamptown had followed her, it seemed. Suddenly she was so happy she forgot her sore feet and started running as fast as she could down the track, stumbling over ties, panting for breath, her hair flying in all directions, but happy, happy, happy—because Lamptown had come after her. . . . She'd go straight to Bauer's and she'd say to Hermann, "I'm going to work for you. I'm going to stay upstairs like Grace and be a waitress—please, please!"

Happy—happy—

Far back on the turnpike her round straw hat sat on the tracks, crushed to a pancake just as the streetcar had left it.

Grace lay on her stomach on the bed and kicked up her heels. She was in a blue cotton chemise and with her glasses off and yellow hair hanging loose she didn't look so bad, Jen thought. Jen didn't want to take off the percale dress and white apron that Mrs. Bauer had given her, so she sat stiffly on the edge of the bed, occasionally stealing a glance at herself in the mirror.

"Men don't respect a factory girl the way they do a girl in a restaurant," said Grace. "I don't know why it is but they just don't. When you've been around as long as I have you'll see."

Jen looked politely interested but to tell the truth she had one worry on her mind and it was not concerned with male respect.

"Do you think Sister Catherine will make me go back to school when she finds I'm here? Because I'll bet the Delaneys will be mad enough to make her do something about me."

Grace snapped her gum.

"Na. You'll get more education right here than if you was in any school. I only went to the fourth grade and I get along, you bet. Some of the smartest men in the world come in this place— they get to talking and if you keep your ears open first thing you know you've learned something. Telegraph operators are usually the smartest. Take Sweeney. Before I knew Sweeney I used to always say 'me and my friends.' Now I know better. I say 'I and my friend is going to do so and so.' Just keep your ears open and you learn enough all right. 'Who's' wrong, too. You should always say 'whom,' but you know how it is, sometimes you get careless, even when you know better."

"I'd hate to go back to school as soon as I get a job like this," Jen said, "with my own room and everything."

Grace's bed took up almost the entire room except for the big golden oak dresser. Jen's room was no bigger, on the other side of the partition; it had a window you could lean out and almost touch the trains as they went by. But usually she was in Grace's room because Grace had her place all fixed up. On her dresser, for instance, was a heart-shaped bonbon box with a huge red satin bow on it, and beside it a blue painted can of talcum powder smelling deliciously of carnations. A velvet souvenir ribbon say with button photographs and little tasselled pencils hung beside the mirror. Over the bed was pinned a big Silver Lake pennant and a passe- partout tinted picture of a full-faced brunette gazing moodily down at her bare bosom.

"Where'd you get that pennant?" Jen inquired.

Grace tittered and leaned coquettishly on one elbow.

"That's what Morry Abbott was always asking, ha, ha!"

Jen stirred uncomfortably.

"Where did he see it?"

"Never mind, he saw it plenty of times," giggled Grace. "I used to tease him about being so jealous. Where'd I get this, where'd I get that, who give me this box of candy and so on. He wasn't going to let me have any friends at all, he was so jealous. Can you imagine that?"

Jen twisted her handkerchief, understanding now. That was why Grace had gotten her to go with her that night following Nettie and Morry. He'd made love to both of them. She didn't see how she could ever look up at Grace—she wouldn't be able to look at Morry again without thinking of this. She wished she hadn't known, now. Knowing things like this frightened her. It made Morry seem so far away from her, somehow.

"It got so bad I just had to stop before it was serious," Grace confided, gazing dreamily at the Silver Lake pennant. "Honestly, Jen, I was afraid he'd do something. Kill himself or something. Crazy kid. . . . You know how he was always following me around."

"I never saw him following you," Jen murmured, a little coldly.

Grace was not perturbed by her skeptical tone.

"You wouldn't. But, believe me, I'd never give in. All a girl's got is her good name and believe me, you got to hang on to that. The factory girls don't care. Remind me to show you the place in the Big Four woods where they take their fellas. Gee, but those girls are awful. Sweeney had one of them up in the Tower during the quiet hour—one to two—in the morning, and a dispatcher walks in and didn't he almost get fired, that Sweeney? Only thing that saved him was the girl happened to have something on the dispatcher."

The fast train tore by and the walls of the house shook, a chunk of damp plastering fell to the floor.

"Isn't it time to go down?" Jen asked, still anxious to make good at her new career.

"Never go down till you're called," Grace instructed her. "Hermann will yell when he wants us. Sunday dinner's always late anyway."

"Do you think maybe Bill or Mrs. Delaney will try to make Hermann send me away," Jen asked, apprehensively, "when they find out I'm here?"

"They'd never dare," Grace declared. "Bill's too anxious to keep on the good side of Hermann. If Hermann says you stay, then you stay. . . . Don't you worry, the Delaneys know you're here. The old woman's peekin' out her window watchin' every chance she gets."

Jen stroked her hair and looked at it again in the mirror, because it was done up like Grace's and made her feel very courageous.

"Yes sir, those factory girls are fast, though," Grace went on. "I'd never get too chummy with 'em and don't you, either. . . . You notice Morry Abbott won't go out with the girls from the Works and they're always after him, too. He can't see 'em, he told me. . . . I tried to get him to be friends with other women but he wouldn't do it. . . . Now of course he's sore at me because I never would give in to him. But I'm sure I don't know what he's thinking of. Men are awful when they're so attracted to you."

She wasn't going to care who Morry liked, Jen thought resolutely, she wasn't going to be bothered about anything. She was back in Lamptown, wasn't she, and safe under the wing of Hermann Bauer, so what did anything else matter? But she could not help listening, fascinated by Grace's experience with life, even though whatever Grace said seemed to have a subtle hurt in it. Even when it didn't concern Morry it hurt, because it hinted of a bewildering world unknown to her, it hinted of things she didn't know, it reminded her again and again that she was left out.

"I wouldn't run with those factory girls," sniffed Grace. "I never wanted a chum. You and me could get along, though, Jen, know that? You're young but you're not so dumb. We can go to picnics together and have dates. It's easier for two girls to get dates than it is for one. It makes it more like a party."

Maybe it was a good thing the Delaneys did put her out, Jen reflected, because now it looked as if she was going to see something of the world.

"Grace! Jennia!" Hermann bawled up the backstairs.

"Oh, all right," answered Grace and slid off the bed to get dressed.

"I'm going to clear out of here one of these days," she grumbled, dumping some powder down her neck, powder that would daintily shower some customer's soup later on as she bent over. "I'd like a job in a Mansfield restaurant. Out in Luna Park. There's a fella runs the rolly coaster there and say, he's good looking. He was kinda crazy about me but you know how it is—I only get over there once a year."

Jen had her hand on the doorknob, impatient to go down because it was Sunday and maybe Morry might come over, as he did on Sundays. She hadn't seen him since the dance night and she wanted to see how impressed he was with her earning a living and having her hair done this new way.

"Wait a minute, I want to tell you about this fella," Grace called her back, slightly annoyed. She picked up the hand mirror to study the back of her hair. "I wish you could have seen him. Those snappy black eyes like Fischer's and slick black pompadour. I was walking along there by the rolly coaster at this picnic—the Baptist one, it was. I had on my blue dotted Swiss and a big milan I paid seven-fifty for at the Bon Ton. I was walking along and this fella says hello kid, all by your lonesome? Then we got to talking and he give me three free rides and after that I had a postcard from him with a picture of a girl sitting on a fella's lap. It's around here somewhere, I'll show it to you."

"Girls!" yelled Hermann. "God damn!"

Jen started running and Grace followed reluctantly.

"He had those black eyes, you know the kind," she whispered urgently as they went down the stairs. "Sort of Italian only not so sad."

Waiting table was much more fun than making beds and washing dishes for old Mrs. Delaney. All the time she swung importantly in and out of the pantry door, there was the awed delight of being on her own, getting a salary, looking after herself, there was the thrill of triumphing over the world. When she saw Morry sitting at the counter Jen upset a cup of coffee in her nervousness. It was gratifying to see his amazement. He'd heard she'd run away—what was she doing here in Bauer's?

"I work here," Jen was proud to answer. "I get three dollars a week and I don't have to go back to school, next fall, either, unless I please."

"Certainly you have to go back to school," Morry said sharply. "Whoever told you you were so bright?"

Jen's face fell.

"I'm tired of being tied to things," she complained. "I want to do things, Morry, instead of just sitting around till I'm old enough. I've been going to school just about all my life and I'm good and tired of it. I want to start in on my own."

"Want to be like Grace Terris, I suppose," Morry sneered. "That's your idea of a great life, waiting table. I thought you were going to be a dancer on the stage and all that. I thought you were going to show this town what you could do. Well, you won't get anywhere quitting school and working in restaurants, I can tell you. Gee, Jen, I thought you had more sense."

Jen hung her head and paid no attention when a man at the other end of the table rapped his fork on his glass for more coffee.

"I only thought if I had to take care of myself I might as well get started," she mumbled.

"Don't you know you can't ever do what you want unless you know things?" Morry scolded her. "You go back there this fall if you know what's good for you."

The man called her then and when she came back Morry had gone without giving her any clue to his indignation. She didn't know that she was Morry's invention, that in some obscure way he expected her to do him credit, her admiration must be more worthwhile than merely flattering worship from a chophouse waitress—hadn't she promised to be a ballet-dancer-on-a-magazine-cover-in-love-with-Morris-Abbott? . . . Jen understood none of these things, she only saw that he had gone away, the way he always did, nothing in the world could make him stay. She saw him in the street turn back to look and their eyes met. . . . Come back, come back, hers said, but he would never come back for her—always she would be left because people didn't care for you the way you cared for them. Your hands stretched frantically out to clutch them but they gained no hold, you were brushed aside, you could not hold anyone to you. Come back, come back. . . . Jen's eyes did not leave him until Delaney's door had swung shut behind him. Then with a sigh she took the catsup bottle over to the Ladies Table.

"I've got to go back to school tomorrow," she told Grace in the pantry.

"Why? Hermann says you don't have to if you don't want to."

"I know it," Jen murmured disconsolately. "But I've got to go back."

Dinner was over when Hunt Russell and Dode O'Connell came in. Jen frantically signalled Grace to wait on them but Grace only winked knowingly and shook her head. They were arguing and neither looked up when Jen set the dishes down clumsily before them.

"What'll you bet she's raising Cain because he went out with us the other night," Grace whispered when Jen came back to the pantry. "I guess she's got her hooks into him good. You'd never cut her out, girlie, you're not the type. Say, I'd like to let him know his party the other night got you kicked out of a good home. Maybe he'd do something for you."

Jen was terrified lest Grace should actually tell Hunt all this, and Grace wouldn't promise not to, only laughed teasingly. She put her finger to her lips and beckoned Jen to stand beside her at the little peephole in the door.

"Sh! Maybe we can hear what they're rowing about. Did you see those rings she always wears? Three diamonds and that big Masonic ring. He never gave her that."

At the corner table Dode slumped back in her chair, ignoring the dishes before her. Hunt smoked a cigarette and smiled lazily at her as she continued her low-voiced accusations. She was leaning her chin on her hand sullenly. She was good-looking in a hard leathery way, her shoulders looked high and powerful and why not, having pitched hay and done chores till she was old enough to get to a factory.

"She's telling him he don't give a damn about her," Grace whispered to Jen. "Says he'll probably marry somebody else and she'd like to see the little sap he'd pick out. Says she wouldn't marry anybody on a bet, she wouldn't want to be tied up with a house and a buncha kids. I notice he don't say anything. I guess she'd marry him all right if he asked her, that's all that's eating her."

Standing behind Grace Jen marveled at the intricate design of gold bone hairpins in her hair-knob; she tried to perk out her own white apron strings into the beautifully stiff wings that Grace had achieved. At least she was proud of her own hair screwed up as it was into a tight knob with hairpins torturing her scalp wonderfully.

"Sst!" Grace clutched her arm in delight. "She's trying to find out who he picked up at the dance last week when she didn't go. Can you beat that? He's not even opening his mouth. . . . Go on in and give 'em their coffee."

"What do you care, you never did anything to her!" Grace gave her a little push as she hesitated. "They can't bite you, you know. Go on."

They stopped talking when Jen approached. Hunt's eyes traveled from Jen's new black silk stockings up the blue striped percale dress to her skinned-back hair. Jen colored and fussed with her apron.

"What under the sun have you done to your hair?" he exclaimed, staring at her, amused and bewildered. "You look ten years older."

"Honest?" Jen was radiant. "I had it on top Thursday night, too, but I guess you didn't notice. It's the way I'm going to wear it from now on."

"Where'd you see him Thursday night?" Dode snapped at her abruptly.

Jen looked at Hunt, speechless.

"I—I saw him at the Casino," she mumbled.

"And afterwards, too, don't kid me," said Dode. "I heard about it all right but I didn't believe it. So this is your new girl, is it, Hunt? Want 'em younger now, yeah? . . . This is who you took out Thursday."

Jen picked up her tray and backed away in confusion, but Hunt blew rings of smoke indolently into the air.

"Well, Jen, if you're working here I reckon I'll have to eat all my meals here, won't I?"

"Oh, you will, will you?" Dode flared up and picking up her glass of water flung it straight in Hunt's face. Then she pushed back her chair and rushed out of the restaurant, her head ducked down so that people couldn't see she was crying. Hunt mopped himself with a napkin silently. At the cash register in front Hulda Bauer allowed herself to turn a fraction of an inch to note what was happening. Jen tried to save his feelings by not watching him but finally their eyes met and Hunt was grinning a little as if he enjoyed Dode's attack. He took down his soft gray hat from the rack and sauntered leisurely up to Hulda at the front counter. In the street a minute later he didn't even glance in the direction Dode had gone but got in his car and drove westward.

"Whee!" exclaimed Jen scurrying out to the kitchen. "Did you see that, Grace?"

But Grace looked at her sourly.

"She threw that on your account—because he was trying to flirt with you. That's why she wanted to throw things. It was your fault."

Then she began bustling about the linen cupboard, quite aloof. Jen was troubled.

"But they were quarreling about something else, Grace, honest."

"It doesn't pay to make trouble, girlie," lectured Grace with a fixed smile. "You'll never get ahead trying to come between couples, just because the man has an automobile, it's something I've never done, I'll tell you."

"But Grace, I didn't do anything. You saw—"

Grace disappeared into the pantry. After that Jen got used to seeing that look in other women's eyes, a veiled, hostile, appraising look. There was nothing to do about that look, Jen found, but it had something to do with men liking you and of course for that women never forgave you. Chilled by Grace's new manner Jen went out in front and sat down idly at the counter. Hulda pointed a warning finger at her.

"Don't let Hermann see you with nothing to do, Jenny. If you're through down here go upstairs and fix Room Twenty for those surveyors. You know your work, child."

She waddled over to shut the piano again; after saving so hard to buy it she wasn't going to have it ruined by people playing on it.

Something was happening to the Lots. Surveyors were busy over it and on the edge of this wasteland men were throwing up a new house. Its skeleton was a familiar one—four rooms down, three up, steep roof sliding off a square indented porch—it was Lamptown's eternal new House. Morry saw it one Saturday noon coming home from work, and he stopped short, incredulous. That gaunt house leapt out of the horizon like his name out of a printed page, at first he could not understand its challenge for him, and his feeling of despair. . . . Why, the Lots were to be turned into a gorgeous boulevard of beautiful mansions (through the vague genius of Morry Hunt Russell Abbott)—chateaux, Hogan called them, with long rolling lawns around them. . . . So long as the Lots were wilderness all this was possible, but the first dinky little Lamptown house going up meant that if homes were to be built, they'd be like all those on Extension Avenue.

The gardens-to-be had become so real in Morry's mind that he was outraged to see the workmen trampling over them as if they were nothing more than the weedy mud they seemed. He stood still, hands shoving restlessly into his coat pockets, staring unhappily at this apparent signal of his defeat. Each night after he closed his eyes he was used to conjuring the Lots before him, acres of tangled clover and scattered bramble bushes changing on his closed eyelids to castles of lordly beauty centered in terraced rose gardens all magically contrived by Morry Abbott. These pleasant fantasies might have gone on forever if the harsh fact of one small frame house had not thrust itself before him. It was unquestionably a challenge, he'd do something about this, he would—he thought desperately of his own ignorance and helplessness—well, then, where was Hunt, where was Hogan, where were all the people who talked of beautiful cities. . . . Where was Hunt Russell? After all, wasn't it Hunt's land? He could stop it all quick enough.

Angrily he looked up at the workmen on the scaffolding. What right had they to do this?

"Who are you building this for?" he called up.

It was for an out-of-town contracting firm, the foreman told him. Maybe, he said, the entire Lots would be built up this year if the factory increased as rumors hinted; two or three at least would be erected on speculation.

"All just alike?" Morry asked with a sinking heart.

"Sure—all just alike—maybe some with the porch on the left, that's all," answered the man. "It's a mighty convenient little house—a big favorite around here."

Morry walked slowly on, depressed. There was that inextinguishable plan in his mind for the Lots, that ridiculous, fabulous plan—Hogan's plan, really, only as soon as he'd heard it Morry had made it his own. But somebody else always did these things first—somebody with money, somebody who knew how to go after things. What were you to do when you didn't know anyone who could help you, no one who could explain the way to the things you wanted—what could you do—you couldn't just take a spade, a few bricks, and a geranium and see what happened. You had to be rich, you had to be educated; you had to be powerful to stop contagious ugliness from spreading.

Walking with his head down, thinking feverishly of desperate steps to take, Morry halted at the edge of the fields; still preoccupied he sat down on the running board of a muddy automobile parked there. He was going to do something all right, he'd go to Hogan—but Hogan was all big noise, just as the fellows said, he never really would get down to doing anything. Maybe if he'd gone to college, Morry thought, maybe then you knew just what way to go at things. . . . Maybe he could go to this contracting firm that was building these houses, for instance, and tell them they were making a mistake in destroying Lamptown's only chance for an expensive residential boulevard. . . . That's what he'd do. Morry stood up and looked uncertainly back at the house. He'd go and ask that foreman his boss's address. . . .

An elderly man with gray moustachios and a wide-brimmed black western hat was scowling gloomily up at the building; this was Fowler, the town builder and so-called "architect," Hogan's father-in-law.

"He's mad, too, I'll bet," Morry thought, "because they went out of town instead of giving him the job."

He sauntered up to him.

"Look at that house, Mr. Fowler!" he appealed. "They're going to be rows and rows of 'em before the summer's over. When the Works enlarge they'll fill in every chink of land from here to the county land with these sheds. Why doesn't somebody put up a good home for a change?"

"Cheap clapboard!" Fowler puffed morosely on a black briar pipe. "Any good storm would blow them down. I don't see why they didn't come to somebody that knows this land and knows enough not to get stung with cheap lumber. Hunt knows better than that."

He spat viciously at a wilting black-eyed daisy.

"Is Hunt behind this?" Morry wanted to know, incredulously. "I thought Hunt was a smarter man than that."

"There you are—Hunt's all right," Fowler agreed. "He'd never take a thing out of my hands, but you see Hunt isn't the whole cheese here at all. It's Russell money, all right, but it comes from Hunt's uncles in the East. Smart men, too. Keep out of the picture till it looks like a boom, then they step in and collect a million on their property. They know all right."

"But if there's a boom," Morry stammered desperately, "there'll be rich men in Lamptown, and they won't want to live in these cheap shanties, they'll want beautiful places different from other people's. Don't you see, Mr. Fowler, this was the place to build mansions—like Hunt's, don't you see?"

Fowler sucked his pipe glumly and then recollected a gift cigar in his vest pocket and offered it to Morry. Morry refused it and Fowler stuck it thankfully back beside the Democratic campaign button without which this gentleman had never been seen.

"They'll buy homes in Avon—people with the money. After all it's only twenty minutes out on the car-line and all residential. . . . Damned poor business for Lamptown, though, you're right about that."

Well, why didn't he do something about it, then, Morry wondered, irritated, certainly he was an old man and old enough to know his own trade, wasn't he?

"Somebody could do something even yet," Morry insisted. "Only one house is up. It isn't too late. Somebody could start on the other side of the Lots with a big place kinda like Hunt's— that's what people want to work for—something different."

"Say a modified Colonial," mused Fowler, and gazed at the fields beyond where the Colonial mansion was to be, "or maybe a Tudor cottage. I wonder. . . . Come on and walk down to the office, Morry, I'll show you a book I've got down there of what they call these Tudor cottages. And there's some pictures of these Spanish type houses like they have in California."

Fowler's office was a room over the Paradise Theatre, and as they tramped up the stairs Milly could be heard in the theatre banging out scraps of new songs on the piano.

"A hell of a business building," growled Fowler, fitting the key into his door. "You'd think it was a conservatory of music, anybody would, with that practicing going on all day. Come in."

The office was a mere closet cluttered with file cases, their drawers half-open and papers dangling out; auction sale leaflets in green and yellow blew frantically across the dusty floor as the door opened and cowered, quivering, against a stack of blueprints rolled up like so many high school diplomas and tied with yellowing soiled ribbon. The rolltop desk leaned dizzily forward, gorged with magazines and enormous photographs of ideal homes, above it a steel engraving of the Roman Forum was slapped in the face by a large cardboard poster announcing a foreclosure sale of the Purdy Property. Fowler dumped the magazines off two chairs and then offered Morry the cigar once more. With a sigh of resignation Morry took it and chewed on it rather unhappily.

"I'd like to show these people what somebody right here in Lamptown could do with those Russell lots," Fowler said, yanking off his coat and vest but keeping on the huge Sheriff's hat. "I'd like to show these people what somebody right here in Lamptown could do with that property. I'd like to show 'em we're a darn sight smarter than their fancy city firms with their cheap little ideas. Maybe I will, too, by golly, I ain't dead yet."

"Here—look these over." He shoved some photographs into Morry's hands, and then leaned back in the slightly askew swivel chair, puffing at his pipe. "I don't know which I'd rather do out there. A row of Spanish type houses, kinda California style, see, something to make Lamptown sit up and take notice, or say these Colonial ones like they do down East. Damn it, I'd like to let 'em know I got ideas, and nothing shoddy, either. I see other towns, don't I, I keep my eyes open everywhere. Just because I've had to keep to a $1800 house for most of the folks here, say, that don't mean I don't know how a $7500 house ought to be built, does it? . . . I'd like to throw up a string of houses that'd knock their eyes out, I would."

"But not just alike!" expostulated Morry, earnestly waving his cigar. "That's the whole point. Each one a special kind of house, see, so that everybody can feel it's his own special home, not anybody else's but his, See? Something worth saving for, something to show off to his friends. . . ."

"Somebody's bound to get rich in this town on this boom—that's as good as settled." Fowler twisted the ends of his thick gray moustache thoughtfully. "In another year there'll be a demand for better houses than anything we've got here right now, and that's a fact."

He kicked the outer door shut as Milly's practicing became louder, and then with his back to Morry stood before a huge map of Lamptown pinned to the wall. He ran a fountain pen slowly across the letters "Extension Avenue" and made a green-inked "X" in the center of a large area marked "LOTS."

"Hunt's share of that property is one fourth." He was talking to himself more than to his visitor, Morry realized, but Morry didn't mind because he was learning something, he could almost see a new door swinging open for him. "If we could talk Hunt into the idea, we'd have enough land and backing to start working on. Let the eastern Russells fool around over there on the east side with their factory houses—we'll begin on the other side of the creek, see, right here, and give the town something to talk about."

"We could call it the Heights," Morry said, and gave up trying to smoke his cigar, allowing it to drop quietly from his fingers into the wastebasket. It occurred to him that it was long past lunchtime and he was hungry, and moreover he'd promised Bill Delaney and some fellows to go to the ball game this afternoon, but it was too late now. Here in Fowler's cluttered office with Milly's desultory piano accompaniment a new Lamptown was being planned, and it was Morry Abbott's Lamptown, even Fowler must know that, for he went on with the "we" plans as casually as if the name on the door was "Fowler and Abbott" instead of just Fowler. The palms of Morry's hands were wet with tense excitement, he was on the verge of something big, something wonderful. He skipped through the pages of a book called *Long Island Homes*—someday even these landscaped estates might be possible, too. Then he got up and looked over Fowler's shoulder at the map. Fowler was marking off a section of the Lots, murmuring, "Lamptown Heights, eh?"

"No—not Lamptown," begged Morry. "Call it Clover Heights."

"Clover Heights," repeated Fowler and inked it carefully in green with an air of finality as if the whole plan was settled by this simple gesture. Then he tapped his pipe on a file case and looked at Morry triumphantly. "We'll put it through and don't you forget it. It gives Hunt a chance to put one over on the uncles, don't you see? That's why he'll be willing to come in with us."

"When can you—we—begin working on it?" Morry asked, struck with awe by the masterful way this man went at things.

Fowler pulled at his moustache with yellow-tipped fingers.

"Well, as soon as we can get hold of Hunt," he answered. "You're there at the factory all the time, you see him every day. Get hold of him Monday, say, and give him the idea."

Morry choked.

"That's the thing," continued Fowler with a faraway look. "You give him the main idea and tell him I'm ready to talk to him about it any time he drops in. Hunt's a nice guy and he's not crazy to have his uncles wipe him off the map. You just get hold of him, say Monday, and outline this Clover Heights idea to him."

"Sure. Sure, I'll tell him," said Morry hoarsely. He was to do all the starting, was he, and not Fowler at all. . . . He remembered his father's sarcasm when he told him of just such a plan, and already he saw Hunt's scornful amusement. It was all right if

Fowler started things but nobody would ever listen to Morry Abbott—and worse yet he could never in this world get up the nerve to approach them. The snappy young Abbott of his fantasies might calmly tap Hunt on the shoulder and tell him just what was what; but nothing, to the real Morry, was worth the anguish of going to a man and quite out of a blue sky telling him your own little private dream of a lovely place to live. Morry wondered how he'd ever managed to sound so casual to Fowler, but he thought hopefully he might drop dead before Monday or the relatives would start building on Hunt's share so that the whole plan would have to be given up, continuing merely as a pleasant dream in the night thoughts of young Abbott.

Fowler took out his watch.

"I've got to get to a farm out east by six," he said. "But see here, Morry, what about you coming down here to the office tomorrow—say around twelve—and we'll talk this over some more."

"Sure," agreed Morry again, who usually slept till two on Sundays then wandered out to the factory ballgrounds to loaf away the day.

"There'll be something big in this for both of us," Fowler thoughtfully pursued. "We'll work on it nights for a while till we get everything all set, understand. You're just the boy for this, Abbott—you've got push and go, not afraid to tackle anybody or anything. That's the right idea."

Morry looked at him alertly to see if he was being kidded, but Fowler's face was serious, almost dreamy. He had push and go, did he?—with his hands already trembling at the idea of approaching Hunt. He wanted to explain to Fowler right here and now that it was all a mistake, the whole plan was just an idea, see, and there was nothing to do about ideas, you just thought about them, that was all. But the big letters in green ink "CLOVER HEIGHTS" across the corner of the Lamptown map made him keep these craven misgivings to himself.

"Tomorrow at twelve, now don't forget." Fowler slapped him on the shoulder. "And you'd better not date up any women for the next few weeks because we'll be working on this every night."

It was dusk when Morry got outside, and the Paradise facade was already lit up, boldly inviting the night to come on. In the drugstore next door and around the barbershops crowds of men were arguing over the baseball game. The Works team had won its first game and this meant a big night at Delaney's, and celebrations all over town, but to Morry this approaching excitement belonged to him, the town was celebrating because at last Morry Abbott was going to do something about it, he was about to break through cloudy dreams into action. He spoke to men here and there but he couldn't stop, he had to hurry home and tell someone. He had push and go, he was going to be a man of power, like Fowler, like Hunt Russell, he would have an office over the Paradise and by merely scrawling something with his green-inked pen the whole map of Lamptown would be changed.

At Robbin's Jewelry Store he slowed up his pace, uncertain of where he should take his news. Hogan was the man to tell, Hogan and Bill Delaney, he thought, so he walked on to Bill's place. The saloon was full of the baseball players and men home from the game, they were singing and shouting, while Shorty, perspiration dripping from his bald head, pushed foaming glasses across the bar as fast as his two fat hands could go. Hogan and his fireman were at the bar and hailed Morry.

"Say, Hogan, I'm going in with Fowler," Morry told him, making an effort to sound as if this were nothing at all, really. "Thought I'd learn building—architecture, you know."

"OK with me, friend," answered Hogan heartily, banging his glass down. "You're welcome to the old man."

A little dashed, Morry went on confidentially.

"We're planning to develop one end of the Lots—build beautiful homes like they have on Long Island, you know, these Normandy cottages with two baths and—"

He had to raise his voice because someone was playing the piano and the men were beginning to sing.

"Mansions for the aristocrats!" roared Hogan. "While the honest workingman eats in his simple kitchen in Shantyville. Mansions for the ruling classes! Why, friend—" his voice became a deep, oratorical baritone—"I would rather go to the forest far away, build me a little cabin, a little hut with some hollyhocks at the corner with their bannered blossoms open to the sun and with the thrush in the air like a song of joy in the morning, I would rather live there."

He paused to wipe the foam off his mouth with a red kerchief.

"Never mind, Hogan'll live in your mansions if the old man gives one to his wife," the fireman winked at Morry. "You don't see him eating in these simple kitchens, either, he's just moved into the biggest house on Walnut Street over in Avon, and he raises hell when his wife doesn't set up the dining-room table."

"That's all right, friend," said Hogan. "You're a single man. You don't understand these things."

It was no use telling anything to Hogan now, Morry thought, disappointed, for Hogan's brightly glazed blue eyes and his rosy nose proclaimed to the world that this was Saturday night and a twelve-hour spree was well under way. As Morry reached the door he pointed an accusing finger at him and bellowed.

"Yes sir, by the Lord Harry, I would rather live there and have my soul erect and free than to live in a palace of gold and wear the crown of imperial power," and Morry slid out the door on the final impressive whisper, "and know that my soul was slimy with hypocrisy!"

Chagrined at Hogan's lack of interest, Morry turned into the alley to go in the Bon Ton's back entrance. He observed the crouched figure of old Mrs. Delaney on her steps, as if she had been waiting for him. He touched his cap, getting fiery red.

"Well, Morry Abbott!" she bent over the railing and scowled at him, one gnarled hand clutching together the black shawl under her chin. "You're satisfied now, I suppose. Happy now you got my Jen out of a decent home and got her waitin' table where all the men can get at her. God'll punish you, young man, God'll punish you as sure as I'm breathing here. You had no call runnin' after that young girl, now, you've got her started on the road to ruin—are you satisfied, hey?"

She hobbled up the steps slowly. Morry, hurrying on home, knew she had stopped at the top landing to glare vengefully at him, and he ducked into his doorway, angry again at Jen for putting him into the role of villain and seducer, a role, to tell the truth, that frightened him as much as it ever did any young girl.

ॐ

Elsinore and Nettie were having tea and sandwiches in the workroom and Morry made himself a salmon sandwich and sat down with them. He wanted to be offhand telling about his new career but he couldn't help it, he blurted it out the minute after he came in. His mother stirred her tea dreamily and for a while he thought she must be displeased. Nettie dropped her spoon and looked at him as if he had confessed to some tremendous sin. He thought, too late, he shouldn't have told Nettie of any good news about himself, for the only news that would please her, after being scorned, would have to be bad.

"Do you mean to tell me you're giving up your perfectly good job at the factory, Morry Abbott?" she demanded. "After you're lucky enough to get in the Works you'd drop it like this?"

"I'm not dropping it—not yet, anyways," Morry retorted. "Not till I'm getting commissions or a salary from Fowler."

"Are you out of your mind, Morry?" Nettie cried. "Do you mean to tell me you're going to do all this work without getting any pay?"

"Well, not exactly," Morry defended himself, sorry he had said anything, sorry that wherever he went he had to defend his triumphs since all that people were glad to hear from him was of his expected defeats.

"Come, now, what did he say? Did he or didn't he say he'd pay you for the work?"

"No, he didn't." Morry was stung into the truth. "But it's a chance to learn something I want to learn and I'm going to do it. Gee, Nettie, didn't you ever hear of anybody being an architect?"

Nettie gave him a long, withering glance.

"Don't be silly, Morry, you have to go to college to learn that, and you couldn't anyway, you haven't got the brains. You stick to something you can do, like the factory work, and don't let that old man Fowler make a fool out of you. Don't you think that's right, Mrs. Abbott?"

Elsinore raised her eyes from her teacup and smiled gently at Morry.

"What is it, Morry?" she inquired, and Morry looked straight at her, not believing she could be so unkind. She hadn't even listened, she didn't care a bit what became of him. His own mother didn't care, she was so busy with her own life. . . . Well, and what was her own life, Morry asked himself resentfully, if she didn't care about her husband or her son, who, then, occupied her mind? The doubt his father had passed on to him returned fleetingly but he shut it out of his mind firmly.

"No, sir, the thing for you to do, Morry, is to hang on to your factory job," advised Nettie, pouring herself some more tea. "You'll never get another like it. Mr. Abbott would be furious, too, if he thought you left the Works."

Morry's throat tightened at mention of his father.

"Aw, what's it to him?" he growled. "What does he care what I do—"

"A young man ought never to make a foolish move like you're doing right now, without talking it over with his father." Nettie's lips were virtuously pursed up. "Or at least with his mother."

She picked up her saucer and went over to the sink. Morry stole a sidelong, unhappy look at his mother. She sat there in her low work chair, sipping tea, staring intently into space. Her thick brown hair was loosened a little and in the blue woven dress she wore it suddenly came over to Morry that his mother wasn't old at all, she wasn't even middle-aged; it made him feel unaccountably lonely, as if a white-haired old mother or even a formless, middle-aged mother like Mrs. Bauer would have been his, his very own mother; but this way his mother didn't belong to him, and he had no right to her, no claim to her attention. . . . She glanced up and smiled at him but he was too hurt and lonely to smile back.

"Did you hear about the big Serpentine Ball the end of July, Morry?" she asked him almost lightly. "I hear it's going to be the big dance of the year and I meant to tell you not to miss it."

"I'll get there, all right," he answered gruffly. "Plenty of time for that."

She didn't care that today an incredible dream had started to come true, she didn't care that he was going to be more than just a factory hand, he was going to be a figure in Lamptown someday, a somebody that she could be proud of; but she didn't care, she hadn't even listened. It would be a long time before Morry's eyes, ashamed for her, could meet her smile.

There had to be someone who thought you mattered, there had to be someone you could tell things to, somebody who thought you were going to amount to something—nobody could be left this way all alone. Desperately Morry grabbed his hat and started outdoors heading almost automatically for the saloon backsteps before he remembered that Jen wouldn't be there, she'd be over at Bauer's. Jen . . . Jen . . . Jen . . . the only person who believed, the only person who listened, the only person who was sure. He hurried across the street, afraid to lose a minute now, afraid that Hogan and Nettie and his mother had so dashed his little triumph that there was none left. He thought it was true that a thing never happened by itself, it had never actually happened until it was related for the right person's applause. He saw Hermann Bauer smoking his pipe and gazing fixedly out the window and behind Hermann's back he saw half a dozen diners and Jen scurrying around them with a tray half her size. He'd better go around to the kitchen door, he thought, it was easier to catch her there than in front with Hermann watching. Hunt Russell's car was at the curb but Morry impatiently brushed by without waiting to speak to Hunt.

"Hey—hey Morry!"

Hunt had seized his arm jovially.

"Want to pick up the Terris woman later on, Morry?" he asked in a low tone. "Lots of room in the back of my car if you want to come along. I'm taking my girl, so speak up if you want to come."

"Your girl?" Morry asked suspiciously.

Hunt jerked a thumb in the direction of the restaurant.

"The kid in there," he drawled. "Thought you might take the other one."

"I don't think so," said Morry, the blood swimming furiously in his head. "I'll pick my own damned women, thank you."

He whirled around and went back home, up the stairs to his room. His whole body buzzed with hate for Hunt Russell as if in blocking his way to Jen he'd done him the ultimate injury, using all of his advantages for this unfair blow. His disappointment in his mother and Hogan faded into this final rage. Very well, let Jen take Dode O'Connell's place as Hunt's girl if she liked; Morry would never fight for her, he'd never compete for any girl, he'd never give Hunt the chance to sneer at a conquered rival.

He tramped up and down his tiny room and when his head hit the sloping ceiling he tore at it fiercely with his fists, and turned his hate for the moment on to tiny houses with low ceilings. Jen's blue eyes fastened worshipfully on someone else . . . Jen listening adoringly to some other hero. . . . All right, he could do without anybody, he didn't give a damn what people thought about him, he didn't care if nobody listened to him or believed in him, he'd show them all a thing or two, he'd make them listen one of these days, he didn't give a damn about anybody.

But in his dreams that night he fought for hours with some enemy, his conquering fists rained on some foe's bent head, a foe who changed under these blows from Hogan to Hunt Russell and then curiously enough took on the features of his father, and ah, what voluptuous ecstasy to blur with his knuckles the significant sneer on this last face!

⸙

If Morry was around the shop when Nettie worked late at night, then she made a great fuss about her preparations to leave, locking drawers noisily, calling loud goodbyes to Elsinore and shrilly exclaiming about the darkness of the night and the long walk to Murphy's. Morry deliberately ignored these hints and Nettie would have to stalk angrily out alone.

"I don't mind going home alone," she complained to Elsinore. "It isn't that at all. But after all, any gentleman would see that I got home safely nights I worked late in his own mother's shop, and was going through a dark street into an empty house. Any gentleman would do that much, Mrs. Abbott—that's why I get so disgusted with Morry."

She swung from such dignified reproaches to vehement denunciations of his character—he was just a bum, the town tough, everyone said he was fast, he chased after bad girls, no decent girl would ever want to marry him, he had no nice friends, just lazy good-for-nothing pool players and Shantyville souses. He'd rather keep company like that than to walk home with a good girl once or twice a week.

Elsinore did not know how to answer these attacks.

"But when the men want to take you home you won't ever let them," she protested. "I thought you'd rather be alone."

"That's just it!" Nettie sputtered. "If Morry was with me, the men from Delaney's wouldn't follow me, they wouldn't dare come up to me if Morry was along."

"I don't understand you, Nettie," Elsinore surrendered. "You weren't cross with Mr. Schwarz—"

"Mr. Schwarz was very different from Lamptown men," Nettie reminded her. "Very different indeed. He took me to the very best places in Cleveland and our seats at the theatre alone were three dollars. Oh, there's no comparison."

She sat down to the table where the crying doll lay undressed waiting for its summer costume. Nettie had given herself a birthday present of a pair of nose glasses from Robbin's Jewelry Store as most of the girls who could afford it were wearing them, and it seemed to her, stealing an approving glance at herself in the mirror, that this was as nice a touch as a lady could wish. She adjusted them with exquisite care on her determined little nose, and squinting a little, picked up the doll so abruptly that its glazed eyes rattled in its head.

"Never mind, I'm going to go over to the Casino before the summer's over," she declared. "I'm sure I could dance well because everyone says I have such high arches. Morry thinks because I don't dance I'm out of everything, but you just wait. He'll be very glad to dance with me someday, you wait and see."

This set Elsinore to thinking. Fischer had a summer dancing pavilion near Cleveland, and if Nettie learned to dance, then the two of them could go out to this pavilion during the summer. She couldn't go alone, of course, but it looked all right for two women to go places together. She decided it would be worth while to encourage Nettie to learn dancing if only for this one convenient reason. When Mrs. Pepper used to speak of having run out to the pavilion to watch the dancing because she "just happened to be in the neighborhood," Elsinore had yearned to ask if she couldn't "run out" with her sometime. . . . Well, if she ever went now, it would have to be with Nettie, that much was sure.

Sometimes she ran into Mrs. Pepper on the street and Elsinore always dropped her glance before the wounded question in the other's eyes. Nettie told her the corsetiere was often lurking in shop doorways waiting for Nettie to pass so that she could pounce on her and pour out her woe. With the passing weeks Elsinore saw that even if Fischer's wife had told him of a strange visitor he hadn't guessed who it was. It reassured her so that no wounded looks could make her feel guilty, and except for the out-of-town customers occasionally asking for corset fittings, the Bon Ton went on as if these extra activities had never been. She thought that she might even, with Nettie's support, be able to face an encounter with Mrs. Pepper at the Cleveland pavilion this summer. After all, there was no reason why his Lamptown pupils shouldn't drop in at his Cleveland headquarters, was there? . . . Still she'd have to have some excuse for being in the neighborhood. She'd have to invent some business in the city for July or August, some extra business, because two buying trips a year were enough for the millinery stock.

"At least I'm glad there's only one of these darned dolls to dress," Nettie grumbled, pins in her mouth and a scrap of blue lawn in her hand. "It's more work than anything in the shop."

Elsinore had an inspiration.

"But everyone asks about it, Nettie. You know how the girls are always trying to buy it from us. I'd thought of laying in a stock if they don't cost too much."

"No!"

"Later on in the summer—I'll run into Cleveland and get a few as an experiment," she went on meditatively. "I think a millinery store has a right to branch out with novelties now and then. Charles is always telling me about perfumes and hose and extra things they sell in the Chicago shops. I think the Bon Ton ought to be up-to-date."

Nettie's mouth puckered into a disapproving pout.

"Of course," Elsinore added. "I'd expect you to help me buy them. And if we had to go into the city we might have a little extra time for an outing."

Miraculously Nettie's disapproval vanished. If dolls meant a visit to Cleveland for her, then certainly every milliner ought to keep dolls.

"We might happen to run into Mr. Schwarz again," she suggested. She began to hum softly, her little finger curved daintily outward as she sewed, already she had marked another notch in her career as a milliner, and certainly a Mr. Schwarz from Cleveland as a "friend" would put Morry in his place.

Elsinore was writing a letter to Charles that night, explaining her plan for selling dolls when Mrs. Pepper appeared quietly in the Bon Ton. She didn't stop to address Nettie in the shop, but walked straight out into the workroom and shut the door behind her. Elsinore jumped up, quite pale, and her letter blew unheeded to the floor. Mrs. Pepper looked at her sadly. Her eyelids and nose were red as if she had been crying and she kept dabbing at her nose with a little lace handkerchief as if this gesture somehow gave her courage.

"You've made a lot of trouble for me, Mrs. Abbott." She didn't sound angry—only tired and pleading. "All I've ever had is trouble, ever since I lost Mr. Pepper. . . . I—I don't see why you did it. I can't understand why you'd do that to me, Mrs. Abbott, it's beyond me."

Elsinore was speechless. She was so sure after all this time that no one had found out about her visit to Cleveland, and this belated discovery found her completely without defense. She rolled her pen nervously between the palms of her hands and looked at the floor. Mrs. Pepper studied her drearily and quite without anger.

"As soon as Harry said the woman wore a black hat with a white feather I knew it was you that had gone to his wife. And then you'd been so strange with me for a long time. . . . At first when he told me—things had to stop—at first I couldn't guess who had told her but then when he mentioned that black hat it all came over me that it was you. I was so upset I had to lie right down to get my breath. . . . I couldn't understand. . . . I just couldn't see why you'd do that to me, Mrs. Abbott."

Elsinore drew a deep breath. Why should she feel so shamed—after all, she hadn't done anything wrong—it was Mrs. Pepper who had done wrong when it came right down to it. She was the one to feel guilty. . . .

"It wasn't right for you to go with him," she managed to say. "You knew he had a wife—you knew you ought not to try coming between them."

Mrs. Pepper's little white hands flew out in a gesture of helplessness.

"I know, oh, I do know it's wrong, but I'm not a bad woman. Nobody could say I was a bad woman. And Harry's all I've had in my life—those few little trips with Harry—once we went to Atlantic City. . . . It began so naturally—both of us traveling through the same towns—but now, I—well, I just couldn't live without Harry. . . . What made you go to her, Mrs. Abbott— what made you do it? You couldn't have just wanted to spoil my life—you couldn't just want that. . . ."

Elsinore kept jabbing the table with the pen and kicking at a ball of colored embroidery silk lying tangled on the floor. She had regained her cool detachment as if what she had done was done, after all, and was no concern of hers any more. She had eased her own steady torment by hurting Mrs. Pepper and was rather surprised to find that she had no more hatred for her. On the other hand when she stole a look at her, the sight of her plump pretty face screwed up into a pitiful caricature of anguish did not stir her pity at all.

"He's had to promise her not to see me again," Mrs. Pepper allowed the tears to course slowly down her cheeks. "It's all right for you—you've got your husband—even if he's only here once in a while—and your nature's different from mine . . . but with me . . . I've lost eleven pounds just worrying over this. I've had to take a 38. See, I've lost it here." She slapped her hips mournfully. "Worrying about what I'm going to do without ever seeing Harry. . . . She's having him watched."

She sat down on a stool and leaned her plump arms on the table. Elsinore kept her face steadily on the embroidery silk on the rug.

"I never did you any wrong, Mrs. Abbott, you know that," desolately went on Mrs. Pepper. "I can't understand why you'd go against me like that. I didn't dare tell Harry I knew who'd told his wife. I didn't want to let him know a friend of mine had done it. I let him think one of the factory girls—maybe Dode—or somebody out of town had gone to her, some woman that was after him."

Elsinore breathed easier and dared to lift her eyes. If Fischer didn't know who it was that had told his wife, then nothing was to be feared—nothing had been lost after all. She had done no harm, really, if she'd merely stopped Mrs. Pepper from being in love with him. That was all for the best.

"If Charles was running with some other woman I'd want to be told," she said. "I'd be glad if someone came and told me. That's why I went to Mrs. Fischer. I wasn't thinking of you at all—I was just putting myself in the position of the wife."

Mrs. Pepper shook her head sadly. She'd never dreamed of being wicked, she never meant to be at all—it was only that after Mr. Pepper went she was all alone, and traveling through the same territory with the dancing master, always getting on the same trains, they just got so they belonged to each other—they got so they'd meet to talk over business in this town and that, and pretty soon they were terribly dependent on each other, almost like a married couple. And that's the way she was, always dependent on the few bright little things in her life, miserable for months at the slightest change.

"For instance I can't settle down at the Bauers'," she confided unhappily. "I have that lovely big room and all, but I was used to the Bon Ton. I was used to you and Nettie running around and Morry always coming in at the wrong time—and the way we'd sit around gossiping. At Bauer's there's no one to talk to— Hulda—well, you might as well try to talk to a piece of pork. . . . That's what I mean, you see, about being dependent."

Cautiously the workroom door opened, and Nettie tiptoed in, glancing quickly at the two women as if she expected to see them tearing each other's hair. She held out the doll, now completely costumed in a wide lawn bonnet and dress, and held it up to Mrs. Pepper.

"Cute? Dode O'Connell wants one like it, Mrs. Abbott. I told her we were going to carry a few so she might buy one."

Elsinore, glad to change the subject, explained the doll idea to Mrs. Pepper. The corsetiere dried her eyes and listened. She bent forward with a spark of revived spirits.

"Let me tell you, that isn't the only thing you'll have to lay in, Mrs. Abbott. When the Works enlarges, like people say it's going to, you're going to have to carry a lot more things than just hats. Or else sit back and let strangers make the money."

"We'll never carry corsets again, believe me," Nettie laughed arrogantly. "Too much work."

Whenever Nettie became possessive about the shop Elsinore stiffened ever so little.

"We might as well carry corsets as dolls," she rebuked her. "At least we're used to the line."

Nettie, flushing, carried the doll into the front room and kicked the door shut behind her.

"Do you know there's going to be over a thousand new men taken on at the factory next fall?" Mrs. Pepper said. "That means more trade for us, you realize that, with all those families in town. Why, Mrs. Abbott, if I had the running of this shop I'd make the upstairs rooms into shops, too, and sell blouses and all the things girls want when they're making money. I wouldn't let the grass grow under my feet."

Elsinore's eyes caught the sparkle in the other's.

"I couldn't ever do it alone," she demurred. "I wouldn't know where in the world to begin."

Mrs. Pepper pulled her stool closer. Her reddened eyes snapped with excitement, and forgetful of her late wounds, she put a tiny fat hand on Elsinore's knee.

"Let me come in with you, then," she begged. "Let me come back and this summer we can plan the whole thing. I'll be looking around in the other towns, see, and picking up ideas here and there. Let me come back. . . ."

"What about Mr. Fischer?" Elsinore asked in a muffled voice.

Mrs. Pepper beat her hands together nervously.

"I don't know. I'll try to get over it—I know you feel you can't respect me because of that, but I don't mean to be just bad the way you think. Now that she's watching everything I'll have to be so careful anyway. . . . Oh, dear, I wish you hadn't gone to her, Mrs. Abbott, I don't see how you could. If it had been you instead of me—"

"It would never be me," Elsinore harshly interrupted. "And if you come back in this shop I'll expect you to behave differently."

"I've got to," Mrs. Pepper confessed. "That's why I want to put myself into a lot of hard work. I don't want a minute to think."

"As you say we'll have to buy more if the town gets larger," Elsinore looked about the workroom appraisingly. "We could use the upstairs for corsets and say lingerie. I could put a cot down here for Morry so we could start right in using his room."

When Nettie came back she stopped short at sight of the two women talking in low absorbed tones, their heads close together. Something in their attitude made her apprehensive of her own prestige—after all, she was part of the Bon Ton, wasn't she, and there was no justice in leaving her out of things this way. She sat down determinedly at the table and started threading an embroidery needle, humming a little tune. Mrs. Pepper turned to her.

"We were just talking of improving the shop."

"Well, we have been improving it," Nettie retorted with no great friendliness. "Didn't you notice we have electric lights now?"

Mrs. Pepper exclaimed appropriately as Nettie switched the lights on and off in demonstration.

"And did you see what Mr. Abbott sent us?" She went over to the cupboard and brought out an electric fan which she placed gingerly on the table; keeping her eyes fixed on it to be on guard against sudden explosions she attached it to the socket. The fan wheezed and whirred laboriously.

"He certainly is good to you, Mrs. Abbott," said Mrs. Pepper politely. "My, I only wish I had someone as kind to me."

Then both she and Elsinore looked idly at Nettie as if she were an intruder, but Nettie set her jaw and sat tight in her chair, sewing diligently. After a few minutes Mrs. Pepper got up.

"Well, I'll see you about that later," she said and reluctantly left.

Elsinore put the fan back in the cupboard, handling it as if it were an infernal device, likely to shoot into skyrockets any minute.

"Well, now we've got her around again, I suppose," Nettie ejaculated nodding towards the door. "I'm sure I don't know where we'll put her and all her junk."

Elsinore looked thoughtfully into space, apparently unheeding. This infuriated Nettie, for it left her outside of things, somehow. She wanted to say something to remind her employer of intimate matters between them, to show that she really wasn't outside at all, but very much in the center of things.

"You know what Mr. Abbott thinks of her and her old stuff all over the place, you know how he hates it," she said reproachfully. "You ought to consider what your husband thinks especially after he sent you that electric fan for a present."

Elsinore whirled around at her almost ferociously.

"I hate that electric thing and you know it!" she blazed. "I hate all of Charles's presents—every single one of them—I'd like to throw them all out into the street this minute!"

"Why—why, Mrs. Abbott!" stuttered Nettie in amazement, so flustered that she dared not utter another word for nearly twenty minutes.

※

"You're never going to be the drinker your father was," Bill Delaney regretfully told Morry. "You come in here and get green on three beers, a big husky like you, too. Why your pap would sit down there with a quart of Scotch and soak it up without turning a hair. Walk out of this place like a gentleman, too. That was Charlie Abbott."

"Lay off the old man's business partner," Hogan warned Bill. "Don't you know my wife's old man is the biggest finanny on prohibition in this country? Morry can't drink and be in his office."

"The old man's all right," said Morry. "We get along. Did you see the plans for those houses we're putting up?"

"Sure, Fowler's going to make a lot of jack out of real estate," Hogan declared. "But watch out for him, sonny, watch out for a man that won't drink. They'll skin you out of your eyeteeth every time. What's he paying you?"

Morry got red in the face and gulped down his drink. Hogan grinned sardonically.

"Nothing, eh? That'd be the old man, all right—promise big money for next year, get you so dizzy talking in thousands that you'd forget to ask for five dollars to keep from starving."

So Morry couldn't explain about the bonuses and commissions that Fowler had promised. Anyway until last Saturday he'd been drawing pay from his factory job so he wasn't starving. True, on Saturday, the foreman fired him. This was for not showing up one day when he was looking at houses outside of town with Fowler. But the bonuses would begin soon enough and he could laugh at a dinky ten bucks a week.

The saloon was cooler than the July outdoors but its damp fermenting coolness was not refreshing, nor was the smell of sweating laborers crowded around the bar swilling beer. Waves of heat blew in at each motion of the door from the melting asphalt outside, a skinny maple tree sprouting from the cracks in the sidewalk dropped a tiny shriveled green leaf on the marble doorsill. When the door swung open Morry could glimpse the Bauers' window framing Hulda Bauer, eyes closed, fanning herself rhythmically with a huge palm-leaf fan.

Morry wandered into the front room and picked up a billiard cue but it was too hot and too crowded to play, he couldn't play with the other fellows hanging around watching, so he went lonesomely back to the bar. There were strangers in Bill's place all the time now, well-dressed men who asked for expensive cigars and conferred in low voices at corner tables, there were surveyors and gangs of workers from out-of-town who were busy on the Lots. Men dropping in for a drink between trains, said, "Hear you folks are due for a boom. Conductor tells me your factory yonder is opening up a big new line this fall. Is that a fact?" Everyone talked excitedly of the new houses being built, of out-of-town money being put into the Lamptown business, of a boom that was sure to come because it was in the air, but no one seemed to know definitely. Strangers were in town, a little Jew from Cleveland started a branch of a ready-made dress chain store on Market Street and called it "The Elite," the drugstore soda fountains began to make chocolate frappes, Hermann Bauer raised the price of a meal to fifty cents, and lounging at a table in Bauer's any day you could see a little sharp-nosed sandy man in a checkered suit plunking a mandolin and humming the latest songs, for he was the actor who did a specialty at the Paradise. To most of Lamptown this gaudily dressed figure strolling about town was the symbol of Lamptown's sudden rise, he represented all the glamour of cities and sudden wealth; factory girls merely humming his songs felt rich and beautiful and in the swim, a town had to be pretty up and coming to have specialty actors at its movie house.

Merchants added expensive novelties to their stock when they saw three prosperous strangers in conference with the bank president one afternoon, and after an evening of discussing these mysterious portents and whispers, young married couples decided to buy a davenport or move to a better neighborhood or do *something* to keep in tune with this vague secret progress.

Even without a salaried job Morry moved along on a wave of optimism, planning more and more daring steps in the development of Clover Heights. He was learning now. When Fowler said, "See Hunt" or "See So-and-so at the People's Bank," Morry didn't suffer the same old agonies in collecting his courage. He "saw" people and said, "Mr. Fowler wants to talk to you about something," and then rushed thankfully away. He understood other matters too. He was beginning to see that the big deeds men spoke of were just dares to each other. All of them—Fowler, and everybody—

were as afraid of starting something as Morry was, and so as soon as you saw they were all afraid it was easy to step up and be a leader, to say, "I'm going to do this"; these quiet boasts awed other men so that with the mere words power came, the thing magically began to take shape, because other men thought, "Here is one who isn't such a coward as I am," and respected and helped him. Men bluffed each other with brave boasts and then their vanity drove them on desperately to live up to their loud words.

It was as easy, if you had no money at all, to talk in terms of thousands as it was to talk in terms of hundreds. It was as easy to call a bare field "The Heights" as it was to call it "The Lots," and once the numbered stakes were stuck in the ground it was simple for an eager builder to vision mansions behind them. Hunt was easygoing and told Fowler to go ahead with his plans; so while the eastern end of the Lots was cut up in little fudge squares and a second house like the first one started, Fowler winked at Morry and said, "Let 'em get their little chicken houses slung up there— plenty of time for us. When we start in on the west end this town's going to sit up on its hind legs."

It worried Fowler, though, that when the two Russells from Hartford came on they stayed at Hunt's house. Bauer's was too dingy for them and when any of their associates arrived they took them to Hunt's too.

"It's too intimate. They'll talk Hunt out of his corner, living together like that," Fowler told Morry uneasily. "That leaves us holding the bag. Hunt's too damned lazy to fight for his share. They're squeezing him out of the Works and out of his own home. It's bad for our business to have them all living with him."

Morry didn't tell him he'd been fired because Fowler might think that was bad for business too. He dug out all of Fowler's books on architecture, and it was a relief seated in his cramped quarters in the Bon Ton to let his eyes feast on pictures of terraced gardens with huge spacious houses sprawling over the page. He

yearned for wide rooms and tall doorways you didn't bend beneath, he argued doggedly the case for great rooms with high ceilings, the manorial against the "cute" type Fowler rather fancied.

"People want a place to breathe in," he pleaded.

"Listen, breathing costs money," said Fowler noncommittally.

He thought of all these homes as steps to a great manor that
was to be his own place, a place for his mother such as she'd
never dreamed. The day he told her a little of this plan, she
said—"That reminds me, Morry, I'm going to enlarge the business here, and we're fixing over the upstairs for corsets and lingerie. I guess we might as well start in with your room, so I'll put
a cot down here in the workroom for you. You don't get to bed
till late anyway, and you're always up early."

Morry didn't mind, he said, and took over one hat drawer for
his things. Late on July nights he sat studying at the long work-
table, his book propped up in the midst of artificial flowers, and
stacks of rainbow-ribboned summer hats. No breeze reached this
back room and perspiration would drip from his forehead to the
printed page as the hot midnights passed. The room reeked with
the dusty smell of long-stored trimmings, of plumes and mari-
bou in mothballs, an old woman smell; but these present irrita-
tions were lost in the magnificence of his future. He pored over
Fowler's books but when he asked him about complicated problems in them, the older man shrugged.

"What's the idea worrying about anything till you come to it?
You know what you want to do in a general way, that's enough. I
figure that when you know what you want in this life, all your
mind focuses on slick ways of getting that one thing without
working too hard at it, and by golly, you get it. But if you plug at it
too hard, understand, with your nose stuck in it the way you got
yours, then you lose sight of the thing you want. Your mind kinda
loses its focus through the drudgery, see, and it's having your mind
on it that lets you out of all the hard work. That's my opinion."

"But I want to know the things I say I know," Morry protested. "I want to be sure and safe in my head, don't you see?"

He checked lists of correspondence courses he found in the trade magazines, and struggled hopelessly with their lessons. No one seemed able to explain the Greek of these Simple Lessons.

"Good God, you don't need to know everything!" Fowler exclaimed. "I got along all right without knowing the whole works."

Morry didn't want to tell him that he was going to be more than any Fowler ever was, he was going to do a lot better than that.

Fowler had never had a drink in his life, he disapproved of saloons, but he needed to know what the strangers were up to, so he was glad Morry hung around Delaney's to listen, later on he might lecture him about whiskey and bad company but for the present he was broad-minded. Morry was swelling up a little with the respectful questions asked him in the saloon, he said more than he knew and talked easily of eight and ten thousand dollar homes, of thirty and forty dollar rents. Even Hogan was respectful but his blue eyes twinkled with sarcastic reservations now that he found Morry was to be paid off in "commissions."

"If I was you I wouldn't stick in this town, buddy," he advised. "I'd bum my way to Akron to the rubber works or down to Dayton to the Cash Register Company or take the Ford plant up in Detroit. I'd go where the big money was."

"Listen, there's going to be more big money in this here town next year than you ever saw," interrupted Bill Delaney. "I got my ears peeled, I know what's going on here. It's a good place to stick around, especially if they start floating stock in the new works like I hear, so's everybody gets a slice. You save up and buy there, Morry, you're young, you got time to get rich."

Morry watched Hogan smacking his lips over his beer and thought of when Hogan had given him the idea for a beautiful Lamptown. There were no two ways about it, he had to do something about that one idea; he had to prove something in the world before he ever dared go to any of those cities. He couldn't ever leave till he'd made a mark here, that much he knew.

"You didn't use to say that, Hogan," he said a little rebukingly. "You said you'd stay here and make over this town."

"That's right," Shorty remembered.

Hogan patted his belly fondly.

"The hell with it," he yawned. "What's a kid like Abbott here want to stick in a little town for? Nothing to do but get some girl in trouble, let her run him to the church and marry him, and at twenty-one he's sunk. Babies, mortgages—what chance has he got? Never dare throw up his job after that and better himself—"

"Well, you did all those things," someone dared to say.

"Sure, I did. I'm telling my story, ain't I? . . . Married twenty years—my wife's a damned fine woman, don't misunderstand me. Lost her good looks but like old Colonel R. G. Ingersoll says, God love him, 'Through the wrinkles of time, through the music of years, if you really love her, you will always see the face you loved and won.' . . . Old Bob Ingersoll."

Hunt Russell's car obstructed the view of Hulda Bauer's window. Hunt, in gray flannels, shirtsleeves, and tennis shoes, slid out from behind the wheel and came in. Morry wasn't afraid of Hunt; he'd been fired from Hunt's factory but vaguely this put him on a level with the employer. Lately he'd made a tense, nervous third to the conferences of Hunt and Fowler—conferences in which Hunt smoked a pipe lazily and said, "Sounds OK to me, Fowler—damned good idea, and if you can do it without getting the family down on me, go ahead—I'm no good on the details. Figure things out yourself and go to it."

"What about it, Hunt—what about this Hartford factory coming out here to hook up with the Works?" Bill Delaney asked the question no one had dared to ask directly before, and men, hanging around the pool tables, edged up to the bar to hear what answer Hunt would make.

"That's about right, Bill," he said casually. "Things getting pretty hot in this town all around. We're bringing all the branches of the Works into Lamptown—taking on fifteen hundred men by the end of October."

"Who runs it, then—you or your uncle Ferd?" Bill asked sharply.

Hunt shrugged his shoulders.

"What's the use of my working myself to death? I'm letting my relatives do the worrying."

"Yeah, and he'll do his worryin' later," muttered Hogan in Morry's ear. "Smarter men'n he is, buddy, you wait and see the big Lamptown cheese king take a spin on his magnum opus, wait till you see what they do to him."

"Where they going to live, for God's sake?" someone yelled from one of the tables. "These fifteen hundred families. Where you going to put 'em, Hunt, eh—let 'em dig holes in the ground and crawl in, maybe?"

"Looks like a swell deal for Hermann," observed Shorty and sent a highball sliding down the bar to stop exactly at Hunt's elbow. "Hermann'll clean up a nice wad renting out his rooms."

"I've got to turn over my house to my cousins and some of the eastern officials, I know that much," Hunt said, frowning. "No place else for them. But later there'll be plenty of places to stay, what with the new houses on the Lots. Then the Big Four has offered their woods to the Works at a figure."

"Now there's a help," Hogan grunted sarcastically. "Why, the boys can live in the trees as snug as you please and practice birdcalls and sling buckeyes at each other, oh sure, they'll have plenty of places to stay. Why, what d'ye say, Bert, we take a coupla boarders in the coal car, and then there's plenty of room in the Round House. Oh sure, there'll be no trouble about housing the bastards, take any of these swell hotels on Market Street, and there's the old pickle factory building, the Bum's Blackstone—"

Men laughed and then stopped uneasily since after all, Hogan was pretty fresh, trying to make a fool out of Lamptown's big man. Morry didn't take Hogan as such an oracle now, he'd begun to be a little cynical, seeing him back down on his big talk so many times; he didn't kid him the way the other men did and call him "Big Noise" because he was sorry for Hogan, sorry for him because he must despise himself a little for not living up to his brave conversation. Morry lowered his glance now whenever Hogan talked as if he was president or God or somebody, because he didn't want to betray the devastating pity in his eyes. No one else listened to Hogan, either, they were crowding around Hunt, firing questions at him, and Hunt, pouring down his throat one highball after another, made half-mocking answers in a shrill strained voice, so that afterward it struck Morry that all this change was worrying him a good deal for some reason.

"Here, Morry, stick this up in the window on your way out," Hunt called to him and handed him a cardboard poster. "There's one for Hermann, too, but I'll take that one over myself, I told Fischer I would."

"I'll bet you will," Morry thought bitterly.

He reached over the green baize curtains in the window and propped the poster against the glass.

EVERYBODY'S COMING

TO

FISCHER'S

SERPENTINE BALL!!

July 31   8:30 PM

LADIES 50¢   GENTS $1

The men crowded around Hunt—Bill ignored orders for drinks and rapped out questions—was it true pay was to be raised, that a guy from Newark, New Jersey, was coming out to run things, that shares were to be sold to the workers; a few who were afraid to address Hunt directly even when tipsy, urged Bill to ask him this and that about whatever worry they had concerning the new state. Morry lingered at the door, listening, so he could report it all to Fowler, since every sensational new step was fuel for Clover Heights.

In the hot tar-smelling street Morry mopped his forehead and then was pleasantly cooled by the idea of widening the creek so that there could be swimming and boating in Clover Heights, maybe a Country Club, yes sir, Clover Heights Country Club. . . .

He looked back in the saloon window to see if he'd got the poster right side up and his mouth curled a little thinking of how Hunt was afraid to let anybody else take the other poster over to Hermann's for fear they'd ask Jen to that ball before he did. . . . Bah, let him go ahead and ask her if that's the way he feels!

⁂

Hot, sticky nights with no breeze in all Lamptown except underneath the Bon Ton's electric fan or behind Hulda Bauer's giant palm leaf. The night men at the factory worked with their sweating torsos bare, behind the honeysuckle vines on the boarding-house porches the girls sat in their kimonos eating ice cream, the factory engines with their now doubled manpower chugged steadily through the hot stillness. A lush yellow moon hung over the Big Four woods seeming to send a glow of heat over the fields, in the stagnant creek frogs croaked and mosquitoes buzzed intently, the sultry wind ruffling the damp clover of the Lots was worse than no breeze at all.

In Delaney's the old pianola rattled ceaselessly, its music was worn out, a nickle dropped in hopefully only set the other nickles to jingling like sleigh bells for three minutes, but the festive tempo was there still and the hint of devilish gaiety. Morry refused its jangling invitation for Bauer's dining room. Here, at ten o'clock, he sat at one of the tables with Jen, and pushed a catsup bottle this way to show her where the Clover Heights Hotel was to be, the mustard here was the club, the relish dish was the Normandy chateau that was now under way, and the trail of the fork he pushed across the table was the boulevard track.

Jen's gingham sleeves were rolled to her shoulders, her black hair was kinky with the heat. She leaned half across the table to watch these fascinating maneuvers and could not restrain a sigh of admiration.

"Gee, Morry, how did you ever dare think of it?"

Morry looked bored with such stupidity.

"Good Lord, Jen, did you think I didn't know anything but crating goods at some factory? I'm not like the rest of these fellas. I should think you'd know that by this time. I got ideas."

Jen hastened to soothe him.

"I know—only I can't get over how wonderful it is, that's all I meant."

"Wait. That's not all," Morry said impressively. "This is nothing. Wait till you see our big offices—maybe headquarters in Cleveland or Pittsburgh—even New York. Can you imagine me in charge of the New York business?"

"Sure, you could do it, I'll bet . . . but, it's far off, isn't it?"

Morry laughed scornfully.

"What—New York? . . . Only a couple days' trip. Not even that. I'd take the morning local to Pittsburgh, catch the limited that night, be in New York the next day."

They were quiet because already he was gone, he was in New York, and Jen was all alone at the table with a mustard bottle for a country club, no Morry—nothing. . . . All right, she would go there, too, she didn't have to follow Morry, but she could do something.

"And when you're doing all that, I'll be in some show—a dancer, maybe, or an actress like Mama. . . . It won't be long now, will it?"

Morry, not listening, shook his head, and watched the sandy-haired little actor from the Paradise lounging at the back table with a frayed copy of a detective magazine. Now the actor abandoned his reading and tipped his chair back against the wall. He tweaked idly away at his mandolin, singing softly to himself—

> Some of these days—
> You'll miss your hon-ey—

He was a tenor with a voice of agonizing sweetness, yet these sugared notes made Morry's spine quiver, they made him desperately happy and miserable at the same time, so that he forgot the red pepper tennis court in his hand and surrendered to this drowsy spell. The singer's eyes were closed, his nostrils quivered holding the high notes, his stiff blue cuffs stuck out three inches from his tight checkered sleeves. He slid further and further back in his chair as he played, winding his legs about the chair rungs to reveal every bit of his purple-striped socks. . . .

Morry sighed. He didn't need to tell Jen any more of his plans—she believed so much more than even he dared believe himself. He was exquisitely contented here tonight, he couldn't imagine why, but it must be the singing. Jen's head swayed to the melody as if always in the back of her head she heard whatever music there ever was, but her eyes stayed on Morry's dark face.

"I've been so lone-a-ly," whined the honeyed voice, "just for-a-you on-a-ly—"

Hulda Bauer's fan slowed up for the long-drawn-out rhythm of this song—if the notes lingered much more Hulda would lose count completely and fall into a doze.

"That's what I'm goin' to do—I'm goin' on the stage," Jen whispered to Morry. "When Lil comes she and I are both goin' to be actresses. Mr. Travers says it's easy. Look here."

She pulled a cabinet photograph from the drawer of the serving table and pushed it across the table to Morry. It was the picture of a young fair-haired girl in graduation dress against a background of painted ocean. Her wide eyes looked straight into Morry's, and his spine quivered again as it had over the song and over the silver-blonde on the magazine. It was her blondness that fascinated him most, except for that she looked like Jen; but he had always wondered secretly what strange things yellow-haired girls thought about.

"Lil," said Jen. "Looks like me, doesn't she?"

"Oh, I don't know," Morry said, and Jen, stiffening a little with unexpected jealousy drew the picture back.

The four legs of the actor's chair suddenly came to the floor with a bang. He threw down his mandolin, stood up and stretched himself elaborately.

"Jesus, what a dump this is!" he addressed the world bitterly. "No place to go—nothing to do—might as well turn in."

Hulda Bauer laboriously got off her stool and approached them.

"That's right, Mr. Travers. Bed's the best place. Goodnight to you."

She waddled somberly toward the stair door, nodding to Jen.

"Better be goin' home, Morry. Jen's got to be up early."

Morry got up. Jen never begged him to stay any more now. Her mouth dropped a little as he reached for his cap. Mr. Travers observed her through half-shut eyes while he put his mandolin in its case.

"Morry, don't you think that's a swell idea—Lil and I going on the stage, traveling all over, seeing everything?" Jen wanted to know.

Morry nodded casually.

"Yeah, that'll be great," he agreed. A flash of irritation came over him that Jen should have plans, too. Part of his own plans was that Jen should always be in Lamptown, always astonished at his great deeds, always breathlessly applauding. He knew a second of cold fear at the thought of this town without Jen, Jen, the one certain thing—but he'd never let her guess that.

"That sure will be great traveling," he repeated, and Jen said no more.

Morry, aching already for a lost Jen, slouched across the street and Jen traced his name slowly with her finger across the glass cigar counter.

"Stuck on him, ain't you, Kid?" teased Mr. Travers. Jen made a horrible face at him for answer and stalked into the kitchen.

Morry didn't go to bed for hours. He got his cot ready, pulled off his damp shirt and threw it over the screen. He sat down on the cot, one shoe in his hand, and thought of how Jen's arms looked with her sleeves rolled up and who would there be to see how wonderful he was if she left town. She couldn't go away, that was all wrong. He was the one who would go away and always remember to write her about cities and strange lands he visited—he'd go away and always remember Jen St. Clair and how much a letter from him would mean to her. Since she was only a girl and had to stay home, he'd gladly tell her all about the outside world. . . . But she said she was going. . . .

Annoyed, Morry dropped the shoe and started unlacing the other one. Lil's picture came before him, in startling detail . . . he'd never seen a girl who looked like that except the girl on the magazine. He couldn't get her out of his head. He made a complete mental image of her, made up of what Jen told him about Lil and what he knew about Jen. This confused image was lovely to think about and he could not shake it away. . . .

An eastern wind came up and blew a few drops of rain into the room. Morry went over to close the window and heard singing somewhere; it wasn't from the saloon and it seemed further away than Bauer's. He strained his ears, it was like a woman's voice far away humming to mandolin notes, but he couldn't puzzle out the exact song or whence it came. Even after the midnight fast train roared by he could hear this music, lingering in the whistle's echo, sweet and far-off like a promise. Finally he gave up trying to catch it, and sat down again. He was happy. He didn't know why this was so, but there it was. He dropped his other shoe. It covered a corner of a postcard that had fluttered from the table to the floor. It was a familiar card and the glimpse of it was to Morry like seeing an evil face peering in the window, destroying every happy thought, making his stomach contract with sick dread, almost before his mind had taken in the words—

THE CANDY MAN WILL VISIT YOU
ON THURSDAY, JULY 31st.

⁂

The electric fan hummed and whirred in Elsinore's room, it sat up on a shelf watching the room, whirring, whirring, it kept the thin blue silk dresser scarf quivering frantically in its perpetual gale; as she brushed her hair it blew her kimono sleeve against her pale cheeks. It was like Charles himself, subtly infuriating, quietly goading her nerves, but she was determined not to let it disturb her self-control. When she picked up her hand mirror she knew what the fan was saying, "So you're wearing a low-necked dress, eh, Else . . . guess this guy's got you running, you never went in for fast clothes before . . . and the silk chemise, too, eh? . . . Well, why not, all the sporting women wear them and if that's you, now . . . no more blue or black dresses, either, I see . . . pink, by George . . . so that's how crazy he's made you, Else, old girl. . . . Pink silk at thirty-eight. . . . Pink silk for the Serpentine Ball—well, well, well."

Elsinore went on brushing her hair, the night was so hot her kimono stuck to the chair, through the little windows came the train smoke and saloon stench, the men singing and carrying on in the street sounded alarmingly near as if they were in the very room. She could hear the orchestra tuning up in the Casino, she heard Fischer laughing, and she wanted to hurry into the new dress but she was afraid of the watching fan. Well, she didn't care now. Let it find out that she hated her husband, very well, let it know everything. In the wastebasket beside the dresser was the box in which a silk chemise had arrived this morning and a note from Charles, saying, "Thought your new lovers might like this."

She had read the card, stunned, while Nettie tore off the tissue papers and pulled out the gift in great delight. All Charles's former taunts had been faint, far-off drum beats leading up to this menacing roll of thunder that could not be ignored. . . . "Thought your new lovers . . ." As Nettie shook out the silk, admiring its lace edge, the cages of Elsinore's mind burst open and hatred escaped. There was no way of locking it back in, there was a fearful joy in facing the truth, that strange blend of relief and desolation in seeing a jewel, long desperately guarded, finally lost forever. She wanted to tear up the note and the gift with it, but her second thought was a perverse resolve to wear the garment, as if she had carried out his savage suggestion. . . . It occurred to her to spray perfume on her hair, just as he had told her bad women did. For the first time in her life she wished for an intimate friend, a woman who knew her secrets, who would come in now while she dressed and say, "Elsinore, you never looked lovelier in your life—not a day over twenty-eight. If Harry Fischer only knew you were through with Charles, he wouldn't hesitate a minute— Mrs. Pepper's nothing to him, really, just a convenience—if he knew how you hated your husband. . . ."

Downstairs Nettie sat in the front of the shop, dressed in prim white embroidery, waiting for Fay and her young man to call for her. Elsinore wanted them to be gone before she came downstairs in her new pink dress, so after she was ready she sat down by her window waiting to see them cross the street as her signal for leaving. There was a tall, black-haired young man standing at the foot of the Casino steps rolling a cigarette. He seemed restless and each time the Bauers' screen door swung open he peered around to see who was coming out. Finally he pulled his cap down over his eyes and slouched into the restaurant. This was Morry, his mother saw, and while his motions stirred no curiosity in her, they irritated the watchful Nettie downstairs, almost beyond endurance. She had almost decided to go right into Bauer's after him, and tell him right before everyone that instead of waitresses he ought to be taking his own mother to the Casino.

The Casino windows gave out a mellow candy-pink glow from bunting-shrouded lights, and Elsinore could not distinguish Fischer from his musicians in the dark group near the window. Then she caught the gleam of a white dress shirt and a humming in her head joined the humming of the fan behind her. It was difficult to sustain, unfading in her mind, the black onyx eyes of Harry Fischer, the white eyeballs spread out and then diminished so that they were now white eyes, now black eyes, the color flickering and changing with the electric fan's insistent vibration. . . .

A man and two girls in white crossed the street—Nettie and Fay. Elsinore took a last look at herself in the mirror. Her hair was too tightly drawn—she took the pins out and did it up again nervously. The pink taffeta dress with its round neck had seemed too low when she first bought it, she had had to put a lace ruching across the front. Now she saw that the ruching was out of place and with her nail scissors she clipped the threads that held it. She picked up her white silk shawl and went downstairs through the darkened shop out into the hot, breathless night.

In her empty bedroom the electric fan whirred and purred, it kept the dresser scarf trembling perpetually, the closet door gently blowing open and shut, the shades on the little windows

crackling, and rapidly it flicked the pages of a mail-order catalogue lying on the bed.

෴

Streamers of colored serpentine fluttered from the Casino ceiling,
men dancing in their shirt sleeves snatched at it and lassoed shrieking girls, they kicked through tangles of the rainbow strips over the
dance floor, under the pink lights all women looked gay and darkly
wicked. In the center of the floor the dancing teacher and Dode
O'Connell two-stepped perfectly, Dode in a skin-tight red dress de-
fying her red hair. The musicians (Mr. Sanderson at the piano) sang
their choruses, their throats bulged and veins swelled on their fore-
heads as they bellowed the words, but even so the shouting and
laughing of the dancers drowned them out, only a phrase now and
then soared through the din, "Some of these days—you'll miss—"

Morry danced with Jen for the third time running, in this up-
roar it would not be remarked, besides she was so light in his arms
he forgot to trade her for someone else. Jen tried to make herself
still and light as a feather so that she could be close to Morry and
not let him notice it, for if he remembered it was only Jen he was
holding he'd drop her and go away. He was so tall he had to
hump his shoulders way over to hold her, and her arm was tight
around his neck. All she could think, dancing, was that this was
the way she wanted to be—always—fast in Morry's arms. On the
visitor's bench by the doorway Nettie Farrell, watching, her em-
broidered dress spread out in stiff petals around her, whispered
something to her chum, Fay, who then stared hard at Jen's feet.
Nettie didn't last very long at the Serpentine Ball for the men
were all hilariously drunk, and they called endearing names to
her as they danced past or chucked her under the chin famil-
iarly—no one respected a decent girl in this noisy carnival, so at
eleven o'clock Nettie indignantly departed.

"I have an announcement to make tonight, ladies and gentle-men," Fischer bawled through the megaphone. "The Serpentine Ball tonight is the last dance of the summer. The first dance of the autumn season will be given here in six weeks on September tenth. I wish to state that I will introduce to my pupils and mem-bers of my studio at that time the Mississippi Glide. This dance, ladies and gentlemen, is the popular ballroom dance of New York City at the present time, and with the assistance of Miss O'Connell, here, I will give you a brief demonstration. The Mississippi Glide. All right, Mr. Sanderson."

Immediately the crowd of dancers backed away, leaving the center of the floor free for the dancing master and his partner. Eyes fastened on the black patent-leather feet (heels never touch-ing floor) and the red satin ($10) slippers as they traced an intri-cate design on the shining oak floor.

"Do you suppose they really dance that way in New York?" Jen whispered to Morry. It hadn't occurred to Morry to ever doubt it, but now he shook his head convincingly.

"Na—they never even heard of it in New York," he an-swered. Jen's hand was hot in his but he did not drop it for Hunt Russell was alone nearby, and Morry thought stubbornly that now he was a business man himself he didn't have to give in to anyone, he didn't care so much about dancing with Jen but he wanted Hunt Russell to understand he had as much right to as anybody.

Fischer was the only man to keep his coat on, all the others were dancing with their shirt sleeves rolled up, their wilted col-lars open, serpentine trailing from their ears and trouser legs, their sweaty palms making smudgy imprints on the light dresses of their girls. The punch bowl in the hall had been filled three times, strengthened more each time with rum. Couples danced dizzily, wearily around, battered by the crowd; girls' heads, peer-ing blankly over their partners' shoulders, seemed pinned there like valentines, their faces dulled with music, their eyes unwinking, hair stringing damply over their cheeks.

Elsinore danced with a big red-faced drummer from Newark with a silver hook for a left hand. He said, "Just catch hold of that there hook, that's the idea," and he said that when it came to carrying sample cases a hook was better than a hand, but Elsinore shuddered touching the cold metal. His big tan shoes scuffed her white kid pumps, he held her so tight that her back ached, but this violence strangely pleased her as the clangor about her satisfied some desperate inner necessity. The jiggling crowd tore the sash from her pink dress, in the frenzy of a circle two-step with the music growing faster and faster her head whirled, and the girls, swinging from one hand to the next, kept up a high, dizzy scream that soared above all else.

"Dance with Number Three," roared Fischer and she was swung into his arms. Perspiration streamed from his forehead, he shook out a cream-colored silk kerchief and mopped his head. His heart thumped against her and confused her, even the smell of whiskey on his breath was rare and exciting. She forgot that he was Mrs. Pepper's, that in little railroad hotels those two met and went to one room. She forgot about the big blonde wife in Cleveland, all of these shadows faded under the pink lights and the hard bright gleam in his black eyes. He called a command over her shoulder, "Dance with the lady on your left!" and she was flung into a new partner's arms. She saw that Fischer was dancing with the Delaneys' girl, Jen—she would always remember that she had been pushed away for that young girl. . . .

She didn't want anyone else to touch her now, so she broke away from the dance and went into the dressing room. Only two girls were inside, big raw-boned girls with red arms and necks thrust out of feathery pink and blue organdie, blonde chickens popping out of Easter eggs. They stood before the dresser shaking clouds of powder over their faces from huge powder puffs, trustfully and intently, as if this witchcraft would instantly compel popularity. Elsinore looked at her face, white and small in the mirror between their two ruddy faces. She looked wild, she thought, with her hair flying about loosely, but she didn't care. Her head was splitting with noise but she wasn't sure if the noise was outside or inside, so many strange confusing thoughts crowded through her head like masked guests at a carnival, exciting, terrifying, shouting phrases they would never dare whisper under their own names. There was something familiar in all these suggestions as if long ago they had briefly appeared and at once been whisked off to dungeons. There was no guard for them now, but a fearful exhilaration in the knowledge that they were too strong for her, that they could overpower her easily.

She saw through the doorway that Fischer was still dancing with Jen St. Clair and she recalled old Mrs. Delaney warning her to keep Morry away from this girl. She would, she thought viciously, or better, she'd tell her to keep away from Morry. She'd say "Morry" but she would be secretly meaning, "Keep away from Harry Fischer!" Because he belonged to her, to nobody else. . . . Elsinore looked quickly at the two girls as if the thunder of her own mind might be overheard. One of them was bending over fixing a red garter on her white cotton stocking but she caught Elsinore's eye and smiled.

"If I bring my last summer's hat back, Mrs. Abbott," she ventured, "could you change the daisies on it for poppies?"

Elsinore smiled back at her but the words seemed no more concern of hers than the girl's knobby knees above her pretty legs, and when the girls went out together one said to the other, "She don't have to snub me twice, believe me." Then at the door they burst out laughing shrilly to show everyone they were having a wonderful time. . . .

Elsinore was glad they were gone, she felt sick from their geranium-scented powder. She opened the window wider and

pulled the moth-eaten velveteen curtains behind her, it was easier
to be here in the next room thinking of Fischer than in the ballroom seeing him with someone else. There was no air stirring
outside, stars and a moon would have looked cool but only the
lights from the Works lit up the sky with a soft red glare. She
could hear the steady chugging of the factory machines going all
night long, and from up here she could see the long dark shadows
of freight cars sliding back and forth in the Yard, the emerald and
ruby signal lights winking on and off. Through the din of the
dance hall the two-four rhythm of the bass drum throbbed triumphantly and punctuated the swish-swish of the engines outside. They didn't need an orchestra for Lamptown dances,
Elsinore thought, holding her splitting head in her hands, the engines and the factory machines could keep two-four time. One
and two and a one and a two and a one—this drumbeat that
could not be silenced was part of Fischer, all of her fantasies were
made to this obligato: they unrolled now automatically, herself
and Fischer on a train going away, away—away from young girls
with smooth throats and light laughter, away from factory girls
with hard mouths dancing with fierce grace, away from delicately
scented, plump women with tinkling voices—only Mrs. Abbott, a
milliner, and Mr. Fischer, a dancing master. Away to what?—
Breathlessly she allowed herself to draw aside this forbidden cur-
tain, to see them alone, he is coming through a doorway smiling
at her, the doorway of her bedroom, she is in the pink taffeta dress
waiting, and—Crowds of girls burst through the door, abruptly
the dream vanished and Elsinore wrung her hands. There could
be no torture like interruption, the brutal ripping of cherished ta-
pestries. If she had one wish in the world it would be to be locked
in a tower to think of one man undisturbed forever. She was nau-
seated again by geranium powder, girls battled for place at the
mirror, giggling they crowded her away from the window, the
room became stifling. She could not endure it any longer. She

pulled her shawl from the hook and a dozen wraps fell in a heap on the floor but she couldn't bother with them. If she could only sleep . . . but she hadn't slept for months it seemed to her. The mad circus in her head exhausted her, she didn't want to face Fischer again tonight. Alone, in her room, he was hers completely, here he belonged to all Lamptown. She walked unsteadily down the narrow hallway toward the steps, she didn't look back once to see him. The dance hall, out of the corner of her eye, was a nightmare of laughter and fluttering colors. She could scarcely wait to get home to think, to plan, to be alone. . . .

In the darkness of the stair landing Morry and Jen and Hunt Russell were standing.

"Well, Jen, how about it, coming with me?" Hunt asked. He was holding Jen's bare arm caressingly.

Jen looked at Morry but Morry wouldn't tell her not to go—if she wanted to go for a ride with Hunt he wouldn't stop her.

"Should we go, Morry?" she asked.

"Do what you please," Morry said distantly. "You wouldn't go if you didn't want to, anyway."

His mother hurried by without looking at him. He started after her but she ran down the steps in almost clumsy haste, so Morry didn't follow her just then, besides he wanted to see what Jen was going to do.

Elsinore's heart was pounding when she reached the street, she felt enormously elated as if she had escaped her hunters so far and was about to gloat over a stolen treasure in perfect safety. Not a soul was out. As far down Market Street as she could see lights blinked on deserted sidewalks, all Lamptown was crowded under the rose lights of the Casino; only Hermann and Hulda Bauer dozed in their windows. . . . She fumbled with her key, but her hands were shaking so she could scarcely fit it into the lock. The shop bell tingled sharply in the darkness as the door opened, then stopped short as the door shut. She turned the key quickly behind her again, she wanted to lock out these nameless pursuers who would harry her, for she was going to be alone, alone. . . . Her head and feet were so light, only her heart was thundering away, it could be heard above the Casino tumult or the engine whistles, she was certain. . . . Now she remembered the feel of his thick white hand grasping hers, the sensation was far clearer in memory than it had been in actuality, she could see the fine lines around his eyes, the cleft in his heavy chin . . . she felt so giddy she leaned against the wall for a moment at the top of the stairs. . . . She was strangely happy as if she were on the verge of something beautiful about to happen, something incredible, she was separated from this triumph by the thinnest of walls, if she could only control the chaos in her head she would know what this lovely thing was. . . . In another minute she could think—she'd be alone. . . . She pushed open the bedroom door and the noise of the fan made her catch her breath with the shock of reality. . . . The lovely thing about to happen . . . she clung to its vanishing shadow, but everything beautiful was fleeing desperately, there was only Charles Abbott, collarless and red-faced, sprawling drunkenly over her bed. She put her hand over her eyes to dispel this bad dream. Charles awkwardly sat up, blinking at her with bloodshot eyes. It was terrifying, the spectacle of the immaculate Candyman with his starched striped shirt rumpled, his black hair tousled and hanging over his eyes, his thin mouth sagging loosely. His coat and hat trailed on the floor, his sample cases were open and bonbons spilled all over the rug. Elsinore shook with blind fury, she wanted to tear him to pieces with her hands.

"Well, who'd you expect to see here if not your husband?" He pointed at her accusingly. "You come in here and turn white as a sheet, cause you see me. Who the hell was you expecting, damn it, stand there shivering away like I was some burglar. . . ."

She didn't dare to look at him again, hate was burning her veins, she wanted to kill him, to destroy everybody who outraged her right to be alone. His thick voice, whatever it was saying, rasped through her thoughts, there surely must be an end to such torment. She wouldn't look at him for she knew tears of rage were smarting in her eyes and through this blur she saw the little heap of silver-wrapped bonbons in the top of the sample case, she saw how cleverly they formed one curious shape, no use steadying her rioting brain to make sure of what her eyes saw there, for silver was in her brain, silver shut out Charles's voice, silver chilled the hatred in her heart, before she touched it she thrilled with the ecstasy of escape that beautiful metal in her hands could bring, wild happiness swept over her, the joy, exactly, of finding an opening in the prison wall too small for her pursuers but for her—final freedom.

On and on the drunken voice droned, accusing her, mocking her, as it had done year after year slowly wearing down her barriers. Facing him, her hand groped among the bonbons for what she had seen there, as soon as she touched the revolver she had a vision of a paradise of solitude and privacy forever. This was one way to shut out words . . . she raised the gun, closed her eyes and fired.

The awful hush of the minute afterward terrified her. She was sitting in a chair, tears slowly coursing down her cheeks. Someone hurrying up the steps, calling out, meant nothing to her. It meant nothing to see Charles sprawled over the floor, his mouth still open in his astonishment. A stream of blood trickled from him across the floor and slowly dyed the little blue doormat. The revolver was lost in the candies that had tumbled over. . . .

She began rocking back and forth in the chair. Her head ached, it was so empty and numb. Back and forth she rocked. Someone came in the room but she could not see or hear or feel, a man lying on the floor was no concern of hers, the only thing that was oddly familiar was the whirring of the electric fan behind her.

꙳

So Charlie Abbott had shot himself, they said.

No one in Lamptown knew why and no one really cared. In Delaney's bar they said Charlie Abbott was a bad egg, he had smooth ways but he was too slick with his women, too damned slick, never doing a thing for his wife and kid in Lamptown, they could starve for all of him. In the backyards of Shantyville women hanging up the wash, their mouths full of clothespins, speculated about what fast woman Mr. Abbott had killed himself for. No good, anyway, running around spending money while his wife worked her fingers to the bone keeping herself and the boy. Mrs. Abbott was a lady, as fine a little woman as you'd care to meet, you'd think after all she'd done the least a husband could do in return was to shoot himself in one of those big hotels instead of messing up her nice little shop.

The reporter from the *Cleveland Leader* asked Bill Delaney how the gun happened to be on the other side of the room after this "suicide," and if it hadn't struck Bill that the wife might have plugged him on account of his other women. Bill Delaney fixed the stranger with an indignant eye.

"None of that funny business, now," he curtly advised. "Don't let anybody in this town hear you say a thing like that or they'll run you out of town. I know that's all in your line, but leave Mrs. Abbott out of it, see? She's a quiet ladylike little body that's had her first piece of luck now with her husband kicking off. You just keep your imagination to yourself, because Lamptown people won't listen to a word about Mrs. Abbott. A plucky little woman, that's what she is."

Only Morry knew. He had known when he opened the bedroom door and saw his mother rocking quietly beside the thing on the floor. He was paralyzed with terror and an awful guilty feeling of having wished this very thing until it came true. . . . Then all he could think was how unhappy she must have been to do it, and such pity came over him for his mother that his throat ached and he was ready to face all the rest of her tormenters himself, and to kill them all. It didn't matter about his father, it only mattered that his mother had suffered all these years, it was as if she were the one who had died, and all his failures to understand or to help her loomed in his mind—too late he would make amends.

But there was little, after all, for him to do now. All Lamptown was taking care of little Mrs. Abbott whose husband had chosen such a tragic end. The Bauers took charge of everything. Hulda slept in the shop and at the last minute there was no place for Morry so he had to stay at Hunt's overnight. He hung around his mother, he wanted her to say she needed him and that Hulda could go home but Elsinore didn't say anything. She stayed in bed, eating nothing, staring at visitors blankly when they asked questions, seeming to recognize no one.

"She's been that way ever since they found him," people whispered.

Hermann knew the story and told everybody exactly how it happened. It seems Bill Delaney was in back of his saloon when he heard the shot, and since Charlie had been in there an hour before, drunk, and waving a revolver, he'd sort of suspected him of something. So he rushed into the Bon Ton and the next minute he was sticking his head out of the upstairs window, yelling, "Hey, Hermann, for God's sake, Charlie Abbott's dead!" Hermann waddled over as fast as he could and by the time he got upstairs Bill Delaney had gone all to pieces—he was on his knees by the bed sobbing and shivering and out of his mind.

"Oh God, Hermann, it wasn't my fault," he screamed, "I swear it wasn't—but look at them spread out all over the tracks—all bleeding and all dead—" They called in Bill's mother to take him home, he clung to her weakly, sobbing against her bent old shoulder that the wreck wasn't his fault. . . .

Girls ran in from the Casino and Hermann finally had to lock the doors. "Well, Charlie shot himself, that's all, now get back to your dance."

Elsinore, all the next day, sat in her chair by the window, wrapped in a blanket, her hair tumbled down, her face sagging oddly, her eyes stupid. Morry kept patting her hand but he didn't know what to say to her, or anything to do for her except vague magnificent deeds that would somehow make her happy. She cared no more for him than for anyone, and she seemed ten times more remote, never talking, looking dully out the window all the time, never heeding the compassionate questions of the neighbors. She didn't comb her hair or change to night clothes when she went to bed, and this bothered Morry more than anything for he could not conceive of a catastrophe big enough to make his mother neglect her person. He didn't think of his father, all he knew was that a terrible thing had happened to his mother, and he was suffocated with tenderness for her. He thought about her every instant, he was going to do something to make it all up to her, he tried to think of something that would astonish and please her, but all he could think of was a little silver bar pin he'd got her from Robbin's for Christmas once.

"That's it—I'll get her another bar pin," he decided with relief.

The blue veins in her temples and white hands moved him almost to tears, and the marble pallor of her face. . . . He knew what it was like to have it all burning inside of you with no way of showing it. If he could only smooth everything for her. . . . He was enraged at his futility, then the whisper came—"You can't help her because she won't let you, it isn't your fault—it's only that she doesn't need you or anybody else."

This wasn't quite fair for her, a woman ought to need her son, oughtn't she? . . . Hurt and troubled, Morry went back to Fowler's office and tried to concentrate on Clover Heights. Everyone he met looked at him reproachfully and said, "Look here, Morry, oughtn't you to be home with your mother?" . . . He couldn't very well explain that his mother didn't want him, so he could only mutter a sullen answer about the demands of his work. He amazed himself by asking Fowler for a salary and getting it.

He was conscious of curious eyes everywhere, and he walked stiffly and proudly so that people would be afraid to talk to him. He'd do something yet, nothing he'd ever planned was big enough, it had to be some colossal achievement now to make Lamptown forget about his father, something so breathtaking that it would swallow up this present scandal, so at the mention of the name "Abbott" the town would not say, "Oh yes, son of the guy who killed himself," but "Oh yes, the young man who owns the Big Four Railroad . . . who built the bridge across Lake Erie . . . the Abbott that put Lamptown on the map." When he read in the paper of some man inventing this or that, or winning a great prize he shook his head and thought, "Better than that . . . it's got to be better than that."

At the moment Clover Heights was all he could work on, and so much depended on other people and money that it seemed not to move at all. He took to wearing overalls and helping out when some carpenter's assistant didn't show up, and found that physical exhaustion soothed his fever to do, to accomplish things.

He fixed up an army cot in Fowler's office because there wasn't any place for him at the Bon Ton. The shop was full of women, and when he would go in the evening to see his mother she didn't talk, all he could do was to pat her hand and finally he shunted off the busy helpers. Hulda transferred herself and her palm leaf to the workroom, and Hermann would bring over great trays of roasts which Elsinore never touched. Nettie and Mrs. Pepper and Hulda and all the visiting women kept the workroom noisy (even though the shop was properly closed) with the rattle of table setting, and eating, while old Mrs. Delaney washed dishes perpetually for these funeral banquets. The constant activity kept everyone happy and the widow's apathetic silence was not conspicuous, it seemed decent and ladylike.

Four mornings after the funeral Nettie came into the shop and found the wreath off the front door. Elsinore, in a big black apron, was cleaning out the closet in the workroom. She'd hauled out half a dozen boxes and her face was covered with soot. Nettie was unprepared for such a quick return to routine. She herself was wearing a black dress out of deference to her employer's grief, and she was prepared with little consolation phrases.

"Mice have gotten into these felts," Elsinore said abruptly. "We'll have to move everything out."

Nettie looked dolefully at her.

"Oh, Mrs. Abbott, you're so brave to pick up things so quickly again!. . . You've been so brave about it all—I don't see what made him do it! I can't understand! Poor Mr. Abbott! And it's all so hard on you."

"Well, there's so much work to be done around here, Nettie, there won't be time to think," Elsinore said in such a matter-of-fact voice that Nettie couldn't believe her ears. "In another two months we've got to have this whole place ready, upstairs show-rooms finished, all ready for business. Mrs. Pepper will be ready to move in as soon as we can have her."

All of Nettie's rehearsed condolences were forgotten in being reminded of Mrs. Pepper's triumphant return. She hung her hat on the clothes tree and silently pinned on her apron. It was true that Mrs. Abbott looked half-sick dragging herself around with heavy feet, but Nettie wasn't sorry for her any more, not a bit. If a woman showed no more feelings than that after her husband was dead you couldn't expect Nettie to have feelings for her. Why, you might even think she was glad about it.

Elsinore was neither glad nor sorry. The revolver shot had blown out some fuse in her brain. She couldn't remember why it had seemed so important to silence Charles, the thoughts that had made her quiver with fanatic delight a few days back were lost, Fischer ceased when Charles ceased, all feeling died with that explosion. Now, night and day, she was only the proprietor of a thriving millinery store, in her numb memory ran color combinations, arrangements of hand-made lilacs on milan, her heart had become a ribbon rosette worn with chic a little to one side.

⚘

"A nice little woman," Harry Fischer said about Mrs. Abbott, "but not very light on her feet."

Mrs. Pepper asked him to be particularly kind to her friend because she'd seen so much trouble, so the dancing master, instead of a mere good-day when he met the milliner, would remember to add, "Is it hot enough for you, Mrs. Abbott?" or "Quite a little shop you have there, Mrs. Abbott, quite a nice little property." It was more than he'd ever said to her before but it meant nothing to her now. She would say over his words afterward in a wistful effort to restore her old romance, but it was gone, it had blown up with its own enemy. She knew that Mrs. Pepper was meeting him again, but she didn't care, it seemed so far away—those years when she had cared. She knew when the affair began again, because for the first two or three months of the enlarged Bon Ton regime Mrs. Pepper had sobbed nightly in bed with her, talked very little, and grew almost thin. Then, after one day on some mysterious business in Cleveland, she began to hum about her work, she no longer wept but chatted optimistically about life, she let out the pleats in her skirts once more and found many important errands out of town, even though she was permanently stationed in Lamptown. She tiptoed radiantly about her showroom over the Bon Ton—the very room where Charles was killed—fondly patting the headless dummies in their gorgeous lavender brocaded girdles, peeping outdoors from time to time to see if any women on the street were admiring the lingerie display in the window, and in mid-afternoon when business was dull she'd go downstairs and say, "Nettie, I wish you'd sing that thing you used to sing, 'Come, come, I love you only'—you know the one I mean—'I want but you.'"

Women from good homes in Avon and neighboring villages began to shop in Lamptown instead of sending to Cleveland or Columbus for their clothes. Two whole new streets were dug up through the Lots by the Lamptown Home Company, twenty-four houses ($2800 apiece) to a street. New families were moving in before the paint was dry on the walls, dozens of strange children played in the street excavations and tobogganed down the rubbish heaps along the torn roads. Officials at the Works rode to and fro in brand new Fords or even Cadillacs and it was rumored that the wives of these eastern strangers smoked cigarettes and played cards every afternoon. Bauer's was crowded with boarders, young men who wouldn't buy homes or bring their families to Lamptown till they saw how they liked their new jobs. So many bigwigs from the east were staying at Hunt's that the old mansion slipped quite naturally into the hotel class. It was called the Russell House, and Hunt, running back and forth to Cleveland nowadays, seemed to think the group of paying guests was a jolly improvement on his old hermitage. The one person who looked upon this change as sacrilege was Morry Abbott, and Morry himself boarded there. When he turned in at the imposing gate every evening he whispered to himself, "My home. . . . Now I know how Hunt used to feel walking under these trees." It was his—now, his, almost as much as it was Hunt's, and the twelve other guests were of no consequence, he swelled with pride of possession whenever he opened the heavy white doors into the dark spacious hallway, he scarcely dared think it was true that he, merely by virtue of nine dollars a week, was able to call this his home. He hoped his mother would see the importance of this step in his life, he said, "Well, I got a place at Hunt

Russell's now, I'll clear my stuff out of that bureau." But all she said was, "That's better than sleeping in Mr. Fowler's office, anyway, isn't it?"

But even the next summer failed to find Clover Heights any further developed than its original three houses—one complete, the other two arrested in the last stage of their construction awaiting the particular demands of problematical buyers. On one side of the Lots scores of tiny houses, Model B, squeezed on to a main road, and dozens of others, neatly identical, paralleled them behind, waiting trustingly for new roads to cross their door stoops. On the other side of the creek, surrounded by untouched meadowland, three large houses marked the beginning of "Clover Heights." One of these was of rough brownstone with a curious rolled roof and this was known as the "chatcau." The other two were brownish-green frame and were referred to as Normandy style or perhaps it was semi-Ann Hathaway, though residents of Avon could boast of similar structures which were merely spoken of as a $7500 home. Lamptown's new inhabitants often spent Sunday looking over these three houses, showing them to relatives from out-of-town, but in the eight months they'd been standing no one had ventured to buy or even rent one. Morry was amazed at this apathy, at first, and reassured Fowler that it would only be a matter of weeks; even the bank officials told him that it was a wise thing to show people they need not move out of Lamptown in order to have a better-class home. But Fowler said, "Uh-huh" and looked longingly toward the rival renting office of the Lamptown Home Company where a steady stream of men and women flowed in and out.

"We could rent for forty, maybe," he meditated gloomily, "but we can't meet their twenty-two fifty. . . ."

Instead of a Country Club, the first big building on the Lots was a huge barnlike place called the Working Girls' Club. It stood at the corner, large, blank, square, with a row of little houses stemming from it east and west. A yard of red earth between its front stoop and the cinder walk allowed a few desperate blades of grass to grow, and a gaunt geranium was on either side of the step, but even these decorative touches failed to entice the old factory girls to live there. However, new girls, answering ads put in state papers, poured in here and were given sets of house rules and introduced to a matron who was to help them with their problems. The chief problem of the girls was how to keep from having babies and the new matron's answer to this was a solemn lecture on the wages of sin, so that better paid girls rapidly took to renting the little neighboring houses, four girls to a house, where they could do as they pleased and work out their own problem. The new officials started a welfare department at the Works with a nurse in charge, who sent girls home who had headaches and wouldn't allow them to return till their health was perfect. For these days of angry rest their wages were docked but it was a very efficient service and admired editorially all over the state. Kindly lectures once a week on the dangers, moral and physical, of women smoking and having too close friendships, opened up a new and dazzling vista to Lamptown girls too busy quarreling over men heretofore to keep up with feminine progress in larger cities.

Lamptown was getting rich. Half the town had accepted the invitation of the directors to buy stock so that you could scarcely find a shoe clerk or a grocery boy in the place who wasn't a shareholder. When strangers made some ribald joke about old Tom, the drunken street cleaner, asleep on the curb in the midst of his work, Bill Delaney loved to amaze them by answering, "Looks like a bum, don't he? Well, that bird sold his shanty and bought five hundred dollars worth of shares in the Works not ten months ago. Know what he's worth today? Twenty-five hundred dollars, yes sir, and it'll be twice that before another year's out!"

Careful citizens who were not going to risk their small savings on that dangerous unknown world of stocks bitterly watched improvident neighbors who had thrown everything into this venture roll by in the automobiles they had bought on dividends. The very shyest men accosted fellow travelers with the news whenever they went out of town, in Cleveland hotel lobbies they stared at innocent strangers over their newspapers until their glance was returned, then they drew close and said, "Have a cigar, sir? Look here, I want to show you something," and they'd whip a Works prospectus out of their pocket. "Lamptown Works. You know our products, I guess. Well, that's my hometown. A year ago I bought a thousand shares in this Works and sir, today, it's worth six times what I paid for it. Why, say, we've got one of the biggest propositions right there in that little town—talk about your Ford plant! Say, what's your name, sir? I wish if you're ever passing through down there you'd look me up. I just want to take you through that there factory. I'd just like to show you something."

Going down Market Street you'd meet dozens of people you'd never seen before, there were four Packards in town owned by men Lamptown never heard of, and when Hunt Russell's car, battered and seedy-looking in comparison to the new ones, drove downtown, an old citizen might remark, "Ah—Hunt Russell!" at which newcomers indifferently queried, "Well, who's Hunt Russell?" And after all, who was Hunt, now? There were Russells on the board of directors but Hunt was only a minor vice-president, he no longer took part in the company's movements. When matters came up needing the signature of a third vice-president Hunt was seldom to be found, unless you wanted to search the grandstand at the North Randall racetracks or keep an eye on the yellow roadster before a Prospect Avenue sporting house in Cleveland.

The new people didn't know Hunt Russell but they knew young Abbott. Everybody knew the young man who showed you over the "chateau," who had for an office a tiny sample house at the eastern edge of the Lots, a small house whose roof was lettered in red and white—"Clover Heights Company. See Morris

Abbott inside or call Lamptown 66 J." The girls on their way home to the Club went round by this little office and if old Fowler wasn't in they stopped by to kid Morry and see if he wouldn't ask for a date. He seldom surrendered to their laughing challenges however. He smoked cigars like Fowler and was considered a cagey young man with a much better business-head than was strictly true. He talked briskly to strangers, helped all the side issues of Fowler's business as notary public, auctioneer, rent collector, and no one could trace the exact beginning of this crisp aggressive manner, though Morry knew he had adopted it painfully, at first, to protect himself from Lamptown's pity and questioning after his father's death. When it was necessary to refer to that event he could say "after the old man kicked off" quite casually without that quick fear of someone suspecting his mother that he had once felt.

Nobody could rattle Morry Abbott, he was armored against everything because he knew it was your business to be hard just as it was the world's business to throw javelins into you. He was intensely grateful to Fowler for opening up his life. It was Fowler and he against the rest of Lamptown and Fowler's frequent moods of depression did not discourage him.

"But look at the place, Morry," Fowler nodded toward the desolate expanse of Heights crowned by its three empty mansions. "We can't get another cent to keep on building unless one of these sells—even old Hunt isn't fool enough to advance us any, let alone the bank. And no work going on makes the proposition look like a dud. And if it looks like a dud it might as well be one, see what I mean."

"Wait till people get used to having more money," argued Morry. "They still have the idea that if they get enough money for a swell home they've got to move to Avon for it. Wait. Why, everyday I take at least two people over those houses. That leads to something, you know."

"Like hell it does," muttered Fowler. "The damn fools steal the fixtures, we got repair bills on those houses as if somebody was living in 'em already, on Sundays folks have picnics in the gardens and break in for souvenirs to show all their out-of-town friends what swell houses they got. But ask one of them to live there! Ha! It isn't that they cost more, rent or buy, it's because they're different."

"But that's the whole point—they've got to be different!" Morry continued to protest.

Fowler shook his head morosely.

"I got people coming to me all the time asking for houses exactly like this one or that one next door, a man's whole aim is to have a place exactly like everybody's, he feels like a fool being different. Take his wife, she says, 'Oh, but you said this house was just like Traumer's and here is the closet on the left of the landing instead of the right, liar!' I got a hunch we're stung, Abbott, my boy—not on houses, understand, but on people!"

"Well, we've got to stick it out until we've proved we're right," Morry said.

"Oh sure, sure, we'll stick it out," Fowler agreed without enthusiasm.

Morry refused to believe the Fowler who had been standing with him against the world was so easily scared. He had felt so secure with the older man applauding each new idea for Heights improvement, it was the two of them against everybody else. Now he suspected he was standing alone, and he was bewildered. How could a man change so completely—the idea was the same idea they started with, wasn't it? . . . Going home, Morry found himself more upset than he had realized. Fowler's misgivings shook the very ground under his future, he hadn't ever dreamed that he would change.

Morry walked down Market Street and in a shop window mirror was surprised to see himself, no use denying it, a big, good-looking young man wearing his new gray suit with an air, his straw hat tilted just so. In this image there appeared no indication of the vague fear in his heart, you would never have guessed that this young man had any doubts as to his own perfection. It was a reassuring image, and Morry was heartened by it. You didn't see a fellow like that out of a job, or working away at some dinky factory job.

He stopped in front of the Paradise to read the bill for tonight. Two vaudeville turns were announced this week, pictures of the performers simpered from the lobby walls. One, a portrait of a slumbrous-eyed Jewess with a guitar proclaimed, "The Singing Salome"; the other photograph showed two blonde girls in white tights and spangled bodices, one holding the other at the waist, both laughing sunnily with an air of incalculable good humor. Morry looked around for other pictures of these "Two Little Clowns from Ragtime Town." He could hear Milly practicing their new songs inside and thought he heard girls' voices, he was almost tempted to go inside and see if the Two Little Clowns were in there, too. He could not get over his old awe of these glamorous stage women, beginning way back with Lillian Russell they were tangled up with his ambition to do great things—why?—in order to come closer, perhaps to be able to touch them. Men bragging in Bill's bar of affairs with little carnival actresses made these no nearer or more easily attainable.

"When do the Two Clowns come on tonight?" he asked the man sweeping out the lobby.

"Eight-ten and ten-ten."

Morry turned away. He thought fiercely the Heights plan had to prove out, then he would turn into a Hunt Russell, he would have a glittering long automobile at the curb here and when the Two Little Clowns came out he would casually invite them to ride. Still, he didn't desire them, any more than he wanted a gold and white yacht, he only wanted to be equal to these far-off splendors, to have no doors locked to him.

Market Street was crowded as it was so often now, strange women in hats and gloves and plain dark silks came out of shops, you turned to look twice at them for Lamptown girls went around town bareheaded all summer. Sometimes one of these foreign women stepped into an auto at the curb and took the wheel herself. Morry was excited by these dashing gestures. Lamptown was beginning to be a wonderful place, he thought, there was no bottom to it now, you saw new things every day as if it were already a city.

In front of the Elite Gown Shop he saw a girl and even before his eye had taken in the black curly hair, the snub nose, and sky-blue eyes, he knew it was Jen. He recognized Jen always by his sudden feeling of embarrassment, here was someone who knew him too well, someone to whom at one time or another he'd told everything, and so when he saw her, his first impulse always was to establish new barriers, to be aloof—show her that he was not such an open book as he seemed. He was surprised, watching her from this distance, to find her so agreeable to the eye, he so seldom really saw her except in relation to himself, someone whose adoring gaze he must avoid, someone who undoubtedly must be so pleased to find herself getting pretty that he would never satisfy her vanity by looking at her. She had an air, too, of being wonderfully dressed, but even Morry could tell it was only blue-checked gingham she was wearing, her proud delight in its newness fooled you at first. She was talking to the little Cleveland Jew named Berman who ran the Elite but when Morry passed she caught his arm.

"Look, Morry, I'm going to work here!"

"What do you mean—sell dresses?"

She waved goodbye to the Elite's proprietor and walked along with Morry. Isaac Berman, dark, bald, leaned against his door with folded arms, his Oriental eyes following her down the street. He turned to his son inside.

"Nice, hey, Lou?"

As soon as she told him of her plan to work in the Elite Morry was whipped again with envy, for he saw it as she saw it, not merely a job in a dress shop but a step toward great things; Cleveland, Pittsburgh, New York, dances every night, music all day, Jen in a silver dress on a magazine cover—while Morry's Clover Heights was crumbling, he was alone in Lamptown, waiting for some great thing to come and pick him up.

"I get nine dollars a week. . . . Say, Morry, Lil's coming to Lamptown. We're going to rent a place, maybe, and keep house."

Morry was always aghast at the things Jen did, he had never ceased to marvel at himself for having got out of the factory, so how could Jen jump so easily out of one thing into another, how could she finally take care of Lil, all of her own doing? His heart beat fast with triumph, as if he had done it, because what he wanted to do and what Jen wanted to do were somehow confused in his head, so this was all his own doing then.

"What will Lil do?"

"Maybe Bermie will give her some work, too," Jen answered. "Not that what I make wouldn't be enough. . . . Nine dollars a week is a lot of money. I'm taking music lessons from Milly. She's going to teach Lil, too, and I'll teach her to tap dance— Mr. Travers taught me. Bermie's son's got friends on the stage, he said when we get something learned he could fix everything, he said I wouldn't lose anything by learning clothes first. Look here."

She pulled a newspaper clipping out of her pocket. It was a photograph of Maxine Elliot.

"Bermie's going to take me to see her, if she comes to Cleveland. . . . You know those Two Little Clowns at the Paradise this week? Lil and I could do that, easy enough. . . . If Lil wants to, of course."

Morry was dizzy from these swift pictures, he was excited by them, and when they reached Bauer's it was he who was sorry to leave, he wanted to stay near this excitement, he was stirred to immense schemes, Clover Heights, Lamptown, was a mere step in this splendid ascent.

"Say, Jen, what about this Berman?" he pulled her away from Bauer's door to ask sharply. "First I hear you're out riding all hours with Hunt Russell—folks say Dode O'Connell quit the Works and left town on account of you. Now you're in with this Berman fella—what's the idea?"

Jen looked at him skeptically, her mouth curled.

"What about Nettie Farrell, and those girls at the Club always hanging around you—what about that girl in Norwalk you always have up at the Casino—what about—"

"Oh, Jen, for God's sake!" Morry, his face red, dumped tobacco into a cigarette paper and rolled it. It wasn't any of Jen's business what girls he ran with, the thing about Jen was that she didn't know men, and somebody ought to tell her who was all right and who wasn't. Now he was furiously ashamed at being taken personally, as he had been the day old Mrs. Delaney delivered the warning to keep away from her Jen.

"I'm only telling you to be careful," he muttered, hating her. "You got to watch out for these foreigners. You've got to remember you're just a kid, and a crazy one at that. I'm only telling you to mind your step."

Jen looked down at the pavement.

"You told me to look out for Hunt and for Fischer and for Mr. Travers and now for Lou. All the fellows I like best," she said slowly. "Gee, Morry, what do you want me to do? . . . Isn't *anybody* all right?"

Morry didn't know what to answer. He couldn't tell her she had no right to like any man but himself, he was ashamed of his jealousy over Jen.

"You're pretty young to be running around, that's all," he said finally. "Somebody's got to keep an eye on you."

"No younger than that girl of yours from Norwalk," Jen answered sulkily. Her eyes met his with a direct challenge and Morry felt queerly stirred and afraid. He lit his cigarette silently, and was relieved to see Hogan waving to him from Delaney's entrance. He dashed thankfully across the street, and the Bauer screen door slammed.

❧

Walking home from the Elite Gown Shop you had to keep your fists tightly clenched to keep from dancing, you could hum softly to yourself but you must remember not to sing out loud, you could whisper it to yourself but you mustn't shout it, "I don't have to wait table any more, I don't have to go to the factory either, I have a real job, next I'll be transferred to the Cleveland store or maybe New York and there I'll be on the stage, I'll sing and dance all day and all night. . . . And I don't have to be helped, I have a home all of my own doing and I can do as I please, and Lil's coming. The Thing is beginning to happen."

Jen actually only had half a home, she rented the upstairs of a house way out beyond Extension Avenue for six dollars a month, she could scarcely wait for Lil to come and be astonished at having a front porch, a yard, a honeysuckle vine, and a lilac bush. Each night she ran all the way home from the store because Extension Avenue was pitch dark. She ran down the middle of the road so that shadows behind trees couldn't grab her, even the thrill of having her own latchkey didn't overcome her daily terror of going into the dark house. As soon as she got inside she locked the door and pushed a table against it. She turned on lights in all the rooms and said out loud, "This is my own home," and she was proud of herself, and then sat by the front window wishing somebody, anybody, would come and see her. She visited the old couple downstairs until they ostentatiously made preparations for bed.

Then she went up to her rooms and said, "My own home—imagine!" and banged the door quickly behind her so the Unknown following her couldn't get in. It was fun walking back and forth through this solitary magnificence, it was fun so long as she heard the people downstairs, but as soon as they were quiet she was afraid of the silence, of crickets chirping eerily in the clover, of dogs barking far off, she was homesick for engines a yard from her window, they must be missing her, their whistles sounded remote and lonely, yes, when she was alone in the home she'd rented all by herself, she dared to wish for the Bauers' kitchen and the darling clatter of dishes and men swearing, and the smell of fried onions. But this was not to be admitted for then someone would pity her loneliness, and she was not a person to be pitied but a child of luck, see, she was only sixteen and had her own home, she could handle wonderful dresses from eight in the morning till eight at night, she could toss a blue satin dress over a rack nonchalantly as if satin was nothing to her, she could even try on twenty dollar dresses for mothers buying for absent daughters, yes, Jen was a girl to be envied and she was sorry for other women and a little awed by her own good fortune. Whenever she saw old Mrs. Delaney hobbling along the street she wanted to apologize to her for not doing so badly as the old woman had hoped, she was sorry for her but she was still afraid of her, you never could be sure when people who once owned you would clutch you again, and this time you could never, never get away.

But only this old woman and the silent night in her own home could chill her now, only these, for the rest of the time an amazed excitement rushed through her veins, something, something was in the air. She wanted to skip, to clap her hands with delight, because this mysterious something was so close to her she could almost touch it, it was like the first rat-a-tat-tat in the circus parade, any minute now the band would begin to play. She could scarcely bear such perpetual delight, it bubbled over so that old

Berman winked at his son Lou, and when Lou pinched her cheek, she had to throw her arms about him and kiss him furiously. When the store closed at night she didn't know what to do but skip down Market Street to see the Bauers, to feast her ears on the music trickling out of Delaney's pianola, to tell a placid Hulda and a jealous Grace every single thing that happened in the Elite that day.

Hulda said she was going to give her something for her place, something nice, you wait, maybe this doily when it was finished, but when it was finished she couldn't bear to part with it, she opened a locked drawer and tried to decide which of these hoarded Larkin premiums she could give away but her heart ached over each decision. When she finally took out a chromo of a white-robed woman kneeling with the printed thought, "Simply to the Cross I cling," Hulda burst into tears because no one, not even her little Jenny, could love any of these tissue-wrapped treasures as she had loved them. After she had given it to her she sat on her stool gazing unhappily at the print now rolled up under Jen's arms, and while Jen leaned on the counter, chattering about what this one said or bought, tears rolled slowly down Hulda's cheek because Jen would not love and save this gift, she would only pin it on the wall where any stranger could look at it.

"I'm going away, too, believe me," said Grace, pausing between the courses of Sweeney's late supper to listen sourly to Jen. "And not to work in any Lamptown dump, either, I'm going to Detroit to work in a big cafeteria. Say, there's a town. A fella was in here the other day, a big bicycle salesman, and he says there's nothing Chicago has got that Detroit hasn't got. He says they got money to burn up there, fellas crazy for a girl with a little life in her, believe me, I'm not sticking in this dump after what this fella told me. He said why a girl with my personality wouldn't have to take nothin' from nobody up there in Detroit, why he says,

Gracie, I've seen girls with only half your personality driving their own automobiles in Detroit and you take this Belle Isle, there's nothin' like it this side of New York City, he was sayin'."

Hulda smiled tremulously at Jen.

"Gracie's always leaving us," she said. "Always going to some big town, but she never goes."

"Wait!" Grace warned her. "You won't see me slinging this tray around here much longer. Not in this hick town, no sir."

It was the way Grace always talked, she did it, Jen knew, to show her how foolish it was to be happy over the simple triumphs of Lamptown when nothing so trivial would satisfy a high-spirited girl like Grace.

"Seen Morry?" Grace called from Sweeney's table.

Jen nodded.

"Ask him why he never comes in any more?"

"No," said Jen, painfully conscious of that matter between Morry and Grace. "I didn't ask him anything."

"Funny," observed Grace. "You and him never seemed to get on, always bickering when you got together. . . . And you won't see him now 'cause he wouldn't drop into a dress store the way he would in a restaurant."

"Morry's a smart young man, now," said Hulda. "It's got to be a mighty pretty girl to catch him."

Jen tried to avoid looking at Grace who was winking broadly behind Hulda's back as a reminder of the intimacies she had so often confided to Jen.

After a little while with Grace, Jen forgot the terrors of Extension Avenue, a home of her own seemed a refuge indeed, and the dark clover lots she had to pass were nothing if she thought hard about something else. So Jen, running home through the darkness, cinders scattering about her heels, her heart thumping with fear, thought about Lou Berman and the curious lure of dark Jewish eyes and olive skin, she thought of Hunt Russell and the way his oldness held yet repelled her, of the dry things he said which seemed to mean so much more than they really did, of how it must feel to be a dethroned emperor (in this light of a lost king he seemed glamorous and sweetly sad to her, she almost loved him), she thought of the doughnut smell of the Delaneys' parlor, of the little gold chair on the mantel which she would never see again. A dim light blinked here and there in an upstairs window, the trees shook dew from their leaves, a twig snapped under her foot and made her run faster. Her heart was as big as her chest now, booming away, it was dreadful to be afraid of darkness, someday she would go to a great city, Detroit, maybe, where dazzling golden lights left no corner for night to hide in, where bands playing day and night crowded out fearful quiet. She remembered that, until then, she must think hard of something else and so, panting down the last few yards of darkness, she thought of Morry, and the thought of Morry was so big, so all-enveloping that there was no wish or feeling to it, it was only a great name, you said "Morry" and it covered every tiny thought or wish, it loomed out of the blackness like a great engine searchlight straight in your eyes, blinding you to everything else, even to itself. Morry, Morry, Morry—you could put yourself to sleep just saying it over and over.

It wasn't the Elite, as Jen had tried to arrange, but the Bon Ton that finally took in Lily St. Clair. Morry saw her first sitting on the wicker bench in the showroom when he stopped in one Saturday night to see his mother. When he went to live at Russell House he was worried about his mother, he thought in her quiet way she wanted him near her and he took care to drop in every evening after he moved. But she paid little attention to him, talking to Mrs. Pepper or Nettie about the new decorations upstairs, and forgot always to ask him about his work or how he liked his new home. If customers came in there'd be no place for him to sit, and after standing uncomfortably around he'd realize there was no place for him in his mother's life, that there never had been, and he'd flush with shame to remember his fierce tenderness for his mother as a frantic lover might blush who realizes in cool retrospect that the beloved was always indifferent to him.

The new independence of his mother bothered him, the change in her taste in clothes, a certain indefinable boldness in her manner, a way of glancing sidewise at men that was disturbingly like Grace Terris. His memory of his mother as a slight, quiet lady was wiped out by the reality of this new knowing, politely aggressive personality. When she and Mrs. Pepper went out together, two well-built, well-dressed women, their hips swaying, he would redden when men standing near him whistled their admiration. "There go the milliners!" And the more stylish Elsinore became, the more Lamptown women remembered that after all Charlie Abbott hadn't been so bad, a waster, true, but what man wasn't? Morry heard these whispers with fear, but as yet there was nothing definite against his mother except that the Bon Ton widow was always on the go with the corset lady. What the town whispered did not bother him so much as the sight of someone he knew so well changing under his very eyes into a stranger, a perfectly unknown quantity.

He was worried over other matters, too, for Fowler was persistently sour and silent, hints came to Morry's ears of the Lamptown Home Co. taking over the Clover Heights area, of the three houses being rented out as boardinghouses, but these rumors could not be tracked down, nor would Fowler divulge any secret plans concerning the Heights. That he had lost interest in the developing of that community was certain, and with its collapse imminent he had possibly lost confidence in his young assistant. Morry dared not face the fears in his own mind, he smoked restlessly all day and wanted to talk all this over with his mother, always hoping for comfort which reason told him would not be there. As soon as he reached the Bon Ton door, a clear picture of what the call would be rose before him—his own eagerness to talk, to tell of his gnawing fear of having to go back to the factory for a job, and his mother listening politely but interrupting with orders for Nettie, exclamations about remote matters to be attended to, and leaving him for the always preferable customer. He wondered, since he knew the whole scene so well, why he stopped in at all, but he reasoned when no comfort came, at least then his need for it was chilled and his defenses against an indifferent world that much strengthened.

No one was in the shop but a girl sitting on the green wicker footstool, with her hat in her lap, and when Morry saw her softly curling yellow hair he knew it was Jen's Lil. She was so obviously something to be stared at that Morry dared not look too long. In his room at Russell House he had pictures of actresses, Billie Burke, the Dolly sisters, Anna Held—and he had never before seen any girl who looked like these gilded creatures, they were not of the ordinary breed of women at all, he was certain they had been whirled dancing and spangled out of some falling comet onto their stage. And here was just such a girl, her yellow hair, her gold-tinged, creamy skin, her clear, violet eyes, the very curve of her lips such objects for wonder in themselves that it was hard to reassemble them into one complete marvel in his mind. She was shy and kept pulling down her shrunken gingham dress to cover her long legs. She must be tall for her age, Morry thought. Taller than Jen. Her own acute embarrassment put him completely at ease.

"Aren't you Jen's sister, Lil?" he asked.

She nodded, coloring.

"I'm Morry Abbott—Jen's told me about you."

Then she talked a little, and Morry was enchanted with her voice, a soft slurring voice using the expressions of the farmers around Lamptown, but he didn't listen to her words, he was drinking in her amazing loveliness. Pretty girls in Lamptown were plump rosy girls invariably handicapped in one way or another, either with thick honest legs, or stringy hair, or an invincible dowdiness, a look of belonging exactly to Lamptown and nowhere else. But Lil had that quality which had struck him from the first in Jen, a quality of not belonging to the place where she was at this moment, of belonging to the place for which she was reaching. This mystified and held him.

She said Jen had left her there because Mrs. Abbott wanted a trimmer and she could sew, really, but she wasn't sure yet if Mrs. Abbott would take her.

"Sure—you bet she will!" Morry said.

The faint blue shadows under her wide blue eyes suggested a seductive frailty, the blonde hair curling at her temples and at the nape of her neck inspired Morry with a persistent urge to touch it and see if it was true. When his mother came in and took Lil back to the workroom he stayed in the shop, smoking and thinking about her, it was as if the silver girl had walked off the magazine cover, he dared not leave her unguarded, this treasure must not be exposed to anyone else. He was certain nobody in Lamptown had ever seen anything like Lil St. Clair, and he had an avaricious desire to set up his claim first, if it was to belong to somebody, then let it be known that he had seen it first. He didn't think of her as a girl, or even as a person, but as a desirable possession, almost an achievement. He couldn't think whether he liked her or not, he felt only awe over her goldenness and wonder that such perfection had strayed into Lamptown. He would have been quite content just to read about it.

Presently Elsinore came back in the shop alone. Morry was leafing over a fashion magazine as if this were his prime interest in the Bon Ton. He planned to stroll home with Lil, but it appeared she was going to stay in the store for a while. A beautiful worker, she was, said his mother, seeming to have a knack with hats. Morry swelled with pride as if he had taught her this gift himself.

"She's a good girl to take Nettie's place," said Elsinore reflectively. "I'll need her when Nettie goes. After all she's no younger than Nettie was when I took her on."

"Where's Nettie going?"

"She's starting a millinery store of her own next season," answered his mother. "Some friend has loaned her a little money. She's going to take that little place behind the Paradise. There's plenty of trade for another millinery store. Mrs. Pepper and I don't mind."

At that moment Nettie herself appeared, and Elsinore slipped out. Nettie looked at Morry defiantly.

"Well, I suppose you've heard I'm starting my own business next fall," she announced. "I suppose you think I can't handle it, too, don't you?"

"I think it's great, Nettie," Morry said heartily, for this meant that Lil would be here right under his eye indefinitely. "I think it's just fine."

Nettie was slightly appeased.

"But you'll be too busy with all your real estate funny business to come in and see me once in a while," she said. "You never see me any more as it is."

"Oh, I'll be dropping in," Morry assured her hastily. "I guess I'd want to see what kind of a store you've got, wouldn't I?"

Nettie's gaze tried to hold him to a promise and he looked toward the door, praying for someone to come in before she trapped him into a definite date. His roving look was misconstrued.

"You've seen that St. Clair girl's sister, that's what!" Nettie cried sharply. "The one I'm teaching to take my place. . . . You'll be running after her next. I'll bet you came to see her this minute!"

"Say, now, Nettie—"

"You did!" she insisted bitterly. "A washed-out little blonde. . . . She looks consumptive to me."

This was the meanest thing you could say about anyone, for everybody despises weaklings. Morry hoped Lil wouldn't overhear. He'd better not wait for her, he decided, Nettie's jealous eyes were too shrewd.

"She's just the wrong type for you, too," Nettie went on. "Just the kind you would pick. . . . You know yourself, Morry, you'd never amount to anything if your mother and I didn't keep after you and when you're that type you ought to get hold of a girl with ambition, a girl with enough business head for two. Some good woman."

Morry felt rising the old homelike sense of guilty incompetence and futile hatred of smug womankind. He started toward the door.

"You know perfectly well she's not a lady, Morry. Neither of those girls. Even you can see that."

At least Nettie was a little lady. Nobody in Lamptown could say a word against little Nettie Farrell. Nobody but Morry . . . and possibly a Mr. Schwarz.

⅀

Supper in the Russell House was a social event still to Morry. There were two big tables in the dining room and except for Hunt's occasional presence, they were filled with out-of-town men, big men who argued constantly about the Works, about running into Pittsburgh tomorrow or down to the Baltimore branch. America was to these men just an area for developing their product, they never knew there was a Lamptown, it was just a factory, the spaces between factories were not towns but Pullman drawing rooms where they planned new arguments with brother officials for factory changes.

They talked during meals, drawing diagrams on the tablecloth with fat silver lead pencils, they argued their way out to the lawn after dinner waving fat cigars, they sometimes drove in Hunt's car after dinner to some crossroads saloon where they continued their discussion over beer and came back, still conferring over the same matters. When they left town duplicate officials took their places at Russell House and in the authoritative ring of their voices, expensively tailored suits, and fragrance of black cigars, sustained the same atmosphere in the Russell dining room.

When the discussion turned to housing problems, Morry often took a part in it and many times talked so forcefully that the strangers removed cigars from the corners of their lips and listened respectfully. Later one would inquire, "Say, young man, I don't think I got your name."

Morry would tell him and the stranger would frown.

"Abbott? Abbott? You're not with us, are you, Abbott? Ah, I don't think I know the name."

Then no more heed was paid to Morry's comments. At these moments he yearned to have accomplished so much, to be such a figure in Lamptown and in all the state that when he gave his name men would start back.

"So you're Morris Abbott!"

Nobody listened to you if your name meant nothing, but on the other hand your name never meant anything unless you forced people to listen. These strangers never heard of Clover Heights, when he said he was in real estate and contracting, they assumed he was with the Lamptown Home Company, part of their own system or else not really in business at all. His three houses at the far end of the Lots had become almost as ridiculous as a full dress would be at a Russell House supper. They meant little enough in the town's development, and only Morry's work on the routine details of the real estate business made him worth any money to Fowler.

But whether Russell House listened to him or not Morry was proud to live there, to dash up and down the great mahogany staircase and tramp casually down the thick-carpeted halls. He had minor panics now and then wondering where he'd go if Fowler's poor business squeezed him out. Supposing he had to live at Bauer's, certainly a comedown, or beg his mother for cot space again in her workroom. . . . These fears could not endure long under the impersonal calm of his new home and the press of his new interests.

There was Lil.

He couldn't explain to himself about Lil. When he went out every night to see her he knew it wasn't because he liked her—you couldn't like or dislike an idea, could you?—it wasn't because he thought she'd be lonely (as indeed her shyness with people was bound to make her), it was for no tangible reason at all, but a certainty that such beauty fell near you only once in a lifetime and whether you wanted it or not you should never let it escape because it was rare. Then the setting Jen had provided for her sister, this little house far out on the edge of town with meadows stretching to the right and behind it, was associated with his dream of a home, somehow, so that Lil was tangled up with the things in life he wanted for himself—glamour, beauty, freedom, a place in which a man could breathe.

Turning from the noise and clangor of Market Street out Extension Avenue he was conscious of a strange expansion in his bosom, the thick hushed trees drew the houses beside them into darkness, the smell of honeysuckle and white clover haunted the air, the flutter of a white dress on a vined porch stirred vague romantic fancy, then the long stretch of fields, hedges settling darkly over yeeping birds, glimmer of a light way off that was Jen's window, all this scented darkness was an avenue to Lil. Here, too, he was lord absolute, with Jen to listen avidly to his boasting, his opinions on this or that, and Lil, frail and lovely for him to admire. Lil seldom talked, when she did she prefaced her comments always with "Jen says—"... She worshiped Jen, and now she worshiped Morry, but he had a disturbed feeling that she would fasten her worship to anybody who was around her steadily.

"Did you hate the Home, Lil?" he'd ask.

"I didn't mind it," she would say.

"Do you like the Bon Ton—is it hard work?"

"I don't mind," she'd answer.

"Are you going away with Jen and try to go on the stage someday?" he'd fearfully inquire.

"I'd rather stay here at the Bon Ton," would be Lil's gentle answer. "I wouldn't want to go away but still I'd want to be wherever Jen was."

He'd hear boys talking about the little St. Clair blondy, he'd ask Lil if she liked this one or that one who had walked home from work with her.

"He's nice," Lil would answer. "I like him all right."

This pale acceptance of life was maddening to Morry, but it kept him constantly intrigued. He suspected that Lil thought he was "all right," too, and he was stirred to more gestures of devotion in an effort to discover some secret intensity in her. She was frightened when he kissed her the first time but after that she turned up her face with the utmost docility. Her intensity came out in her work, her fingers flew over her sewing, they never hesitated over the design of a hat, Elsinore and Mrs. Pepper marveled over this dexterity, and Nettie, who was supposed to be teaching her the trade, sat back with jealous wonder. Here in the Bon Ton workroom Lil attained the pitch of intensity that Morry hoped to arouse in her. He waited to find Jen's furies in the younger sister, but they weren't there. He needed both girls to make up the one necessary for him. When he found Jen out for the evening he grew restless alone with Lil, he'd start to tell her about something concerning his work, and then he'd remember that it must be told to Jen, he couldn't have the news spoiled by Lil's sweet cool, "That's awfully nice, Morry"; he must have Jen's breathless reaction so that the whole affair became tremendously important and himself, by his connection with it, made more important.

In Lamptown, which had made its own dark conclusions over two pretty girls living alone, Lil quickly became classified as Morry Abbott's girl. Lil knew this and accepted her role as she accepted everything, sweetly and casually. She loved trimming hats and she loved her sister Jen, and the rest of life was pleasantly negative. She was glad Morry liked her because Jen liked Morry. When the two girls were busy cooking their supper, she told Jen everything Morry said and did, until Jen would harshly tell her to keep still and watch the potatoes.

~

So Jen was no longer lonely in her new house because Lil was there. When she came home from work at night Lil and Morry were always there. At first she was glad that she had something—say it was Lil—to make Morry call every night, but after two or three weeks she somehow didn't want to hurry home, she lagged around the shop, helped Isaac Berman with the books or talked to Lou about the stage because Lou had seen all the plays and all the actors that there were. When Hunt Russell, always slightly intoxicated, always carrying some magic in his insolent lazy manner, drove up to the shop door occasionally and ordered her to drive with him she was glad to go and put off her homecoming a few more hours. But no matter how late she got home Morry would still be there, sitting on the porch adoring Lil.

"I didn't want to leave Lil here all alone," he would say reprovingly to Jen.

"Thanks for looking out for her," Jen would answer in a hard voice and call a gay farewell to Hunt. She said to herself that she was glad Morry liked Lil, but she knew that nothing had ever cut her so deeply as this persistent devotion. When Lil mildly questioned her about Hunt—"wasn't he awfully old and wasn't he bad?" she knew Morry had said something of the sort, she knew he thought she was taking Dode O'Connell's place with Hunt, but she didn't care. Most of the time she thought about places Lou Berman talked about, of what Vaughn Glaser said to him once, of the party a friend of his gave for Blanche Ring, and every detail of her costume, of the time he saw Marguerite Clarke walk into the hotel ("Baby Mine" she was playing), and of so many trips to New York City he never even counted! . . . All these people belonged to her, now, they had places in her brain, and in her dreams they accepted her as a fellow artist, even Lou Berman himself boasted of knowing her. (Why, that little Jennia St. Clair—used to work right here in Lamptown!) Now it changed to Morry boasting of her, but no, Morry must be in the theatre watching her perform, see there he is now. . . . But then that leaves no one in Lamptown to say they knew her once. . . . Dreams were very difficult to control. Anyway she would look into the audience and see Morry . . . no, she would have to be unconscious of his presence for in or out of dreams as soon as she saw him she'd be bound to rush down to him and say "Look at me, Morry, look, see, I did it, just like we used to plan. Isn't it wonderful?" Then it would merely end with Morry reaching for his hat and saying, "It sure is, well, goodbye." And that would be the end of that. . . . In despair Jen decided there was nothing to be done about Morry, and she must sooner or later do things without keeping his possible applause in mind. She went out with Lou Berman sometimes, to the theatre in Cleveland once with him and often to the Paradise. Lou's approval of her became important, because he praised seldom and was scornful of Lamptown girls. When he called to take her out he'd look her over from head to foot critically.

"Are you going to wear that?"

Then she would know it was all wrong, that her new silk dress was not the thing to wear even if it was the prettiest thing she'd ever owned. He was always patting her arm but she learned this was not a caress but a prelude to pulling the sleeve to a tight fit.

"There's the way your sleeves should set, honey. Fix that before you wear it again. You can wear clothes all right but there's things you gotta learn, hey, papa?"

Lou was sleek, slim, foppish, silent, enviably poised. He fascinated her for he represented the City. But when she looked at old Isaac Berman she saw Lou cartooned with age, paunch-bellied, fang-toothed, bald, greasy, only the dark fathomless eyes eternally romantic in silence no matter what price cuts were being calculated behind them. Lou never tried to make love to her, and Hunt Russell was far too conceited to risk a rebuff, but Jen had a waiting feeling inside, a heavy sense of dread, that if either of these men decided to take possession of her she would have no chance of escape, for you couldn't set yourself against Hunt because he was Lamptown, and you couldn't betray your provincial fear to Lou because he was the City. With Morry so enthralled with Lil she was afraid for herself. No longer was the thought of him any protection to her.

She was terrified at the envy she suffered when she saw him sitting with Lil silently on the porch steps, she had a fleeting lust for revenge, the revenge of throwing herself at Hunt or Lou, of being easy like Grace. But this was no revenge, it was punishment for herself. She listened to Lil's talk of the Bon Ton and when Lil broke out—"You're cross with me, Jen, you're sorry I came to Lamptown!" she answered carefully, "No, I'm not. Didn't I always say we'd live together, didn't I say I'd send for you to come? I wouldn't have said that if I didn't want you, would I?"

But jealousy was gnawing at her constantly and for this illness there is no rest, day and night veins burn and somehow do not burst with the fever, there can be no peace in remembering a past moment of security, such moments are gone for ecstasy leaves no mark, pain alone cuts deep.

"If I could only see Morry as he really is, then the ache would be gone," Jen reasoned, "because look at him—he isn't so different from anybody else, when you think of it, he isn't so good-looking, he certainly isn't kind—yes, he is, remember those nights on Delaney's back steps, yes, he was kind, then."

If there were only some operation that could destroy this perpetual ache, if you could go to a surgeon and say, "Will you please cut out the Morry section of my brain?" But then what would be left? Because he wasn't just in her brain, he was in her blood, he was part of her. If she could sleep nights instead of thinking, she reflected, then she might be strong enough to wish to be free of him, but wounds from him were better than nothing at all from him, that was the awful part of loving someone. Worn out with thoughts that ran round and round forever in the same little circle, she would at last wearily admit that what she wanted most in the world was to be desired by Morry, but this was not possible because it was so plain to him that he could have whatever he wanted from her and no man ever desired something he knew was his.

She was afraid her mind was getting all crooked, she had to go over the words, "Isn't it fine that I did get Lil out of the Home?" Inside those words she knew the truth, because until Lil came Morry was potentially her property—Nettie Farrell and Grace and the girl from Norwalk and the little peroxide blonde from the Works, they didn't matter, these women changed but she remained. She thought if she had brains like Mr. Hogan or Lou Berman she would know how to reason Morry out of her life.

At least now she was determined to do something tremendous with her future. If Lil hadn't come she might have waited around

Lamptown for Morry all her life, but now—let Lil have Morry and Lamptown! As for Jen, she was going to climb every wall and every ladder until she was so high up that she could look down on loving Morry Abbott as nothing at all. And when she was up there at the very top she would thank him for preferring Lil and she would be glad Lil came to Lamptown. These thoughts passed in clear review in her mind while Lil lay sleeping beside her. Oh she'd leave town, Jen thought, wide awake, you bet she'd go. There'd be no place where trains went that she wouldn't go, no city too big for her to conquer, but the next instant, all the cities in the world conquered, she ached for Morry and buried her face in the pillow. Oh Somebody . . . Somebody . . . Somebody help. . . . She remembered the broken rosary in her top drawer but she made no move to get it after her first impulse. No rosary was going to help you. Nothing could help you but yourself, there was no help from any other person or from any Somebody. This was all right . . . in fact as long as she would live, any unexpected service from outside would be regarded by Jen not as luck but as a sinister unnatural phenomenon to be paid for one day or another in blood and tears. . . .

Along about four o'clock she got out of bed and looked out the window on the clover fields. The sullen gray sky gave no hint of sunrise. It was still smudged with night and a few weak stars. Jen tiptoed to her dresser and got out her manicure box. She sat down by the window with it and in that dull pearl light began earnestly on her fingernails. An actress, Lou Berman said, must have beautiful hands.

❧

"Morry's a fine-looking man," said Mrs. Pepper to Elsinore every time Morry called at the store, "a fine-looking man, indeed."

They were always saying that about somebody. On their trips

to Cleveland, at one time or another during the day Mrs. Pepper was bound to nudge Elsinore and say in quite a dignified low voice, "Isn't that a fine-looking man over there—that big man in the Palm Beach suit?"

If there were two Fine-looking Men in the hotel lobby or the Union Station or in the parlor car going home, then Mrs. Pepper was likely to lean toward Elsinore and whisper, "They think we're sisters—can you imagine that? It's on account of these hats."

In summer both women wore big milans heavy with flowers set ever so slightly toward the right eye, just as the wholesaler had advised, and in winter they wore big black velvets with two superb plumes curling under the brim. Elsinore, since Charles's death, had grown much heavier, her face was full and blankly white, though Mrs. Pepper sometimes coaxed her to use just a touch of her vegetable rouge and her curling iron. The Bon Ton, hats, corsets, lingerie, gloves, hosiery, was prospering steadily and the two proprietors used the cream of their stock for their own persons. When they sat discreetly together on excursion boats to Cedar Point, their dotted veils drooping from their big hats, their long gloves demurely on their laps, men shifted cigars to their fingers and one was bound to observe, "A couple of swell figures, there. Classy dressers, eh? We'll pick 'em up at the Point, what d'ye say and take 'em over to the Beer Garden."

They usually wore rustling black silks, black for smartness and discretion, but certainly alluring enough when cut snugly for a perfect 40, accented with dangling long gold chains, heavy musk scents, and modestly revealed openwork stockings. They went to matinees together in Cleveland to see what new costume touches were in vogue, not so much for the Bon Ton clientele as for themselves, they worked hard for the Bon Ton but they lived for their "trips," the whistles of admiration, the whispers, "Gee—what a figure!" the perfect applause of a man stopping in his talk to stare attentively as they passed. It was always Mrs. Pepper's gay little laugh that answered bolder men's invitations, a silvery little tinkle that slurred over every situation, made the whole business just jolly fun and not at all horrid. If the two women ever got separated by their chance male companions, they never confided to each other details of this interim any more than they talked of their "trip" when they returned to Lamptown. What they talked over was the success of their new costumes, a new hair retoucher, and a plan for even more breathtaking ensembles next time. They were two very discreet women, ladies both of them. Even Nettie, jealous and unhappy under the new regime and waiting impatiently for the autumn to launch her own business, could not actually put a finger on anything to talk about except long-distance calls that came from time to time, so cautiously conducted that even Fay, toll operator and Nettie's bosom friend, could not find cause for scandal.

"You know, Elsinore," Mrs. Pepper said as they sat in their pink nightgowns one night patting lotions into their faces, "Harry Fischer says I've completely changed since we started this new store. He gets so worried about me—he says you have a bad influence over me."

Elsinore saw herself in the mirror over Mrs. Pepper's head, her full white arms reaching down for a lost juliet, her dark hair flying, her plump breasts bursting through the lace top of her nightie. The picture was strangely like the image of Mrs. Pepper right beside it, save Mrs. Pepper's bosom, without a corset's support, settled cozily into her "tummy," the waistline completely vanished, and Mrs. Pepper's blue eyes, set in the same sort of round white face, were definitely merry where Elsinore's were blank and cold. Sleeping together, though, Mrs. Pepper's fat arm trustingly encircling Elsinore's waist, her cheek confided in slumber to Elsinore's smooth back, they were like sisters, so close to each other under the pink comforter that they needed no words for their secrets.

"We ought to go over more to Harry's dances," Mrs. Pepper said, regretfully. "He says the inspectors have condemned the Casino, so it may be months before he can find a new hall in Lamptown. He and Hunt may build a new pavilion, and that will take time."

"We went over when we could," said Elsinore. "The Casino seems pretty tame, though, after you've been around."

She tried to think what it had been that she used to see in Harry Fischer, but it was no use. That romance was dynamited out of her brain and in the vacuum a strange new Elsinore had grown. When she thought of Fischer she could only recall with distaste how he perspired in dancing and she even shuddered remembering his hot wet hand on her back, and the ever so faint odor of onions from his breath. She listened to the dance music on Thursday nights but it no longer meant Fischer to her. It was only a reminder of a trip to the Hollenden Grill with two B. & O. officials, or an automobile ride from Cleveland out to a Willoughby roadhouse. When he came to the Bon Ton to see Mrs. Pepper, it was Elsinore who whispered with the latter behind the screen, advising what excuse to give for not meeting him next Wednesday in Cleveland—say they had a dinner of wholesalers to attend, or no—yes, say anything so they could meet those two drummers at the Hofbrau as they'd promised.

"You do make me be mean to Harry," Mrs. Pepper gently protested. "Honestly, I don't feel right about him when I've always been so fond of him. But then I hate to give up a good time and you and I do have good times together, don't we? I'm sure Harry oughtn't to begrudge me a little pleasure after the way I've worked all my life. He surely ought to understand that."

"He does as he pleases," Elsinore answered coldly. "You can't tell me he doesn't with all those young girls always crazy about him. I notice he never got a divorce for you."

Mrs. Pepper's mouth trembled. She still wept over old wounds, over candy denied her as a child, over scoldings remembered from her long-deceased husband, over Harry Fischer long, long ago refusing to divorce his wife for her. So, reminded of this, she became happier in her digressions, not to be revenged on Harry, she was far too gentle for that, but because she thought it wouldn't really hurt his feelings after all.

"That Mr. Kutner from Chicago was so surprised," she murmured to Elsinore, "when Nettie told him you had a grown son. He couldn't believe it, he said."

"Nettie talks too much, anyway," Elsinore exclaimed angrily. "I don't see why the salesmen have to be told all my family affairs."

"She told him about Charles's killing himself, too," said Mrs. Pepper. "Mr. Kutner said he'd read about it but never knew it was your husband."

"I'll be glad when Nettie leaves and gets her own shop," Elsinore burst out in extreme annoyance. "She's much too friendly with strangers. She talks all the time—she's too much of a gossip."

Mrs. Pepper made no reply for in the depths of her amiable soul she was as jealous of Nettie's position in the Bon Ton as Nettie was of hers. And as for her being a gossip, that, to the corsetiere, was her only virtue. She hurried down to the workroom every time she heard Nettie's girlfriend, Fay, come in, for between Fay and Nettie you were bound to get a good hour of fascinating tattle. Fay told everything, every telephone call that came for the Girls' Club, what every vanished factory girl said who called up her Lamptown girlfriend from a tough hotel in Pittsburgh, what women were called up by slightly tipsy visitors in Bill Delaney's saloon. Once Fay stopped her chatting when Mrs. Pepper apologetically stole in the room.

"She'll tell," Fay explained her reticence to Nettie. "I'll tell you some other time."

Mrs. Pepper pouted.

"It's about Dode O'Connell," Nettie told her briefly, "and

you'd go right and tell Harry Fischer and he'd tell Hunt and Hunt would get Fay in dutch at the telephone office."

Mrs. Pepper clasped her hands pleadingly.

"But I wouldn't tell! I wouldn't really! I never see Hunt to talk to any more—I wouldn't tell a soul! What's happened to Dode—is it true she got married to a man in Grand Rapids?"

Fay's lip twisted scornfully. She adjusted her turban with a left hand grown much more adept since it flaunted a diamond solitaire.

"Dode isn't married to anybody. Hunt wouldn't marry her and that finished her. Well—you're sure she won't blab, Nettie? . . . it isn't anything. Only Hunt calls up Toledo last night and when I was getting the party Toledo says to me, 'Say, Lamptown, you know the party you're calling, don't you' and I says no, it's a hotel, ain't it, and she says, 'Some hotel,' she says, 'it's Lizzy Madison's, the biggest sporting house in town. Better listen in if you want to hear something good.' So I says, 'Say, Toledo, think I'm so darned dumb you got to tell me to listen in?' Anyway Hunt gets the party and it was some woman answering so Hunt says is Miss Dolores there. All the time Akron was trying to get me, but I let her buzz, I hung on to Toledo, you couldn't have pried me away. Well, this Miss Dolores says, 'Hello, who is it?' then, and Hunt says, 'Hello, Dode, this is Hunt. I want to see you.' She says 'Who?' and sorta gasped as if she couldn't believe her ears, and he says 'It's me, Hunt. How are you, Dode?' Well, she didn't say another word, so he kept saying, 'hello, hello' and still she didn't answer, only sort of a funny noise, I heard, sounded like somebody crying. He kept it up—'Say, Dode, hello, can't you hear me,' he says, 'It's me— Hunt.' And no answer from her just that funny moanin' sort of, gee, it got my goat coming over the wire that way, and then she clicked off. So he says to me, 'Operator, operator, I was cut off.' And I just told him. 'Oh no you wasn't cut off, Mr. Russell,' I says, 'the lady hung up.'"

Mrs. Pepper listened sorrowfully.

"She was so crazy about him!"

"Well," said Nettie, threading a needle, "she's where she belongs now, I guess."

"I'll say so," said Fay, and flicked a raveling from her dress with her engagement finger.

Mrs. Pepper told Elsinore about Dode in their room that night while they took turns manicuring each other. Wasn't it a shame, she said, the way Dode turned out?

"There's worse things," Elsinore said.

❦

Coming out of Bill Delaney's Morry heard a "Sss-t!" and saw old Mrs. Delaney at the alley entrance. She jerked her head toward him commandingly. She was in a dry brown calico dress, her shawl pulled over her head, one brown twisted hand grasping an egg basket. She seemed shrinking more each day into old brown goods until someday you could pick up this antique bundle and find no more bones or body to it than to a dried leaf, if you shook it two shriveled hen feet and a wrinkled yellow mask might fall out but no more than that. She clung to the stair railing as if the languid breeze might blow her away.

"Evening, Mrs. Delaney," Morry said uncomfortably. He could not meet her fierce old eyes, he knew she was ready with accusations and he had no wish to hear them, other things were pressing on his mind.

"I told you she'd turn out bad, didn't I?" she sputtered. "Didn't I say there was bad blood there? Got her own place now, she has, where she can carry on and nobody see, she's a smart one, nobody can deny those bad ones are the smartest and you, young man, you got yourself to thank for it, I could've handled her if you hadn't hung around, letting her think you was soft on her, it's you that's ruined that girl's life and don't you forget it, someday you'll have a daughter of your own and you'll find out, then, you'll be the one to worry then, young man. . . ."

"I never hurt Jen, you're all wrong about that," Morry protested, wishing there was some weapon for dealing with old women.

She sniffed scornfully.

"You can't lie to me. I know my characters. I knew your pa and I knew her mother. Didn't that woman come here time after time trying to find Jen and didn't I run her out of town as fast as she could go—didn't I call the police for her not two months ago when she came to my door?"

Morry hadn't known this.

"Did her mother come again, really?"

"I'm tellin' you right now. She come here not two months ago sayin' she'd heard both her girls was here workin' in town and she was their mother come to make a home for them. You make a home for them, hah, I says, you want their salary and you want them to keep you now you've shirked 'em all your life. Well, she says, they only got one mother and it's my duty to be with 'em now when they need a mother's care. Hah, I says, one mother is one too many and I called Bill up here and he got her ticket right back to Cleveland without her even seeing the girls."

"She'd better keep away from those girls," Morry exclaimed angrily. "Throwing them away when they were born—the way she did . . . she's got no right to them now."

The old woman turned on him.

"If she hasn't who has? You, maybe. . . . I hear things. I hear Jen went from you to Hunt Russell and from Russell to that Jew, but you're responsible, you gave her the start, young fella, and you'll get your punishment, glory be to God."

She hobbled up the stairs and Morry, disturbed, went on toward the Bon Ton. He was always supposed to be Jen's keeper, he reflected, even if he never saw her, Bill's mother or Hulda Bauer would always be giving him old nick for letting Jen do this and that. . . . As if he could stop Jen from doing anything she'd set her mind on. . . . He thought of her plan to go away. He hadn't talked to her much about it because she wouldn't really go, he felt. But what made him so sure? After all Berman had promised to help her go, and there was nothing to hold her in Lamptown. Nothing but Lil. . . . Lil and—well, face it squarely—himself. He didn't like to think about Jen loving him—it was such a violent, possessive love, not what he wanted from a girl, such fierce, unreasoning love made a man instinctively cautious and sensible—somebody had to be. He could have made love to her, there were times he remembered, but he was afraid of losing himself. Oh yes, somebody had to be sensible. As for being in love—well, he loved Lil; but loving Lil was like loving prestige or an idea, not like loving a person. If he allowed himself to be drawn to a strong person like Jen she would inevitably crowd into the romance and be equal to the hero—this was disturbing and not romantic, romance was between a man and love, not between a man and woman. . . .

Morry found himself caught up in the puzzle of his own feelings. . . . Could Jen really go away and leave him? Even here waiting for Lil to come out of the Bon Ton door, he grew sick with fear of a Lamptown without Jen. The Delaney backstairs, the Bauers' kitchen, the Casino, the house on Extension, these places were Lamptown and they were barren with Jen ripped out of them. And Lil, pale and sweet, was nothing without Jen coloring her. . . . It was silly of him to be so sure Jen would not leave him, she went around with other men, he'd never been jealous because he was sure of her, so certain of her that he had no desire for her. . . . No, be truthful, there were moments when she was adoring him that he wanted desperately to possess her, but then he would be lost, she would know he belonged to her, there could be nothing casual between him and Jen. . . . But if she should go away he'd have to go, too. He had to. He couldn't let her prove superior to him. That was settled. . . .

He leaned against the Bon Ton window and smoked. It was too early for Lil to go home to supper, he'd have to wait a little while. He observed the newly painted doorway of the Bon Ton—no doubt about it, his mother was a good business woman, she'd done a lot for herself since his father's death—all right, call it "suicide." He could certainly use that word if his mother could so casually. Maybe, if she thought about that event at all, and sometimes Morry doubted if she did, she really thought it was a suicide. Anyway the further back in your mind you pushed those things the better it was for you.

He stepped back to study the show window. A gold fringe ran across the top of it and propped against a little gold silk screen was the crying doll dressed in black velvet, its blue eyes staring out under its huge black hat, a duplicate of the life-size black hat on the stand beside it. One hand was held out stiffly with a tiny purse hung on it, the other hand was concealed in the folds of the dress because the fingers were broken. Morry felt curiously guilty before the doll's glassy stare. He wished his mother would get rid of the damned thing. It made him think of his father.

*

It was a fact, Hogan told Morry in the barroom, that Fowler had made a deal with the Lamptown Home Co. to continue their little houses all over Clover Heights. When Morry demanded what Hunt said to this, Bill explained that Hunt was selling everything he owned in town, shares in the Works and everything, and that he was going in with Harry Fischer to build a dance pavilion somewhere in this county.

"Outside of that old Hunt has set up a little drugstore blonde in a swell apartment on Euclid Avenue in Cleveland," said Hogan. "I give him two years to get down to his bottom dollar."

"But I don't understand about Fowler—why didn't he let me know what was going on?" Morry wanted to know. His head was swimming, he was afraid his face had paled, something stuck in his throat. . . . Fowler had fooled him, everybody had fooled him, there never would be any Clover Heights, but this was not so terrible as finding out how people used you, fooled you, always kidding you along as if they meant what you did.

"If the old boy didn't tell you, then he's got something crooked up his sleeve, Jesus, those Fowlers never had a straight thought," Hogan answered. "Every goddam one of my wife's people, the same. . . . You wait, there'll be a dirty deal in it somewhere, that's why he didn't tell you. Sell you out for a nickel, that man would. Won't touch liquor, won't look at a woman—say you never can trust an abstainer, boy, if he's abstaining from pleasure it's so he can put all his strength into some shady business deal—you mark my words."

Morry steadied himself at the rail, he drank fast to dispel that choked feeling in his throat. There was nobody you could believe in—your father, your mother, nobody.

"I don't see where Morry's stung," Bill had objected. "He's not going to be fired. He'll go over with Fowler and work for the Lamptown Home Company, that's all."

Morry found his voice returning at last.

"I wouldn't do it!" he snarled. "You think I'd spend the rest of my life doing nothing but see how many of those shanties I could squeeze on to an acre of land? Why, I wouldn't work to put a thing like that over on this town, this town's got as much right to be a decent place to live in as Avon has, right next door. I'd feel as if I was spreading smallpox, honest I would. If Fowler's giving up Clover Heights, then I quit Fowler, that's all. You got to believe in what you're doing, Hogan, you see that, don't you? A fella's got a right to work for something he believes in, hasn't he?"

"Maybe," said Bill. "But a fella's got to work at something, believe or not believe."

"The prettiest thing this town will ever have," observed Hogan, "is the Yards. You'll never see anything prettier in this burg than those old black engines pushing up and down the tracks. Boy, you might as well make up your mind now as later that people don't want anything pretty, and damned if they want anything useful, they just want what other people have. You take these cement porches—"

"You never used to talk like that," Morry reproached him.

"I wasn't this old," grinned Hogan.

"All right, then," Morry said, "the hell with Fowler."

He swung out to the street and walked rapidly and dizzily toward Extension Avenue. He forgot about Lil waiting in the Bon Ton. His head buzzed with Hogan's words. Fowler had sold out, gone over to the rivals, he hadn't believed in anything but piano boxes for homes from the very first, he only loaned himself to the Clover Heights enterprise because the bank thought it was good business and because the Works directors hadn't asked him to build their workmen's cottages. As soon as they did ask him he dropped everything and went flying over to them like a child going to whoever extended the most candy.

Hogan said the three houses were to be fixed over into a boarding club for the company officials, a big flower garden was to be laid straight across all three front lawns with huge letters in red and white gladiolas, "LAMPTOWN WORKS OFFICIALS CLUB." And Fowler had worked all this out with the Works people without telling him, thinking he'd be glad to go over to them, too. That's the way people were. Nobody believed in the things you believed but yourself, nobody believed that even you were really sincere about it, people believed whatever was good business for them at the time. Nobody believed in anything but good business. Clover Heights was blown up, the world was blown up, by good business. Everybody knelt to good business. No use counting on anybody having faith in an idea for its own sake.

Restlessly Morry walked on. What was going to happen to him, then? Fowler wouldn't fire him, he'd expect him to go cheerfully over to the rival company, but he wouldn't, he'd be damned if he would. Well, what would he do, then—go back to the factory? Give up living in Russell House and beg five dollars now and then from his mother, "till he got something good enough"? Either he fell in with the Lamptown Home Company for a little while—oh, just a few months, say—and worked to see that every citizen had his rightful portion of ugliness, or he went back to the factory. Damned if he'd go back there. He'd leave town, go to the city. Cleveland—Detroit—Chicago—What would he do there? He'd never dare go. . . . Still, Jen St. Clair wasn't afraid to strike out. He knew a second of despair, thinking that all his life it was Jen driving him to do things, he never did anything without that lash, he never would. He had to do the things she expected of him. She would be a big actress on Broadway, she said, when he was an architect in New York. So that's what he had to do, that was all there was to it. Maybe Pittsburgh first, work it somehow to study at Carnegie Tech . . . then New York. Jen would be there because she always did the things she set out to do, and he—well, he had to be what Jen thought he was. . . . He stopped to roll another cigarette. His hands shook. He dared not think of going away, but if Jen had the nerve to go he wouldn't be afraid, he'd never dare let her see how perilous it seemed to him. . . .

It was nearly six. He could go back to the Bon Ton now for Lil or he could go on to the house, since he was nearing it, and see Jen, who went home earlier. He needed the reassurance of his own voice boasting to Jen about what he was going to do. He needed desperately to be told he was wonderful, that there were far bigger things for him than any Clover Heights, he needed Jen's eyes worshiping him and he forgot Lil.

The sun withdrew and drained all color from the trees, they looked gloomy and ragged, their branches were too skinny, he thought; in the unbecoming twilight the old gray houses of Extension Avenue crowded beside their trees looking dowdy and unloved like the wives of executives. Good-bye, Lamptown, Morry thought, hurrying along, good-bye. . . . This was the moment of curious lull when it was neither day nor night, it was time for the six-o'clock whistle to blow, then warm darkness would smudge these sharp edges and let shadows invent their own town.

The factory siren suddenly shrieked through the air, cutting the day in two, and boardinghouse kitchens responded with an obedient clatter of pans and dishes, the smell of frying potatoes mingled agreeably with the fragrance of fresh-mown lawns and strawberry shrubs. Good-bye, good-bye to all this, Morry whispered. . . . He'd go straight to the house, then, he decided, and when Jen came in he'd tell her, he'd say, "What would I do in the city? What's there to be afraid of? Don't be foolish, Jen. I'd just walk into an office and get a job, that's all—there's nothing to that, is there?"

Now the evening fast train roared through Lamptown, its triumphant whistle soared over the factory siren, in its vanishing echoes the beginning of a song trembled, a song that belonged to far-off and tomorrow. Yes, yes, he would come away, Morry's heart answered, now he was ready.

A NOTE ON THE AUTHOR

DAWN POWELL was born in Mt. Gilead, Ohio, in
1896. In 1918 she moved to New York City where she
lived and wrote until her death from cancer in 1965.
She was the author of fifteen novels, numerous short
stories, and a half dozen plays.

A NOTE ON THE BOOK

The text for this book was composed by Steerforth Press using a digital version of Granjon, a typeface designed by George W. Jones and first issued by Linotype in 1928. The book was printed on acid free papers and bound by Quebecor Printing~Book Press Inc. of North Brattleboro, Vermont.

Also by Dawn Powell

ANGELS ON TOAST

COME BACK TO SORRENTO
(OR THE TENTH MOON)

TURN, MAGIC WHEEL

THE LOCUSTS HAVE NO KING

MY HOME IS FAR AWAY

A TIME TO BE BORN

THE WICKED PAVILION

THE BRIDE'S HOUSE

THE HAPPY ISLAND

THE GOLDEN SPUR

DAWN POWELL AT HER BEST
Including the novels DANCE NIGHT
and TURN, MAGIC WHEEL *and selected stories*

THE DIARIES OF DAWN POWELL: 1931–1965